MW01382565

Outro

A NOVEL BY

Michael J. Vaughn

iUniverse, Inc.
New York Bloomington

Outro

iUniverse books may be ordered through booksellers or by contacting:

iUniverse
1663 Liberty Drive
Bloomington, IN 47403
www.iuniverse.com
1-800-Authors (1-800-288-4677)

ISBN: 978-1-4401-1140-2 (sc)
ISBN: 978-1-4401-1141-9 (ebook)

Printed in the United States of America

iUniverse rev. date: 12/30/2008

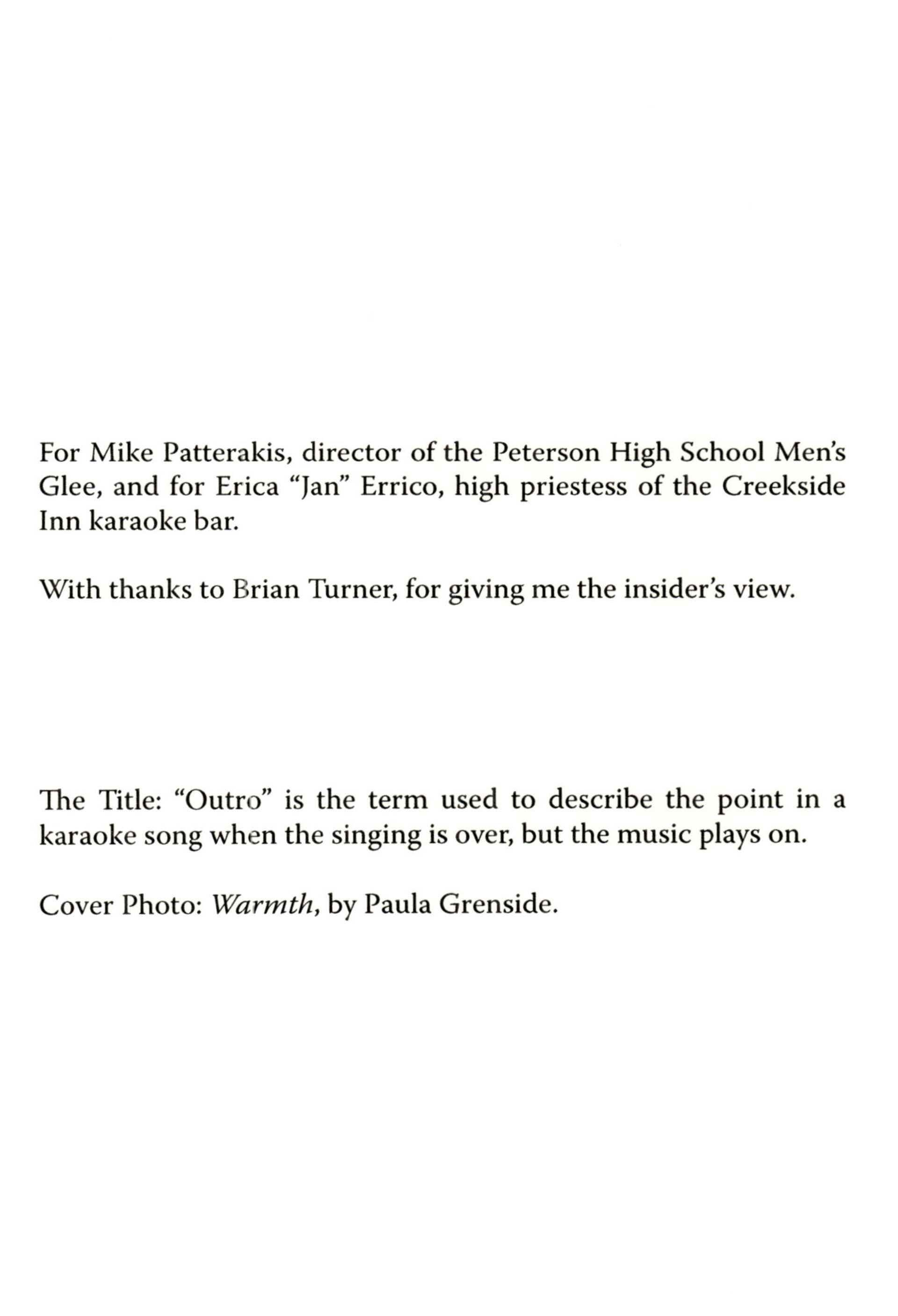

For Mike Patterakis, director of the Peterson High School Men's Glee, and for Erica "Jan" Errico, high priestess of the Creekside Inn karaoke bar.

With thanks to Brian Turner, for giving me the insider's view.

The Title: "Outro" is the term used to describe the point in a karaoke song when the singing is over, but the music plays on.

Cover Photo: *Warmth*, by Paula Grenside.

One
Channy

Traditionally, when someone leaves my hometown, there's drama. Big family arguments, occasional fistfights, two or three stabbings. I was the exception. We weren't the closest of families, but my folks were elated that I had gotten through school without the common surrender to boredom and drugs. The reason for my success was largely a mystery. Whether instilled or innate, I possessed an iron sense of self-worth, and a horse-trader's notion that I could swap the mediocrities of today for the glories of tomorrow. Once graduation arrived, a journey Outside (which is what Alaskans call anywhere not in Alaska) was seen by all as my just reward.

Because of my patience and choosiness – and the slapping away of several pairs of hands belonging to drooling jock lotharios – I earned a reputation as a prude. The few times I did give away the goodies, this served to elevate the pleasure and surprise of my happy recipients. Surprise was a natural reaction, anyway, because my candidates were *not* on the roster of Boys Who Get Laid. He had to be nice, he had to be someone I could control, and he absolutely *had* to use a condom, because my autobiography would not be titled *Knocked Up in Anchorage*. Most importantly, although some attraction was necessary, I didn't want it to reach the narcotic level – because, the day after graduation, I had a date with the lower

48 (I used this phrase so often that my friends began to sing-song it back to me).

Looking back on my patterns (as more people should do), I realized that most of my boys were musicians. The last was James Kitagawa, who was also the best musician. He was a stocky Japanese boy with a broad Buddha-like face, skin the color of a toasted marshmallow, and a grin that could light up the whole quad.

The highlight of our graduation ceremonies came when the choir sang its commencement song. The song was chosen by a vote of the senior choir members, which always carried an element of suspense. After four years of Rodgers & Hammerstein, Brahms and madrigals, they were usually anxious to do something pop or rock, and I always expected some particularly squirrely class to do something like "Sympathy for the Devil."

For the class of 2001, the choice seemed obvious: "Beautiful Day" by U2. It had an anthemic quality that seemed naturally choral – like *Carmina Burana* with guitars – and the hook was celebratory and hopeful. The bonus came in the verses, which contained all these references to being stuck somewhere, aching to get out – muddy roads, small towns. Because really, those *were* our hopes. Singing them out loud to our parents (knowing that most of it would go right over their heads) was the perfect gratuity to our teenage sense of rebellion.

Problem was, choral arrangements were not exactly on U2's priority list, so we called on our resident Mozart (in fact, that was his nickname, "Mozart"). James had his own after-school jazz ensemble, so surfing this musical no-man's land was right up his alley. He already had the basic rock 'n' roll lineup – drums, bass, guitar, himself on keyboards - so all he had to do was throw some of The Edge's ringing guitar explosions to his horn section and then get to work on the vocals.

Bono is one of those classic double-gear singers who likes to start low and then jump the octave when things get exciting (think Orbison, Isaak, Prince). James gave the low intro to the bass and alti, then handed the chorus sforzando (that's "sudden forte") to the tenors and soprani as the lower voices supplied echoing harmonies.

The master stroke arrived with the accelerated lines that Bono sings in the bridge (U2 always has these – they're masters of construction). James worked these into a counterpoint fugue, like a damn Haydn in leather pants. From there, he built it to a climax by repeating the chorus with verse lines draped over the top, growing in volume and chaos until he cut us off, leaving the horns, drums and guitars to finish it off with three big crunchy chords, so like *Don Giovanni* that I figured it was James' private joke, sort of a nickname signature to his high school thesis.

I'm sorry if I go on about this, but being a part of that performance, standing in the alto section in the middle of our football field on a bright spring afternoon, might have been the single event that hooked me on music for good. *And* I was screwing the arranger.

I almost got all the way through school without meeting him at all. I met him two months before, during Breakup (which refers to the ice in the rivers, not to relationships). I was lollygagging on the senior lawn, where underclassmen are allowed only by express invitation, when two ideas came into glorious collusion in my head: 1) the baseball-like hardness of the oranges that came in our box lunches, and 2) the inexplicably deep and dangerous hole that was drilled into the ground at the far end of the lawn. I sprang to my feet, struck a classic bowler's pose and rolled my orange across the grass. It traveled thirty feet, took a slight left-to-right break, and dropped into the hole with a thud.

James, who was crouched over a chessboard directly behind the "green," looked up from his bishop just in time to witness the entire thing. When he saw what happened, he jumped to his feet and yelled "Genius! Fucking *genius*!" Then fell to the lawn and disappeared most of his arm so he could retrieve my orange and roll it back. Thus are Olympic events and friendships born.

James was a classic nerd – all that much cooler because of the way he reveled in it – and extremely surprised, two weeks later, when I added a friendly crotch-rub to our makeout repertoire. I assumed he had heard the stories about Channy the Chaste (also Miss Tightzipper, which, I had to admit, was pretty clever).

"Don't get me wrong," I said. "I *am* picky. But the kind of boy I pick is also the kind of boy who keeps a secret. Am I understood?"

"Small price," he said, and smiled. I undid his buttonfly and removed my chewing gum.

After commencement, I waited for James at the senior lawn. He arrived in his gown, too rushed by loading his keyboard and accepting praise to bother changing. He strode my way exactly like a man with a freshly inflated ego, grabbed me by the waist and swung me in a circle, then planted me with a kiss. I don't know if it was good hygiene or natural chemistry, but I could kiss that boy's mouth for hours, he was like human candy. After a minute, though, he deflated a bit and gave me a sad look.

"You're absolutely sure."

"What did I tell you?"

"Yeah – 'day after graduation.'"

"Don't say I didn't give you an expiration date."

"Let me go with you! I'll go home and pack right now."

I kissed him on his broad nose.

"No way. It's the trip of my life, and it's strictly solo. Besides, you've got a muse to chase."

"Yes." He smiled. "And her name is Ann Arbor."

"Does anyone from here ever go further south? Like, I don't know – Arizona State?"

"You kiddin' me? They'd melt!"

I ran a finger along James' upper lip and finished it with a kiss.

"I see that you still have one punch left on your ticket, Herr Mozart. Is there anywhere you've always wanted to…?"

I stopped when my customary crotch-rub landed on something unexpected.

"God, Jimmy! Did you have an operation?"

After a spell of epileptic laughter, Jimmy reached under his gown and pulled out a pair of rock-hard oranges.

"That's not all," he said. "I also have the keys to the music room, which I neglected to return after our last rehearsal. I have heard that Mr. Paris's grand piano is capable of supporting quite a bit of weight."

"You know, Freud would have a field day with *you*, Maestro. And so would I."

That's the last time I saw him. Late that summer, a landscaper was driving the freeway outside Minneapolis. A rolled-up tarp fell out of his truck. Just behind him, a tow-truck driver pulling a transit bus swerved to miss it and jumped the meridian. James was driving the other direction, on his way to the University of Michigan. He never had a chance. "Beautiful Day" shows up on a song slip about once a month, and I still have a hard time listening.

I'm sorry. I'm getting ahead of myself. The day after graduation (my personal Valhalla), the contiguous 48 called me from bed at six o'clock. My dad was already downstairs, drinking his coffee, and he helped me pile all my belongings into the truck. When I was all ready, he rousted my mother from sleep so she could anoint my jacket with tears. Perhaps we didn't realize how close we were until that moment. I warmed up the engine and drove off, the two of them standing arm-in-arm on the porch, popping up in my rear-view like some misty coming-of-age movie.

Dad was a mechanic, and had given the truck a thorough check-up. He was well-acquainted with the damage that could be inflicted by the Alaskan Highway (what we call the Alcan), and had also prepared a large box of emergency supplies. By the second day, I had already made use of the spare fan belt and one of those epoxy hypodermics that keeps a windshield crack from crawling toward Juneau like a spiderweb.

By the fourth day, the damage was mostly to my exhausted body (which had started out sore to begin with, thanks to my Jamesean concerto). Lord knows, they had made lots of improvements to the old road (and still were, judging by all the construction delays), but there were still all these rollercoaster dips where the permafrost had given out, and long stretches of gravel that pik-pokked their way into my brain. I made a mental note to get some new shocks once I reached a city.

A couple hours past Teslin, Yukon, I was just enjoying my first glimpse of the Canadian Rockies when my view was rudely drowned out by a bombardment of fog. And not just any fog – freezing fog. As I slipped into the brief summer night, microscopic ice crystals danced across my headlight beams, creating a fairyland aura that was putting me right to sleep. I had sunk into the more desperate stages of Auto Wakefulness Therapy – self-slapping, knee-knocking, the occasional Fay Wray scream – when another set of fairies, orange and blinking, appeared on the shoulder. Hazard lights on sawhorses, leading me into a rest area that said *Watson Lake.*

This was the home of the Signpost Forest, something I had always thought of as an artful myth. Back in World War II, the U.S. had some real concerns about Japan attacking military outposts in Fairbanks and Anchorage, which were wholly dependent on air and sea for the delivery of supplies. (The Japanese actually *did* make some attacks on the Aleutian Islands in 1942.)

So they sent 27,000 workers – 11,000 of them soldiers – to work on the Alcan, and they built all 1500 miles in eight months, working non-stop in awful conditions. One day, an Illinois soldier named Carl K. Lindley expressed his homesickness by putting up a sign from his native state. There are now almost 50,000, from all over the world, covering a grove of telephone poles just off the highway.

I know. I sound like a freakin' tour guide. But I was enjoying a free cup of coffee in the interpretive center, and I'm a compulsive reader. When I finally wandered outside, the freezing fog was snaking in and out of the signposts, which added to its mythic qualities. I touched a few of them, just to make sure. The variety was amazing. I found a single pole with signs from The Netherlands, Manitoba, Michigan, Switzerland and Yorba Linda, California. I was running my hand over a handmade sign from Bob and Mary Stetson of Texas when I heard footsteps, and turned to find a striking young man headed my way.

"Hi," he said. "Have you decided on a destination?"

He was tall and lean, a classic Jimmy Stewart type, with dark, intense eyes like Gregory Peck (my whole senior year, I was on a classic-movies kick). In any case, he had read my mind so precisely that I had to laugh.

"I've been so occupied with getting out of Alaska, I hadn't figured out where I was getting out *to.* Where are you headed?"

He smiled mischievously. "Wherever my next ride takes me."

"You're hitchhiking the Alcan? Are you insane?"

"My friends seem to think so."

"And here I was thinking I was so reckless and brave."

"You're a girl. You get extra credit."

"Well thanks."

We stood and talked for another hour, but it didn't seem to matter what we said. We were locked in a mutual study. He spoke in clear, careful sentences – almost like an actor – and his voice was smooth and baritone, like a radio newsman. He had thick, jet-black hair, with a single renegade hank that would slip over his forehead when he laughed. He had a wide mouth, and generous lips that would almost seem girly but for a small scar on his right upper that set things fetchingly asymmetrical. When he told a story, he would insert little questions so I could take part ("So then we headed for Prudhoe Bay – have you been there?").

In short, he had all those gentleman qualities that I had always screened for in high school, but he also seemed like a Boy Who Got Laid. This was a combination I had never encountered. The attraction was so strong and natural that I had to remind myself of the hard, external facts: *strange boy, middle of nowhere, traveling alone...*

His name was Harvey, which fit rather comically with the Jimmy Stewart vibe. Harvey Lebeque, son of Cajuns who left New Orleans to work on the Alyeska pipeline. His dad worked in maintenance, which meant constant travel, but also a comfy existence for his family. That was the part that drove him out.

"People who come from poor families, and then find themselves with money, they go all security crazy!" he said. "If I had to listen to one more of my dad's pep talks about 'doing the smart thing,' I was going to have a freaking seizure. It's my theory that the only way you ever learn is by doing the *stupid* things. So here I am – ha-haah!"

He seemed to save that laugh for things that really broke him up. The second syllable was open and joyous, a touch of a James Brown shriek. Only an hour, and I already knew that. *Strange boy, middle of nowhere.* I also knew that the one thing he needed the most had remained conspicuously absent from the conversation. I ran my hand along a license plate from Montreal.

"How do you rate as a driver, Harvey?"

"Four years, no tickets, no accidents."

"No car," I said, and laughed.

"No, I've got a car. I left it in Fairbanks."

"Wait a minute. You're hitchhiking by *choice*?"

"Stupid things? Learning? Besides, I wanted to break out of my shell. I've always been a little shy."

"Shy?" I said. "Talking to strange girls in sign forests?"

"I'm not talking to strange girls. I'm talking to *you*."

I was desperately fighting off a blush. Perhaps it was cold enough that he wouldn't notice.

"Okay," I said. "Here's the deal. You drive, I sleep. And none of this macho crap about driving forever – you get tired, you let me know. And I'm reading you as a gentleman, so I'm trusting you to stay that way."

"Yes, ma'am."

"Can you chip in for gas?"

"I can *pay* for gas. I'm stupid, not broke. In fact, um..."

I don't know if he was trying to prove his previous statement, but this seemed to be his shy side. He buried his hands in his jacket and looked groundward, like a soldier delivering bad news to his commanding officer.

"I hope you'll take this the right way, but I already got a room at a hotel down the street, and I would be more than happy to sleep on the floor if you would share the room with me, because I've already paid for it, and because, frankly, you look exhausted."

"Oh," I said. This was getting trickier by the minute. I chewed on a thumbnail.

"Not to discount your attractions, Channy," he said. "But a hitchhiker can hardly afford to lose a long-distance ride by making untoward advances. We can... buy some jingle bells and string them around your bed. You can handcuff me to the radiator. Provided... you have handcuffs."

"Geez, Harvey, I just..."

"Did I mention that this room has a clawfoot bathtub? With hot running water?"

"Sold!"

We walked to my car and drove half a block to the Watson Lake Hotel. When Harvey opened the door and waved me into his room, I realized I was in big trouble. There in the far corner, balanced across an easy chair, was an old, beat-up guitar case.

Two

So here's my thought on cover songs: if you're not going to make the song your own, don't bother. You're just a hack with a record deal, looking to milk a twenty-year-old hit.

Pretty funny, coming from a KJ (that's Karaoke Jock). But six months after someone records that cover song, the wake rolls into my bar. A few months ago, I started getting requests for "Drift Away." Once a night, three times a night – when it got up to six, I had to call a moratorium. One of my college kids informed me that the latest acoustic grinder hunk had covered it for a soundtrack --probably with that grungy yarl that everybody ripped off from Eddie Vedder.

I make my living through the good graces of pop culture, so I engineered a compromise. At the end of our third round, I take out all five of our mics, and anybody who's up for it gets to sing along. Over the weeks, it has almost become a beautiful thing. Kevin the Cop contributes a high third, Harry Baritone constructs something mysterious but effective down below, and Shari Blues has come up with a full gospel descant. I turn down whatever mic Caroleen is on (poor old gal), and me, I'm strictly melody, 'cause I'm the KJ, that's my job. I call it the Karz Bar Korale, and we are occasionally magnificent – especially when the CD knocks off and we finish with a bonus a capella chorus. There are times when karaoke is downright spiritual, like church with cocktails. Whoever's left in the audience (at least Alex, who's only here to dance) gives us a nice round of applause, and I gather up mics like a teacher collecting homework. Except for Kevin, who waits as I line up his salsa track, "Suavamente," a disc that he brings from home. I guess I'd get tired of the thing, except for the stimulating effect it has on the hips and buttocks of its listeners. It doesn't hurt that it's Kevin, of the sunny smile and brown sugar tenor – he who spends his days shaking down meth labs in Lakewood. You wouldn't guess that he was half Puerto Rican – not with a name like Connaugh, and that Caucasian face. But a couple of rolled R's and hip swivels and you can see where Mama's genes had their way.

When the song hits the percussion break, the rhythm gets too much for me, and I escape the bonds of my station to join Alex and his latest hottie on the floor. My pelvis is just beginning to loosen up when I hear a rolling thump on the entranceway and turn to find Supersonic, human train wreck, reeling our way. Oh, man.

Super is the Kitsap Peninsula's primary freak, a position he endows with a distinctive visual style. His name comes from his wardrobe, composed entirely of paraphernalia from Seattle's basketball team. Tonight it's a jersey with the number of Ray Allen, recently traded scoring machine. Super's other outstanding feature is a head of outlandish Einstein hair, completely gray on one side, completely red on the other. You could draw a line down the middle.

Sadly, there's no stopping him now. He reels up to Kevin's mic and lets loose a string of crackles and grunts in a crude approximation of the melody. Kevin pivots, blocking Super with a shoulder, but I can tell this won't hold him for long. I dig under the soundboard for the cheapest mic I've got and hand it to Super, let him babble for a few seconds and then fade out his volume. Once he figures out that I've cut his sound, he protests with a trio of full-body stomps and hurls the mic across the room. It barely misses Doc Mendelssohn, but not his martini glass, which explodes in a shower of crystals. (Fortunately, Doc's wearing a thick tweed coat, which deflects a couple of scary-looking shards.)

For Kevin, that cinches it. He tosses me his mic, whips Super into a headlock and rams him against the bar.

"Rule number one," he says. "You do *not* impede an officer in the performance of his favorite tune."

Super sputters an answer: "Fucking spic!" He kicks at the bar and convulses in a full-body shiver, forcing Kevin's ribs into a barstool.

"Asshole!" cries Kevin. "You've done it now, buttboy." He cranks down on the headlock and rides him toward the back deck, pushing the door open with Super's flailing, scrawny frame and steering him outside. The dancers plug up the doorway to see what happens next, while everyone else gathers at the window.

Kevin brings Super to the railing and forces him to look.

"That's some mighty cold water, Super. Now apologize, or you're goin' in!"

Super looks back over his shoulder, drooling with defiance. His next words come out like the quack of a duck, or maybe it's just a similarity of consonants.

"Fuck you, cocksucker!"

Kevin smiles. It's just the invitation he's looking for. Keeping one arm on his headlock, he spins the other around the backs of Super's legs and hurls him upward, like a Hefty bag headed for the Dumpster. Super phases through several hieroglyphic postures before striking the drink and sending up a long fishtail of water.

Even in August, the water of Gig Harbor will turn your testes to Popsicles, so it's no surprise when the next sound is something like an old-school Michael Jackson yelp. Kevin peers over the railing and grins.

"You want out of there, Super?"

Super yodels back: "Yu-yu-yes!"

"You'll behave?"

"Yes! Yes!"

"All right. Grab onto this and shut the fuck up."

"Yes sir!"

He tosses a life ring, then fetches a dock ladder from the other end of the deck. Meanwhile, I figure I'd better coax the evening back to normal, so I call up Harry to do "Delilah." As I turn back to my song slips, perched in business card holders on my table, I discover *Engine #9* pulling in with a drink and a note: *Thought you might need this.* I turn to salute Hamster, beaming from the bar, and I bring the sweetness of rum and Coca-Cola to my lips as Tom Jones' horn section blows forth.

It's a pretty good crowd for a Sunday, thirteen singers, four full rounds. At the end of each round I allow myself a song, and then I ring this old sailing bell to signal another circuit. I can't even remember where I got that thing – but we are on a harbor, after all. At the end of the fourth round we're nearing one o'clock, so I finish with my usual, Marc Cohn's "True Companion" – simple chords, simple thoughts, a nice reflective tune to send everyone out into the night.

My songbooks magically appear, neatly stacked, on my table (usually the work of Harry Baritone, if he isn't fondling some young chickie), and all I have to do is pull on my dust covers and nudge my speakers against the wall. I'm a lucky girl. Most of my fellow KJs have to lug their stuff around to two or three bars a week. Me, it's all Karz Bar, four nights a week. I am blessed. That's what I tell myself on Sunday nights, when it all begins to hit home. I am blessed.

I'm not crazy, however, so I lug all one thousand CDs to my truck, in three large metallic cases. CDs are a KJ's lifeblood, and a ten-thousand-plus songlist is nothing to sneeze at. Multiply that one thousand by fifteen bucks, and you've got enough for a new car.

I lean back in to give Hamster the high sign – he's whipping chairs onto tabletops like a short-order cook flipping pancakes – then I take my weekly stroll down Harborview Drive. I turn at Jerisich Dock, past the bronze statue of Samuel Jerisich, catcher of fish, marrier of native women, founder of Gig Harbor. What was a Serbian boy doing here, halfway around the world?

The thing I especially like about Jerisich the Bronze is that he's tossing a real net, tied down at strategic locales, replaced on an annual basis. In a more frivolous town, this would be an open invitation for buffoonery – I picture spiderwebs for Halloween, ensnared effigies of rival football players for homecoming. But the youth of Gig Harbor are not fishers of fun – they are fishers of SAT scores and university admissions. Princeton. Pepperdine. Purdue.

I stand beneath Samuel's determined stare and feel a coward - retreater from the frontier, refugee from my native Alaska. I lift the loose corner of his net and bring it to my lips. This is corny (and a little unsanitary), but Jerisich protects me from ghosts, and I am grateful.

I slide down the walkway to the long, narrow public dock, shiny new, lit with knee-high theater lamps like a high-fashion catwalk. A single small yacht, the *Auntie Maim*, is tied up midway, hailing from Ballard, forty miles north. It might be Peg and Bill, the uninspired fortysomethings who signed up for nothing but Eagles songs and doubled their crime by drinking nothing but tequila sunrises. They'd be just the type to live in Ballard.

Forty strides later, I reach my retreat, a dock-ending square with two wooden benches. During the day, you might see a family here – or a spouse, a girlfriend, a cousin – waiting for their true companion to return from the sea. It gets me, sometimes. Tonight, the water is black as crude oil, the dock lights stringing out cotton candy trails of red, yellow and white. I spend much of my time in blackness, and it's not all that bad – even comfortable, if you resign yourself to it. Someday when I'm ready, I'll grab onto those colored strings and yank myself out – but not yet, not now. I watch the darkness with steady eyes; the lapping of the water tickles my skin, the tender chink of metal as the boats jostle their moorings, thoroughbreds anxious for the starting bell. A truck whirrs into second gear, downshifting the incline of Pioneer Street.

When I have wrapped the dark around my shoulders, I reach for the inside pocket of my leather jacket and pull out a pack of Swisher Sweets cigarillos, the little ones with the wooden tips. I clamp one between my teeth, always a little surprised at the cherry-flavored coating, and light it up. I hold it in for a second, then I open my jaws and let the smoke find its way. It hovers in a scrum over the dock light, then lifts one finger after another into the blue-black ceiling.

Swisher Sweets. Super Sonic. The world is ripe with esses, full of steam, escaping in a hiss, and Sunday night the only time I peek beneath the curtains and chew the sadness in its raw form. The blackness wells up inside; I coach myself to breathe between the puffs. In, out, there you go, just like that.

Something landward begins to flash. The crosswalk across Harborview has yellow blinkers half-embedded in the asphalt. When you press the Walk button and those lights go off, it makes you feel like royalty. I do it sometimes even when I don't need to cross. Then I wait a minute and come back the other direction. This time it's a man, not too tall, clean lines. I can tell from his gait – light-footed, graceful – that it's Kevin the Cop. Did he press the Walk button at two in the morning because he's a cop, or because he, too, enjoys its Vegas dazzle? Three puffs later, he arrives at my little island.

"Hi Kevin."

"Hi Channy. Can a cop get a smoke?"

"Sorry, sailor. Last one." I hate to lie to a guardian angel, but you do what you gotta.

He joins me on the bench and sniffs the air. "Is that a cigar?"

"Cigarillo. That's why I smoke 'em out here." More lies. One step closer to hell.

"Hope I didn't make too much of a ruckus tonight. I hate to pull that off-duty-cop shit."

I laugh, little walk-lights tickling my head. "Are you kidding me? I've been *dying* for someone to take care of that guy. I wish he'd get off whatever he's on."

Kevin slaps the side of the bench. "There's your big surprise. Judging by those superhuman moves he was throwin' at me, I was guessin' PCP. Turns out Super is a bona fide schizo."

"No shit!"

"Yep. They took him off to Steilacoom for observation. You shall probably not see him hence."

"I won't miss him a bit."

"It's all for the best. I see too many wack jobs wandering the streets when they should be getting help somewhere. It's also kind of refreshing to run into a case where the chemicals are internally produced."

It occurs to me that cops probably care more about these problem children than we do – simply because they spend more time with them. I give Kevin a pat on the knee.

"You're a good man, Kevin. One hell of a professional wrestler, too."

He looks at me, but he doesn't smile like I expect him to. Uh-oh. I've gone too far.

"You know, Channy, if you wouldn't mind, I'd love to..."

"Kev. I'm sorry. You know how much I like you, and how much I enjoy having you at karaoke. But I've seen too many K-bars turn into seething pits of gossip, and Karz is the best place I've ever worked. I can't be seen anywhere outside the bar with a regular."

"What about right now?"

"*This* has an explanation. We had trouble tonight, you took care of it – you came by to tell me how it turned out."

He cocks his head and considers it. I mean, really considers it. He's such a sweet boy. "I'm sorry," he says. "I guess I knew that. But we all adore you, Channy."

I am immensely grateful that he has chosen the words *we all* instead of *I*. Otherwise, I would now be doing an extremely chilly Australian crawl across the harbor.

"Thanks, Kevin. And thanks again for tonight. Come talk to me anytime at the bar, okay? I'd really like that."

I'm overdoing it again. *Shut up! Shut. Up.*

"Okay," he says, and stands up. "Well, I think I'll get out while I'm behind. See you Thursday, Channy."

"Good night, Kevin."

He traverses the catwalk, much slower this time, hits the button and splits the magic flashers. My black, black heart swells in his direction. I'm not ready for cotton candy trails, and "True Companion" is a memory, not a wish.

Besides, he's a hero. I don't do heroes.

You can imagine how KJs are plagued by the Great American Songbook. The next morning, as I dangle my legs off the edge of my back deck, overlooking the Carr Inlet, my internal CD changer clicks automatically to "Dock of the Bay." I'm soon into that whistling solo that my singers are chicken to try – and whistling guarantees the end of my solitude. The blackberry vines give out a rustle, and out from his tunnel pops Java, world's tallest standard poodle. He lopes my way on basketball player limbs, and I put him through the standard drill.

"Sit Java! Okay. This hand. Now the other."

He sits and whacks my palm with either paw. It's a poor imitation of a proper handshake, but this is the only trick he's got. I grab a hank of his coffee-colored dreadlocks and reach down to thump his ribcage like a ripe melon. Then I go for the look.

"Listen carefully, Java. If someone – say, a poodle – wanted to describe the mass of an object, what unit of measure would they use?"

He peers down his long snout, but refuses to take the bait.

"Why a newton, silly! Now, a lot of people think the newton was named after Isaac Newton, but I happen to know it was Wayne Newton. You know, 'Danke Schoen'?"

I sing a few bars, but still, nothing.

"He also invented the fig newton."

Ah, that did it. Java cocks his head to the right like he's actually, humanly puzzled. I'm sure it's a trick of evolution – a hundred canine generations figuring out that humans dig the tilted head thing – but I wouldn't trade the illusion for the world.

"Good Java!" I yank his moptop, and he gives me that slightly fierce V-shaped grin.

Another rustling comes from the human entrance, a trellised archway covered in passionflowers. It's Floy Craig, and naturally she's got baked goods, a plateful of apple turnovers.

"Floy!" I complain. "How am I supposed to keep this weight off if you keep tempting me?"

"Ha!" says Floy. "'This weight,' she says. I am surrounded by skinny people who don't realize they're skinny."

This is all ritual, of course. If Floy opened a bakery, I would be first in line. But female custom demands protestation before piggery.

All the interaction gets Java barking, a lyric "woof!" that sounds exactly like Lassie.

"Now Java," says Floy. "Don't even start. This is not your carbohydrate of choice. So cliché," she tells me. "A poodle who loves French B-R-E-A-D."

"Come on up," I tell her. "Dangle your legs off my deck. I'll get you some tea."

"That's a deal." She engages the steps as I head inside for a mug.

Everybody needs a guardian presence in their life, and the Craigs are certainly mine. John's a retired Navy pilot out of Whidbey Island who retains his military discipline, fighting off Floy's baking with daily commutes to the Navy gym at Bremerton. He's in ridiculously good shape. Floy works as a maternity nurse and is, by any standard, the first person you want your kid to see on her entrance into the world. She's got curly gray-blonde hair that thickens and thins with the weather, and an animated face forever touched with pink, as if she's been out sailing. I return to the deck and hand her a Ruby Mist.

"Thanks, Channy. You're a doll."

"That's what they tell me."

"Oh! Another suitor?"

"Yeah. One of my regulars. Great guy, but I do have my rules."

"That's very smart of you. We've had some affairs at the hospital, and believe me – you may as well make a video and put it on the Internet. Still, it must be nice, surrounded by all those handsome crooners."

That gets me laughing. "Most of them are just handsome drunks. But I guess they make a decent substitute."

She flashes her pale blues in a thoughtful way. "Substitute for what?"

"Well, I, you know..." There is no way in hell I'm finishing this sentence.

She takes a long sip, giving my embarrassment time to vaporize. That's one thing I love about Floy: she plays fair. Not that she's letting me go scot-free.

"Well, Channy. You know John and I love having you here, but sometimes I feel like we're hiding this great, beautiful secret from the world. And we worry about you. Especially..."

"Especially" is a word containing far too many newtons to leave dangling in the air, but Java is unhappy with the way this conversation has left him out of the loop. He pries his snout under Floy's hand, demanding a head scratch.

"Well!" she says. "All right, sillydog. Um, well… the other night, Java started that nervous muttering of his…"

"I love that! He sounds like an old Jewish man."

"Well, yes," says Floy. "But then he worked into a howl, which he never does. So I went out on the balcony to check and, well… We try not to be nosy neighbors, Channy, but you *are* just below us, and I heard you moaning. It sounded painful – and believe me, I know pain. And then you let out sort of a half-scream, and I guess that's when you woke up."

"Oh." Now I'm really embarrassed. I hold my mug higher, hoping it'll hide my face.

"I'm sorry, Channy. We both understand that there's something you can't tell us about whatever it is that brought you our way. But if you're having nightmares… well, we're just concerned, is all. And you certainly don't have to tell *us* about it, but I do know some excellent counselors at the hospital."

Again, Floy knows when she's made her point, and when to let off the gas.

"By the way, a little fair warning: the little terrors will be by this afternoon."

"Joey's kids?"

"Yep."

"Thanks. I'll make my usual foster aunt appearance, and then I'll do a little boating."

"Good plan."

Floy's like me – she loves the grandkids, but she also knows her limits. And today, mine are pretty low.

I take a back trail to the waterline, carrying visions of Kylie and Jo-Jo in their Cubs outfits (a family affliction). My visits to the boat shed became so regular last year that I concocted a deal – sort of my own season pass – with Manny, the teenage ranger. When I enter, he's outfitting a couple of twelve-year-olds, so I nab a paddle and life jacket and head for the dock. My regular vessel is Blue Pistol, a sporty fiberglass number small enough for single-pilot navigation. I paddle backwards, swing around with a right-hand stop and head out. Halfway across the inlet I gaze into the clear water and find thousands of sand dollars, fuzzy purple Frisbees scattered along the blue-green stones. What they're doing here, I have no idea, but then I could say the same about myself.

Two years ago, a young woman sails out of her shock across the Tacoma Narrows Bridge, drives into Gig Harbor and finds a bakery called Susanne's. Settling at the back table with green tea and a lemon scone, she looks across the harbor and discovers a bald eagle, sailing on enormous wings, his spiky white head slicing through the evergreen background. On a nearby bulletin board she finds two ads: an apartment on the Carr Inlet, a bar looking for a KJ, and she knows that she is part-way home.

Three

I interviewed with Hamster the same day I spotted that ad on the bulletin board at Susanne's. We got past the business part in ten minutes, and then I got his life story. Not as bad as it sounds; Hamster's storytelling carries a pace that any Hollywood filmmaker would envy.

He grew up on the Texas panhandle and developed a profound fascination with trains. But a black man in a small town had to take any opportunity he got, so he took a job busing tables at his uncle's saloon. Within a year, he was behind the bar, serving drinks.

"But *that* is where I got my break," he said. "Bartending is a gateway job – you can do it almost anywhere, and it's always in demand. A couple years later, when my cousin Gerald moved to Dallas, I went with him, with one goal in mind: to tend bar on a big cross-country train."

He worked the southern line for ten years, running to one coast and then the other. The West Coast won out. He transferred to Los Angeles so he could work the Coast Starlight, an Amtrak line from LA to Seattle.

"The money was excellent," he said. "But that was the least of it. Being the bartender got me into late-night conversations with white businessmen – conversations that your average black man was not privy to. Place a man in a trainbound isolation, provide a steady flow of liquor, and you'd be surprised how much financial information comes out. Privileged information. So I started sending my tip money to Wall Street."

Approaching fifty, Hamster had quietly become richer than most of his customers, and began to study alternatives to his ever-mobile occupation. This time, the battle was between north and south – and the north was winning.

"Texas panhandle to Los Angeles," he said. "I had suffered enough heat for three lifetimes. In winter, I would step off the train in Klamath Falls, Oregon, and that cold air would cut right through me. It was thrilling. I wanted more."

Once he earned his pension, Hamster packed up his things and headed for Seattle. On his way there, however, he was sidetracked by an old curiosity.

"Almost ten miles north of Olympia," he said, "the track enters into a dramatic squeeze. On the right, you've got these forested cliffs – a glacial cut from the Ice Age. On the left, there's the Puget Sound, so close you could hook a salmon out the window. And just when you feel like you're on the edge of a vast wilderness, here comes the Tacoma Narrows Bridge. It's a classic two-tower suspension, a cable draped over them like a loopy M. The tracks go directly underneath, crossing at a perpendicular. It's a dramatic perspective, and I always wondered what was on the other side. It looked so dark and green and lovely."

On his post-retirement drive, Hamster headed west off I-5 and finally crossed the bridge, spotting a long freight on the tracks below. He turned off as soon as he reached the other side and immediately got lost, following whatever bits of water he could sight through the evergreens. This took him, eventually, to a wide, beautiful harbor, and a sign that said *Restaurant For Sale.*

At this point in the story, Hamster let out a broad grin. "It was all so perfect. I halfway expected that sign to start talking to me."

At the far end of a year-long renovation that depleted most of his savings and taught him more about building codes than he ever cared to know, Hamster paid a visit to the local model train society and hired two of their best craftsmen. These were Mack and Heath – both of them retirees from the Army Corps of Engineers – and they spent the next three months building the tracks that loop the interior, delivering drinks via HO-gauge locomotives. The trains exit the bar through a scale model of Mt. Rainier, suspiciously similar to those produced by the Army Corps of Engineers.

Hamster is one of the few owners I've seen who insists on tending bar himself. This might be because he's the only one who can operate the complex track system without causing three-martini pileups. More likely, it's because his presence is good for business. He exudes a lean, elegant bearing that has fueled more than a few Nat King Cole fantasies among his older female patrons.

Walking me to the door after that first interview, Hamster asked me for a suggestion.

"About what?" I asked.

"About anything. I became a successful man by knowing how to cultivate advice. So any time I meet someone who appears to have a head on their shoulders, I ask them for a thought. So, young lady – what do you have?"

"Well, I don't..." I began, and immediately interrupted myself. "No. Actually, I do. Do your trains have names?"

"Not really. 'Santa Fe,' 'Union Pacific.'"

"Well, since you are now going to be a karaoke bar, name them after songs. Like 'Engine Number Nine.'"

Hamster snapped his fingers. "Roger Miller."

"Bingo."

He unleashed that smile again. *Definitely* Nat King Cole. "And that," he said, "is why I ask for advice."

Oh, and the name? Hamster? I have no freakin' idea.

The *City of New Orleans* pulls in as I'm doing my sound check, hauling a Seven-and-Seven. I don't know how I got on this high school booze-and-soda thing, but it's thoughtful of Hamster to make them extra weak so I don't get loopy.

"Harry, are you ready to kick us off?"

Harry is my prize pupil. He's a high baritone, with a ballsy lower edge that you just can't teach. (One night when he sang "It's Not Unusual," a pair of panties somehow ended up at his feet, though no one ever confessed to the deed.) The only item in his debit column is an absolute lack of adventure. Here we are, three paying customers in the joint, and still he's doing "Suspicious Minds," one of his twelve tried-and-trues. I'd bet he sings the same twelve in the shower.

About a year ago, I borrowed a recording system from a friend and we turned Thursday into Studio Night. Slip the KJ a five, walk away with a live cut of yourself on a CD. Harry refused to go anywhere near it. The idea of setting down something permanent just petrified him. One night his girlfriend, a hyper, sexy number named Sheila, slipped me a five and a wink. I thought for sure that Harry would find us out, but I managed to fake some technical difficulty as I lined up the levels, and four minutes later we had a note-perfect cut. When I called him back and handed over the CD, he broke into a flop sweat – *after the fact*. I'll never fully understand the effects that singing in public can have on people.

Harry and Sheila didn't last. Sheila was an attention whore, and dating a guy who gets panties thrown at him wasn't cutting it. The breakup was ugly, and Harry had a bad reaction, lying in wait for college girls with father issues and snapping them up like a Mars flytrap. There's a steady supply from across the Narrows (University of Puget Sound, Pacific Lutheran), and Harry is pretty powerful bait. He drives a tow truck, which has the triple effect of keeping him fit, supplying him with interesting stories, and endowing him with a white-knight aura. That and the manly beard, the surprisingly soft blue eyes.

Okay. I'm giving myself away. But I've seen too many of Harry's shenanigans to answer *that* doorbell. And I'll give him credit – he hasn't been ringin'. Karaoke is therapy for many a mid-life crisis, and Harry knows better than to get involved with the psychiatrist. He's happy to tip me excessively and collect all my books at closing time. A girl could do worse.

I note that Kevin's not here, which makes me nervous. I don't want Sunday's offer and turndown to be an issue. I don't want *anything* to be an issue. I got enough issues for a lifetime, bruddah.

Harry hits the big finish, receives a three-person ovation and makes way for Caroleen. She is nearing sixty, pleasantly gray and doughy, the way women used to age before we all got obsessed.

When she first took the mic, a year ago, I thought the poor thing would have a heart attack. She had not the least idea of rhythm and tone, just sort of mumbled the words as they changed color on the lyric screen. I thought I'd never see her again, but she returned the next three nights, and each night she sang the same song: "Mama, He's Crazy" by the Judds. A year later, she's still singing it.

I know what you want to hear: that Caroleen has learned how to sing that one song beautifully. Sadly, no. She still sounds like a rusty gate – but a rusty gate that no longer mumbles. I think that's all she really wanted, to tell people that yes, I go to this karaoke bar in Gig Harbor and I stand up in front of people and I *sing.*

Three months ago, Caroleen ordered up "Hit Me With Your Best Shot" by Pat Benatar, and I nearly fainted. Not just because it wasn't "Mama, He's Crazy" or because it was so against type, but because it holds a special place in karaoke phenomenology as the Most Frequently Butchered Female Song. The male equivalent is "Brown-Eyed Girl" by Van Morrison, and in a real bass-ackwards way this is the highest of compliments. What Benatar and Morrison managed to do was to take difficult songs and make them seem easy – leading many a neophyte to think, "Oh, I can sing *that!*" I get a deeply guilty pleasure from this, and I work hard not to snicker as I call them to the mic.

Perhaps Caroleen understands this, because she insists that I sing along. Sometimes I give her a subtle nudge, backing off from the mic a half inch at a time, but I swear at exactly two-and-a-half inches she gets this look of vertigo panic and I have to dive back in.

It's looking like a pretty routine Thursday. Shari Blues arrives to rip her way through a Bonnie Raitt tune (Shari is so *Janis* sometimes it scares me). Alex reels in with Sofia, a long-limbed Italian lady from tango class (the boy does know how to work it). But then, about ten o'clock, we're interrupted by a bachelorette party, nine twentysomething chickies who ride in on a wave of giggles. This presents a slew of dissatisfactions for the regulars, but some serious monetary benefits for Hamster's till and Channy's tip jar.

The thing about this randy nonet – or for that matter, any sizable group of karaoke turista chicas – is that they're here strictly for each other. They will sing horribly. They will giggle uncontrollably at the phallic possibilities of the microphone. They will sing four at a time, and no one will be close enough to the mic to be heard. When the girl who did high school musicals crawls her way through "Hopelessly Devoted to You," they will scream and hoot as if they have just witnessed the second coming of Patti Lupone. Directly after, as Shari Blues is snaking her way through "White Rabbit" like the second coming of Grace Slick, they will chatter amongst themselves like mad raucous chipmunks until they work up to those awful Girls Gone Wild glissandos. Lastly, after they have consumed mass quantities of Hamster's liquid assets, they will declare eminent domain on the stage and rub their bodily parts along each male performer until they have reduced his singing to mere sideshow.

Not that the guys seem to mind – like Harry, who finds himself at the center of a five-woman Bob Fosse choreography during "Delilah." Kevin shows up soon after, and you can just imagine the Carnaval reception afforded his "Suavamente." (The KJ offers secret thanks, but suffers a surge of irrational jealousy when the bride-to-be flashes her impressive breasts.)

Once the hubbub dies down (the flasher gone to the women's room to puke her guts out), I'm on to my next song slip, which reads *Amber.* The song is "Little Girl Blue," Rodgers and Hart, a tricky arrangement purloined from Nina Simone. Nina would play a spare, flowing "Good King Wenceslas" on the piano, then gather it into chords and reveal the way they matched up to the old jazz tune by singing the words on long, slow lines. I don't even know what it's doing on a karaoke disc. Karaoke's supposed to be easy.

It's hard to believe I didn't spot Amber before. She's a pageboy redhead, like something from the forties, wearing slinky silk pants of mustard yellow. The top is white cashmere, flecked with threads of gold and copper, a neckline just low enough for intrigue. Her name is in her jewelry, a chunky necklace of amber, dangly oval earrings of same. The face is a little hard to catch through all the glitz, but certain features stand out: plump cheeks, cushioned lips in a natural vee over perfect, showy teeth – she could kill you if she smiled. The eyes are round – liquid turquoise – the nose wide, with a playful lift at the tip. She has a stage face, and apparently she's here to use it.

She slides a stool to the lyric screen and pulls the corded mic from the stand. (I can read these details like a gypsy reads tea leaves: freehand means you're a performer; corded means you're old-fashioned, a traditionalist.) She looks my way, expecting the music. I take a step to tell her but she waves me off.

"Wenceslas," she says, flatly. "I know. Thanks."

So I press play, and here's another clue. To the average singer, I would say, You've got a long intro with no clear point of entry. Your best bet is to wait till the first lyric turns color, then swing a late entry (hell, Sinatra made a whole *career* swinging late entries). But Amber's got her eyes closed, and she comes in perfectly.

The song is about torment, and crushing loneliness. The singer is talking about Little Girl Blue, but really about herself. And then, the neatest trick of all – to reveal searing anguish in quiet, half-whispered lines of music, and to do so in a bar filled with horny, drunk bachelorettes and the middle-aged men who lust after them. It's a tremendous act of faith, and it's working. The flashy outfit has the boys' attentions, anyway, but now the girls are listening, too. A bridesmaid shushes her friend: "Listen! She's really good."

By the ending verse, the bar is a wall of anxious silence. Amber is inhabiting the song, eyes still shut, and, you would swear, on the verge of crying. She lets her last note die of its own accord, leaving a fragile void of sound hanging in the air. Harry breaks it with a throaty "Yeah!" and opens the door for everyone else. One of the bachelorettes is weeping.

"That's Amber!" I say. Amber unleashes half of that smile, and replaces the mic on the stand. The next song is "Drift Away," so I duck under the soundboard to dig out microphones. When I look up, the front door is clicking shut, a mustard cloud drifting up the stairs.

Harry leans over during the intro, one eye on the parking lot, and says, "What the hell was that?"

Four

I'm too damn nice. I am the Good Samaritan, tractored by circumstance. But that's a copout, and we all know it. What I lack is intestinal fortitude, an appetite for conflict. *Huevos.* (Can women have huevos?)

Wild Birds Unlimited sits way back between two old buildings on Harborview. The old brick walls shadow a lawn scattered with rockers and benches, birdbaths and topiary. As a late-night worker, it takes me till noon to catch the flow of the general populace, and in this case I wasn't quite there yet. I stood before a propeller, transfixed by spiraling ribbons, sipping an herbal tea. Any reasonable person would've guessed I was high.

A crow floated by, drawing my vision to the left, and I landed on a swath of wide-ribbed corduroy, color of ketchup. In the passage of five seconds I realized that these were pants, worn by a woman on the porch above me, and that this woman had the finest ass I had ever seen – shape of an upside-down heart, endowed with recipes of line and circle known only to Michelangelo and a single family of Greek mathematicians. My Inner Lesbian understood, for a moment, how it is that the female body is capable of driving men to literal, clinical madness. I wanted to slither between those railings, a momentary python, and press my cheek to those luscious red apples.

She shifted to one side; the apples winked at me. From this one gluteus movement, I could extrapolate a dozen others above the railing. She wraps her right arm across her abdomen, supporting her left elbow. Her left hand cups her chin, three fingers folded at the knuckle, index finger tapping out thoughts beneath the left side of her left eye. She is window shopping, studying an object of desire. I peeked at the storefront window to confirm, and found myself looking at Sheila.

"Channy?" she said. "Is that you?"

I wanted to say "No," but she flew down the stairs and assaulted me with a hug.

"Channy! Oh my Gawd! It's so good to see you. God, I *so* miss my karaoke fixes. I'm up in Redmond now, and it's such a drive – but I had the day off, so I thought, what the hell. And here you are! Is this kizmet or what?"

"Yes," I said. I was still trying to get over lusting at her derriere. All sorts of unwelcome cinematography.

She came closer, meaning to evoke confidentiality. "Do you think it would be okay if I came by tonight? I mean, assuming you're still at Karz – you are, aren't you? And, you know, I mean... if you think Harry would be okay with it."

I'm not hosting anymore. Harry would be really uncomfortable if you showed up. You're a conniving little bitch, and if I hear you sing that fucking song again I will have to stuff those goddamn boots down your throat.

Blink. Blink.

"Sure. That would be terrific. I'm sure everybody would love to see you."

She attacked me with another hug. Yikes.

"That's fantastic! God, I can't wait to see the old place. Well listen, I gotta meet someone at the Tides for lunch, but we'll catch up tonight, okay?"

She squeezed me on the elbow and shifted all that jitterbug energy down the garden path, rolling a Minnie Mouse finger-wave as she rounded the corner. I held up a limp hand.

Yeah, the girl's got a nice ass. Perhaps someday I'll have a chance to kick it.

Which leaves me standing here, looking up that familiar disc as Shari Blues masticates a Stevie Ray tune (this is my only complaint about Shari: she needs to occasionally sing something as if her life *doesn't* depend on it).

I do not, as a rule, dislike "These Boots Were Made for Walkin'." In fact, I like it quite a lot. With its low range and half-spoken lines, it's a great beginner piece, and its vengeful, kiss-my-ass lyrics carry a special appeal for the bitterly divorced female market (the one that keeps karaoke bars in business). But Sheila ruined it for me, by singing it night after night, and then ruthlessly acting it out, leaving my favorite singer in its wake.

At the moment, I'm not even sure where she is. She came in early to sign up, swore me to secrecy, and went off to hide in some corner booth. I put in a mental order for Harry to arrive with the waitstaff from the local Hooters, but no such luck; he waltzed in stag, a half hour after Sheila. I've been too busy with microphone batteries and needy singers to send him a warning. What's worse, it's really busy, which means that Little Miss Bitch will have a huge audience.

The moment is here – the fifth singer on my list. I am condemned by the KJ code to shoot down one of my best friends. I hate this job.

"All right. We've got a little surprise for you. Would you please welcome our next singer: Nancy!"

I start the disc, per instructions, and Sheila vamps across the dance floor. I recognize the outfit immediately. It's the very getup from Nancy Sinatra's album cover: the ribbed black-and-gray hose, the tight gray sweater, the blood-red go-go boots and miniskirt. She whips the microphone from the stand, right on time, and punches the first line. I remember why the song is such a good match. Sheila's voice is no prizewinner, but the girl can act – and that's what the song is about. I can't see Harry, but I know where he is – sitting in a booth with Shari and Caroleen – and that's precisely where Sheila is aiming her words.

I'm trying to stay cool, but I'm also wondering, What is the fucking message here? *I dumped your sorry ass, and now I've come back to pound my go-go boots into your testicles?*

There are women, I know, who are capable of carrying their spite this far. Who are bent on destruction. But *this* is vulgar, and I'm pissed. I need to do something to save Harry, but nothing that makes it look like he *needs* saving. I'm running my hands along the gain levels (Sheila's close enough to swallow the mic – insert your own joke here), when I spot my team of second-hand mics, lined up in an old wine box.

The horns kick into their groovy finish – sounding all the world like a surf band – and Sheila does the Pony all the way across the floor. Those who don't know any better give a rousing applause; those who do give a polite golf-clap. I try to lend a gracious commentary as I polish the plan in my head.

"That is Nancy! Also known as Sheila, to you Karz Bar veterans. And you know what this means. From now on, I will expect thematic attire from everyone. Dark glasses for Roy Orbison songs. A Burmese python for Alice Cooper. Miscolored eyeballs for Marilyn Manson. But seriously, I don't know how late Sheila will be here tonight, so I wanted her to see one of our new traditions. Harry, get up here and lead us."

Harry heads across, looking like a high wind has blown out most of his brain cells. But the music seems to kick him into focus. He gears into the first verse of "Drift Away" as I dole out mics to the Korale. I flip on all my tracks, and the singalong chorus comes off with nary a hitch.

During the second verse, however, something unexpected. People are coming to join us who don't usually sing: talky barfly Bob, Alex and his latest Ginger Rogers, a sultry Irish redhead – and, unless I'm hallucinating, Hamster, who has never shown the least interest in singing. This motivates a second wave, folks who have no idea what's going on but can't resist the gravitational pull: a yachtload of Norwegians from Port Angeles, a trio of seminarring lawyers from Seattle, and some guy who was just delivering a load of Budweisers. Just guessing, I'd say we've got forty singers. It's like a a rerun of "We Are the World."

Come the repeat, Harry's in top form, throwing a Tom Jones ripple, busting a porkchop growl at the lower end. I am mighty proud. As we near the fadeout, I snatch a conductor's baton from my prop box and race out in front to pull us into the final chord. There's really no audience left, so we content ourselves with hoots and backslaps as we migrate back to our places. Harry's getting high fives all around, working the crowd like a politician. A minute later, I'm finally back at my station, throwing switches, harvesting microphones, getting back to business.

"Wow! Was that a trip, or was that a trip? I..."

I can usually talk my way through anything – but not the ghost of Nancy Sinatra, standing on my dance floor, streams of mascara tracking either cheek. She holds her arms out to her sides like a condemned woman pleading with her captors. I assume that it's me – that she's read the bitchslap intentions behind my little show – but then I see Harry, still on stage, frozen by the sight of her.

I'm feeling the need to break up this little melodrama, but I know what the next song is, and it's killing me. Still, I have to do *something*, so I return to the mic and speak in a half-voice: "Doc? It's your turn."

Doc Mendelssohn comes to the mic, nudging his way past Harry, who still doesn't know what to do. The music begins. Nancy raises her arms, beckoning Harry forward, and forward he comes. They begin to dance, cutting slow circles in the half-light as Doc sings "I Can't Stop Lovin' You." Alex brings out his redhead, perhaps to siphon off some of Harry's embarrassment, but it doesn't matter, because a second later he and Sheila cross the floor, stop at Sheila's table to collect her purse, and slip out the back door.

A minute later, as Doc takes his applause from a distracted audience, the *Chattanooga Choo-Choo* pulls in with a ginger ale and vodka. Hamster's note reads, *You know I'm not one to traffic in gossip, but I'm dying to know what just happened.*

Despite a late-morning drizzle, I am out on the back deck with Java and a cup of same. We're playing fetch, but with Java it's never that simple. He fancies himself a wide receiver, and is ruthlessly devoted to the offsides rule, refusing to leave my side until the "ball" (a bone-shaped pillow) has departed the quarterback's hand. This leaves me with two options: lift a lame popup, giving him a chance to run beneath it; or give him the classic pump-fake, wait till he runs ten feet and looks back, then loft a pass further downfield. The latter is much more satisfying, much more *You, too, can be Peyton Manning.*

Sadly, he only buys this trick a handful of times. Then he stays there on his haunches, giving me a look that says, *Come on! I'm a poodle, remember? I'm not that dumb.* So now I'm standing, hoping to add some leverage to my popups, while my coffee sits on a statue of Artemis, going cold. From this new vantage, I can see the distinct track that Java has burned into my lawn. Perhaps I spend too much time at this.

I reach way back for a good, high throw, but I louse up the release, sending the bone pillow too far. I fear that Java will end up in the brambles, but instead he veers right and bullets the passionflower archway, barking like crazy. I can swear I hear another dog barking back – and I'm close. Harry Baritone steps up the trail, Java leaping at him with joyous abandon. Once they clear the archway, Harry grabs him around the chest, leaving his head and front legs squirting out the other side of Harry's looped arms.

"I remember this one," he says. "*Loves* to wrassle." He lets Java go and thumps him on the back. "Macho poodle." Java's all worked up now, panting in a half-growl, but Harry grabs his collar and smooths his mop-top. "There now, Mister LeBark. Settle down. Mom and Harry need to talk."

I'm suddenly self-conscious, hoping my lounging clothes don't look as grubby as they feel. "Wow, Harry. So weird, seeing you out of context. Um… want some coffee?"

"Yeah. That would be great."

"Have a seat. I mean, an edge of the deck. Dangle your feet."

I cheat my grubbiness by trading my sweatshirt for a clean windbreaker. I return to find Harry and Java playing tug-of-war with the bone pillow.

"This dog is tenacious."

"Yep. And if you like your coffee warm, you'll just have to give up."

Harry looses his grip. Java takes his pillow to the lawn for a light-but-thorough chewing.

"I hope I'm not being invasive," says Harry. "But I had an hour's break – and I remembered your house from that tow I gave you last spring."

"No, not at all. I was just easing into my morning lollygag."

"I hate to butt in on people. But I thought I owed you an explanation."

My own response surprises me: "Why?"

"Well, because it was nice, what you were trying to do for me. And I'm assuming it turned out a little differently than you expected."

"*Oh* yeah."

"But here's why. And you're a singer, so I think you'll understand this. If you take 'Boots' literally, it looked like Sheila was rubbing it in my face – especially the way she was putting the goods on display with that getup. But what you don't know is this: the first time I ever *saw* Sheila – in a Mexican restaurant in Tacoma – she was singing 'Boots.' And she sang it every single time we went out for karaoke."

"I know."

"Well, look at it this way. 'Mack the Knife' – song about a homicidal thief, right? But how much you wanna bet that some couple, somewhere, thinks of it as 'their song'?"

"So Sheila's message wasn't 'Fuck you...'"

"It was 'Fuck me.' Less crudely, it was 'I miss you and I'm lonely.'"

I'm feeling overexposed and awkward, so I get up and practice some evasive pacing. Harry's not letting me; he stands to join me, forcing me to stop.

"Look. I've already told you too much. But what you did last night... it was the nicest damn thing anyone's ever done for me, and I didn't want you to think I was ungrateful. In fact, this morning, when Sheila started spinning all this shit about us getting back together, it was *you* who gave me the power to say no."

I turn, and he's smiling. With his blue service shirt, he looks like one of those over-happy plumbers in a commercial for drain opener.

"Go Harry!" I say quietly.

He kisses me on the cheek; the whiskers tickle.

"I gotta go."

Harry bounds off the deck and through the archway, shouting over his shoulder.

"See you tonight!"

Java runs after, barking. I pick up Harry's coffee, barely touched, and give it a slow sip.

Five
Channy

My proscription of improper behavior barely made it out of Canada. Taking my first-ever step into the lower 48, the aura of adventure lit me up like a Roman candle. We booked a motel in Bellingham, Washington, and I just plain jumped him.

This I was used to. I had made a high school career of being the aggressor, the stealth riot grrrl. But this time, the boy aggressed right back. The meeting of two such electric forces sent me to places I didn't know existed. Animal places. It was true: sex in the contiguous United States was much better.

At the denouement of our third mutual assault, I found myself in a position better suited to Cirque de Soleil, not certain which limbs were mine. When I located Harvey's face somewhere near my left foot, we both burst out laughing, which caused intense pain in my left elbow. It was true: sex was better with Boys Who Got Laid.

The next morning, I drove us toward Seattle, enjoying all the little scratches and bruises that tickled when I moved. As we approached the center of town, I thought there must be some mistake – I-5 was headed directly into a huddle of skyscrapers. What a trip when it shot beneath them, a mile-long stretch ceilinged by a web of city streets and overpasses. I felt like a space probe digging into a concrete planet, and I kept having to merge left in order to keep going south. I was thinking, also, that I should wake Harvey, but when I looked over he was up, dark eyes reaching into the vista.

"Is this it?" I asked.

"No," he said. "*Way* too much. We need to do this 'civilization' thing a little bit at a time. Keep going."

"Are you going... the same place I'm going?"

He smiled and put a hand on my knee. "I guess so."

That was our big talk – and, as it turns out, the offramp to the rest of my life. Soon after came the tiny alchemies that turn sex into love. He started to call me *darlin* and *honey,* took my hand as we walked into a restaurant, rested an arm on my shoulder as I slipped a hand into his back pocket. Our momentum was building.

But first, we climbed a long hill, bore to the right, and discovered a luminescent presence.

"There," said Harvey. "Let's go there."

Such was our youth and alien status that we didn't know what this presence was. But we trusted in signs. Rolling past a roadside amusement park, we saw the words *Enchanted Parkway/Mt. Rainier* and exclaimed the last word in unison.

A half hour later, we were headed right for it, splitting a long, semi-peopled valley bracketed by high treepicket ridges. We were nearing the foot of one of these ridges when Harvey slapped the dash and said, "Hey! Pull over. Take this ramp."

I was looking forward to an explanation, but getting only directions. Left under the freeway. Left at the light. Left into a turnout. He got out and beckoned me to follow. I caught up to him at a tall wire fence and followed his gaze to the center of a wide pasture, where stood two haystacks with legs.

"Bessie and Ben," said Harvey.

"Bison?"

"Brown, boisterous bison. Bessie and Ben."

"You know their names?"

He took my hand and guided it, as you would a blind person's, to the sign against which we were leaning. The one that said, *Bessie and Ben Bison – Please Do Not Feed.*

Once we had enough of watching two bison who refused to move, I turned and saw another sign, *For Rent,* in front of a small clapboard house across the street.

"There," I said. "Let's go there."

Two days later, we were in. I yanked open the chimney flue and brought in some logs from a woodpile behind the house. As I wadded up pieces of newspaper and stuffed them under the grate, I spotted an article.

"Hey, honey!" I said (enjoying the sound of *honey* in my mouth).

He called from the next room: "What?!"

"We're on a mudflow!"

He peered around the corner. "What?"

"The last time the mountain collapsed, it left a mudflow that was thirty feet thick. And *we* are sitting right on top of it."

"Well thanks!" he said. "I feel much safer now."

"Says if we live here thirty years, there's a one-in-seven chance we'll be buried alive."

Soon after the word "alive," I found myself drifting over the earth. Piecing it together afterward, it appears that Harvey hit me with a flying tackle, wrapped his arms around my midsection, then spun himself beneath me so he could take the brunt of the impact. I landed on top of him and went about reinitiating my lungs to the concept of oxygen. Then I swatted him on the head.

"Are you nuts?!"

He spoke between snorts of laughter. "A demonstration... of the everpresent dangers... of living."

I straddled him and delivered a theatrical kiss. (Why was I rewarding bad behavior?)

"So when are you going to play for me?"

"Play what?"

"Guitar, silly."

"Guitar?" A cloud of puzzlement passed over his face. "Oh! Guitar!"

He rolled me to the floor (gently this time) and dashed into the bedroom, then returned with his guitar case. He opened it to reveal rubber-banded bundles of plastic cassettes, padded at the perimeters by rolled-up socks.

"Video games," he said. "I figured I would get the console once I settled someplace. But these... these are a major investment."

As much as I tried to hide it, I couldn't help feeling deceived. Harvey wasn't one of my nice nerd-boys at all – he had proved that much in Bellingham. And now he wasn't a musician. I pictured the molten vaults of magma miles beneath us, ready to break enormous chunks of Rainier and hurl them down the slope. Then I lit a match.

Six

The signals get too heavy. The circuits overload.

I'm descending the long pitch of Pioneer, a steady drizzle, eight o'clock. Exactly the time my first singer should be picking up the mic. The traffic on Highway 16 backed up like a sewer, splattering refuse into my path. The Narrows Bridge is a fragile conduit – one stalled Mini Cooper and you've got a parking lot all the way back to Bremerton. (I have always feared being the cog in this deviltry, the object of so much hatred. I spend each crossing holding my breath, casting prayers to the mystic regions beneath my hood.)

Nevertheless. Punctuality is the one absolute I demand of myself, and I have committed a sin against karaoke. In my frantic state, I become absolutely convinced that I have forgotten something. My brain, having turned into a shit-seeking missile, latches onto the worst of all possibilities: my CDs. If I have forgotten those, I may as well call it a night, because I would be forced to penetrate that 16 backup twice more. And I wouldn't get paid. And my rent is due.

I steal a glance at the cab space behind me, and there's the big silver case, swaddled in beach towels. Of *course* it's there. Would the third king forget the myrrh? I bring my eyes forward to find a pearl-white bumper rearing up at me like a Hitchcock quick-zoom: brass trim, multicolored magnetic ribbons, personalized Washington license plate with a red registration sticker.

The last thing I see is a pair of brake lights. I don't know when it is that I became a Hollywood stunt driver, but my extremities have taken over, fluxing into a ballet of navigational logic that simply should not be there. I tap the brakes, veer right as much as I dare, dodging the pearl-white bumper by three inches. My poor pickup is then forced to gallop the water-puddle ridges of the roadside, steamroll a couple of squat bushes and plunge into the Key Bank parking lot. When I spy level asphalt, I hit the brakes, bringing us to a skidding, hydroplaning halt.

For a half-minute, I am content to breathe heavily. Then I look around, and there's just no one. I'm out here performing feats of Nobel Prize-winning proportions, and not a single eyewitness. I peer to the left and find the pearl-white car, shape of a wing, as it rolls to the intersection and turns.

For a second, I can recall the letters on the license plate. Then I cough, and they're gone.

She enters the bar, plagued by shame (referring to herself in third person). When she apologizes to Hamster, he erupts in laughter.

"Ten minutes late, once every six months. What do you want me to do – send you to the principal's office? Besides…" he nods at the big-screen. "The Seahawks got the Sunday night game. I was going to ask you to wait, anyway."

She doesn't feel right, getting away with things. She retreats to the corner and lines up her song-slip holders with extra precision, soldiers in their ranks, hoping to atone for her pedestrian sins. (The words *atone* and *atonal* mix unexpectedly in her head.) The *Orange Blossom Special* chugs into her personal siding with a brown drink on ice. The note says, *Drink first, then read other side.*

The taste is purely awful. She flips the card.

Root beer and gin. What do you think?

She turns to the bar and forces herself to smile. Hamster gives a USO salute, then she takes a boisterous swig and chokes it down.

This, she thinks, *will be punishment enough.*

Punishment number two is low attendance. My only regulars are Harry, Shari and Caroleen, although they're sitting with a couple,

Mark and Sandra, who turn out to be good singers. Harry tells me they're dedicated karaokephiles, friends from Boise. Mark is partial to sixties rock: Doors, Who, Kinks. Sandra is entrenched in the sub-category of feminist disco: "I Will Survive," "She Works Hard for the Money," "Gloria."

We're speeding into round three, each of us pulling heavy duty, when I hear these words: "Wanna try suicide?"

It's Harry. His meaning escapes me.

"Well, since it's kinda slow," he continues, "we thought it would be fun to... You do know suicide, right?"

I've got nothing. Harry seems to read my silence as disapproval. He's fidgeting.

"Everybody puts a song into the hat, and you take one out, and you have to sing whatever you get."

"Oh," I say. "Yeah. Sure."

"Cool! You'll play too, right?"

"Yeah. Sure."

Mark's got a baseball cap, so we dump in the song slips and go by the order we've already established. Which means I'm first. I draw "Only the Lonely," one of my favorite songs and (thanks to Roy's supernatural pipes) directly in my range. Not very challenging, but amusement is right on my heels, as Harry pulls out "I Feel Like a Woman," by Shania Twain.

"Caroleen!" he complains. "This has your fingerprints all over it."

Caroleen confesses her guilt by giggling, but Harry hams it up nonetheless, playing the a capella hook as gayly as possible. Then it's Caroleen's turn: "It's Now or Never," which comes out more spoken than sung. I help her out by loaning her my Elvis sideburn sunglasses. Sandra pulls out her own song, so she has to put it back. She gets "My Sharona" instead, another guy song in a girl range, and does pretty well, especially with the jungle screams.

Mark seems *real* hesitant, and I think it's because he's done the math. The only slips remaining are his and Sandra's, so feminist disco it is: "What a Feelin'," from the movie *Flashdance*. He gets a little lost picking an octave – trying and failing with a Mickey Mouse falsetto – but for a Boise boy he certainly shakes that booty.

Sandra gets up at the instrumental break and threatens him with a glass of water, but the dangers of electrocution hold her back.

"Sha-ree," I say, tauntingly. "Only one slip leh-eft."

Shari takes a look at the slip and smiles. "No sweat."

She hands it to me. "All Along the Watchtower." My hand tightens up. Mark is leaning over the soundboard, holding a CD.

"I didn't see it in your book, but I had one in my personal stash. Track seven."

I take it, praying for Dylan, but the silver surface is etched with a 'fro and a buccaneer headband. Hendrix. I manage to center it on the changer, and bring up the track, but then I'm stuck. Shari looks up from the lyric screen, puzzled. The pearl-white bumper charges me like a rhino.

I step to the stage, take Shari's mic and pretend to inspect the battery as I speak sotto voce.

"Feminine difficulties. Need a bathroom break. Could you wait ten seconds, and then press play?"

"Sure, hon. I gotcha."

I hand her the mic and hurry off, afraid to look up lest I meet someone's eyes. When I get to the restroom, I head for a stall and start flushing. Jimi's guitar finds a seam in the rushing water, crackling through like a roadside bomb. So I flush with one hand, clap the other over my left ear, and press my right ear to the side of the tank. The car was a Thunderbird.

When I return, it's much too quiet, but perhaps this is a consequence of my ruse. The suicide gang is constructively ignoring me, replaying the cross-gender comedies of their little game. I'm stuck by the vision of Harry, my least adventurous singer, mimicking Shania Twain. What's gotten into everybody? I load up the Sheryl Crow that I was going to sing before, and I work through it carefully, tiptoeing the higher passages lest they trip a lever.

Singers talk about a "break" in the voice. This is where the point of production, the spot through which the tone resonates, switches from the throat to the sinal cavity (you'll hear the phrases "chest voice" and "head voice," but the former is more metaphorical than accurate). The break is a real trouble spot – a choral reef, difficult to navigate. A singer is likely to have a harder time with a melody that hovers along her break than one that operates a third or even a fifth above it.

But there's a second break point – an emotional break point. This one hovers near the top – the highest note you can sing without feeling undue stress on your throat. This places you in such a free, untethered stratosphere that it leaves you vulnerable, literally sticking your neck out. Given the right lilt, the right set of heartbreaking lyrics (thank you, Patsy Cline), the proper minor-chord progression, this note will yank a wire in your lachrymal glands, and there you are, Pagliacci, mid-aria. Singing is either speech emancipated or sobbing controlled.

Fortunately, "Every Day is a Winding Road" is no "Bridge Over Troubled Water," so I'm safe. Harry follows with "You Make Me So Very Happy," and we're back to a normal evening.

Two rounds later, still an hour from closing, we're joined by a band of 16th century villagers. I am back to my thin grasp on reality until I flash on a poster at Susanne's Bakery: the Renaissance Pleasure Faire, just over the hill at somebody's farm. Damsels with bubbly cleavage and raucous hairy men in pantaloons dive into my songbooks. This could be very good for my tip jar.

"Zounds!" I say. It's the only bit of archaic English I can muster. "What's going... on here, fellows? What... say you?"

A young man in hunting leathers and a Robin Hood cap is about to produce a snappy Shakespearean reply when he meets my eyes.

"Channy?"

I'm back at the wheel of my pickup. I ease myself to the mic, and when I speak I feel an odd vibration at the back of my throat.

"Hey, um... Since we've been fooling around tonight, and the, um, revelers need some time to pick out their songs, I've always wanted to try something. I'm going to put on "Miss American Pie," and I'd like my regulars to do the whole thing, one singer to a verse.

At eight minutes, 33 seconds, Don McLean's epic tune is the longest selection in the catalog, and I keep it in a special slot in my

CD case for just such an occasion. I slip it out, jam it on the changer and hit play. Harry's already there, ready for the first verse.

I hop off the stage and meet Kai near the entrance. He goes to hug me but I grab his arm, pulling him through the front door and into the parking lot. The first thing I see is the Thunderbird, license plate STRYKER2. I brace myself and turn around.

"Channy!" he says. "God! I heard you went back to Alaska. I was just... well, I guess it's obvious what I was doing. For God's sake, don't tell the guys about this or I'm dead meat. I can't tell you how much grief I would catch for the tights alone! But I was heavy into theater back in high school and..."

Bunches of Kai are coming back to me as I try to follow his chirpy, mile-a-minute digressions. The burnt brown sheen of his skin, the fierce beauty of his white teeth, cheekbones like Mayan carvings. He's a Sherpa – the tribe, not the occupation, though I have a hard time not picturing him on a snowy peak somewhere, one hand on a flagpole. He's second-generation American, and his parents have taken great pains to remove him from the stereotype. In fact, that's what he's talking about.

"...and I thought, first thing back in the States, I'm climbing Rainier. That'll cheese 'em off. I mean, we're the greatest climbers in the world, born and raised at ten thousand feet! Is that something to be ashamed of?" He laughs, and then pauses. "God, Channy."

Uh-oh. He's giving me that look.

"Are you okay? Are you doing all right?"

At which point, voice control once more becomes an issue.

"Just okay. Nothing special."

He grips my shoulder, a clumsy attempt at reassurance.

"I understand. I've got some things in my head right now that I'd rather... weren't there."

He seems to recover, and his eyes flash.

"Channy! My God! I've got something for you. I've been saving it like, forever. Ya got two minutes?"

I cock an ear toward the bar. They haven't hit the slow part yet.

"Yes. But hurry."

He jogs to the T-bird, then reaches in and shuffles a hand under the passenger seat. The car is one of those new retro models, more bulk in front than the back, like a cross-section of a wing. A gift from his parents for graduating college. He paces back and hands me an aluminum box, one of those little cash boxes you might see at a bake sale. I accept it, but I hold it at arm's length. Kai looks fidgety, un-Sherpa-like.

"I'm thinking you shouldn't open it... until I'm gone," he says. "I'm thinking that would be best."

My voice is a whisper: "Okay."

"I'm... I'm really sorry, Channy. And I'm sorry if my being here, well, you know..."

He looks inside, where Shari is handling the final verse – naturally, the one about Janis.

"I better let you get back," says Kai. "But, I'm in the book, okay? Spanaway. Look me up."

I pat him on the shoulder, one awkward gesture for another.

"You're a dashing Robin Hood."

"Thanks!" And the shocking white smile.

We break through the doors just as the choral ending is trailing away. The Elizabethans have littered my tray with song-slips.

The Ren-Faire folks are drunk but good; probably they're all drama clubbers like Kai. A willowy damsel, complete with conical hat and dangling veil, does "God Save the Queen" by the Sex Pistols. A bulky, long-haired gentleman in a purple cape and silk doublet does "Paradise By the Dashboard Light" (a buxom serving wench filling in for Karla Bonoff).

Singing is apparently not on Kai's resume, because the next time I see him he's sending me a courtly bow before he troops out with the others. We don't need any more words.

But then there's the box. It sits beneath my soundboard, a radioactive presence. I try to ignore it as I slip on all my dust covers, but I know if I don't open it the night will be sleepless.

A half hour later, I wave off Shari, my final regular, as she strolls across the lot. She lives a few blocks up the hill, which gives her the option of getting drunk if she pleases. Hamster has burrowed into his office, conducting his cash-out before he gets to the cleaning. I've never known an owner who scrubs his own floors, but maybe it gives him peace of mind when the inspector comes.

I open the door to my pickup and hoist my CD case inside, wrapping it with the beach towels and bracing it against the back of the passenger seat. Then I open the driver's side door, center my danger box on the seat and click the metal tab that releases the lid.

The first item feels like a life sentence. It's a box of Swisher Sweets, sealed in a plastic bag. The second item is a small cloth sack, blue fabric worn at the edges. The object inside is a polygon, solid and smooth. I feel a vague recollection, like the first hint of a familiar cologne, but it takes too long to set down roots. The string comes loose, the polygon hits the seat, and a flash of silver buckles my legs.

The wet asphalt bites into my knees. I grab onto the steering wheel, and cry and cry. I hear footsteps, far away then closer, quicker. Long-nailed fingers rub my shoulders, strands of wheat-colored hair sweep across my forehead. I hear a voice like Etta James after a long night, saying something about everything's gonna be okay.

"I'm really sorry, Shari. Really sorry."

"Nonsense," she says. "Tell me why we're here?"

Here is the end of the Jerisich Dock, my waterborne synagogue. The drizzle has returned, and we're huddled beneath a huge umbrella that I keep in the truck.

"We're here to smoke really bad cigars," I say. "And, to forget."

"Amen, sister," says Shari. I hand her the first of the new Swisher Sweets. The last of the old is for me. I extract the silver polygon and fire it up with a roll of my thumb. First time, like magic. Shari's first drag fills the dome of the umbrella.

"Whew! Nasty. Nice lighter, though. Whatcha call that flowery thing?"

"A fleur de lis." I give myself a light and breathe in the familiar toxins. Raindrops smack the cloth above us.

"So hey," she says. "I understand if maybe... you don't want to tell me about..."

"Good," I say, then I laugh, so I can pretend I'm joking. "Honestly, Shari, it's just a bunch of little things, piling up all day long."

"A straw/camel's back situation?"

"Exactly." (She has purchased the fabrication.)

"Okay," she says. "But Channy. Could you tell me something else about yourself? I feel sometimes like I don't know the least thing about you."

I consider my options, watching the little spits of water jumping from the harbor surface.

I say this: "Chanson."

Shari looks puzzled.

"That's my name."

"Song," says Shari. "Wow. That's beautiful. Can I tell?"

"Ain't no state secret. But it was the primary reason I got beat up in third grade."

"Aren't kids awful?"

"Yeah. But they got theirs. I grew six inches that summer."

Shari lets out a raspy Janis cackle, wrapped in tobacco.

"Tell *me* something, Shari. Sometimes when you sing, I feel like you're just gonna bust. Is there something behind that?"

She cackles again. "Absolutely nothin'. But I get that a lot. 'Why, that girl musta had a turrible life. Just *turrible*."

"Exactly," I say.

She smiles. "In truth, I have had a mundanely happy existence. I think I seek out weepy, heart-wrenching ballads so I can balance things out. I think our emotions are like our skills. Use 'em or lose 'em, right? When I found you back there casting tears all over your parking brake, I was actually a little envious. I mean, ya feel better now, right?"

"Yeah," I say. "I guess so."

"I've got this friend who gets real bad PMS. And she decided to scour her CDs for sad songs, and listen to them, one after another, till she made herself cry. 'Cause she knew it would make her feel better. After a while, she went ahead and made a PMS mix tape."

"That is fucking beautiful," I say. We laugh at my sudden obscenity, and I'm thinking, *It would be so good to have a sister.*

But there's something else in that box. And it might be years before I look at it.

Seven

"So what is this place?"

"The Russell House."

"Chan*son*," says Shari, as Frenchly as possible. "Zees most clearly eez nut a house."

"More of a building. Private offices."

Shari scans the general area. "Where?"

I point a thumb at the ground. "Down thar. We're on the roof. It's a family foundation eco-thing. Those wooden arches there? With the black iron fittings?"

"Yuh-huh?"

"Nothing but windfall, not a single tree chopped down. The garden out front uses drought-resistant plants. These cement blocks beneath our tootsies have gaps between them – no sand, no mortar – so the rainfall can seep directly into the soil, and not into the drainage system."

Shari flicks away a strand of hair – more golden than ever in the light of day.

"So how come we get to sit here and eat sammiches on their roof like we own the place?"

"'Cause they want us to. And they want to give back to the community."

Shari narrows her eyes. "That is suspiciously nice."

"Hardass."

"Honey, in case you ain't looked back there lately, I am anything but..."

"Baby Got Back!" I shout. It's a peril of KJ'ing: you find yourself talking in song titles. But Shari seems to enjoy it.

I take a big crunchy bite of my sandwich and let the overripe flavor of the meat smoosh onto my taste buds. I forget where I picked up this thing for braunschweiger, but it seems to soothe a rough patch deep in my being. So much that I have missed Shari's question.

"Honey? Did you hear me?"

"Oh." Smack-smack. "No. What was that?"

"Where were you born?"

I scout the question for dangers; it comes out clean.

"Anchorage, Alaska. Well, a town just south of there. Tiny, tiny place. When we got a Fred Meyer's, it was like the high school science club had landed a rocket on the moon. Boh-ring. Boring! Did I mention boring? The only recreation in town was recreational drugs. Heroin, acid. Suicide. Suicide was the favorite. I went to thirty funerals before I graduated. Had three different outfits, just for funerals."

Shari looks captivated; more tragedy.

"Is that why you left?"

Another fork in the road: fabrication or vagueness? I'm going for vagueness.

"I couldn't see *becoming* anything up there. It was leave or stay exactly the same, forever. How 'bout you?"

"How 'bout me what?"

"Where ya from?"

She smiles. "Iowa. I was a big ol' corn-fed jockette – pitcher on the softball squad. Then I went to college to learn how to crunch numbers. Married the college sweetheart, turned out to be a cheatin' son-of-a-B. We divorced after four years. I figured a financial analyst could work any damn place she wanted, and we didn't have any kids, so I headed west."

"Why Washington?"

She waves her cherry red fingernails at the harbor. "Water! Big, fat, oceanic stretches of water. Why do you think I live on Soundview?"

"I'm gonna take a flyer here, but, so you can have a *view* of the *sound*?"

"You're a smart chick, girlfriend."

Girlfriend. I like the sound of that. Shari runs her gaze along a high stone wall bisecting us from a private garden. The wall is constructed from thousands of thinly hewn stones, like sugar wafers.

"I know I should be happy with this lovely public area, but why do I have *such* a desire to see what's on the other side of that wall?"

"I'm gonna take another flyer here, but, because you're human?"

Channy's Karao-Courtesies
(A Karz Publication)

1. Don't ask the KJ to start the song over. If you miss the first line, just come in on the second. No one will care. Also, if you discover that you have ordered up the wrong song (say, Marvin Gaye's "What's Going On?" when you wanted the 4 Non-Blondes' "What's Up?"), you'd better just fake it, because you're *not* getting a do-over.

2. Don't hang out on the back deck until your name's called. Hey, I'm sure it really *is* all about you, but could you at least pretend to care about the other singers?

3. Don't scream into the mic. As you pack your lungs with oxygen for the jungle yell on "Immigrant Song," back that puppy up a couple inches. You'll save everyone a lot of pain.

4. Don't get falling-down drunk. Remember how great you were, singing "Bohemian Rhapsody" after six tequila poppers? Neither does anybody else.

5. Don't hassle the KJ. It's hard enough keeping all those raging egos in check without you coming up to bitch about the lack of Neil Diamond selections. KJs are the sacred priests of music – treat them accordingly.

6. Do *not* horn in. Perhaps your backing vocal to "Sex and Candy" really is God's gift to harmony, but you pick up that second mic without prior permission and you will die a terrible death. (This is not to discourage a planned harmony jam, which can be a beautiful thing.)

7. Don't milk the applause. Even if you deserve it – *especially* if you deserve it – nothing looks cooler than a humble "thanks" and a quick departure. If you are offered a high-five, however, slap away. Also, if you have just performed an Elvis tune, you are required by law to mumble "Thankyouvermuch."

8. Do not change your song selection within three singers of your turn, unless you're willing to add substantially to the tip jar.

9. Try to avoid singing a song that has already been performed that evening. If you sing it badly, your effort will look that much worse in comparison. If you sing it well, you will appear to be showing up your predecessor, who will then be entitled to throw a baseball at your head in the following inning.

When I report to Karz, Hamster is standing at the bar with a songbook, reading my Karao-Courtesies yet again.

"Don't you ever get tired of that thing?"

"It's not just that it's funny," he says. "It's that it's so completely out of character. It's so...edgy!"

I take a stool across from him. "I never would have written it for the customers. I did it for a KJ newsletter out of Spokane. Strictly in-house. Somehow Harry got a hold of it, passed it all around the bar, and they loved it. And do you know why? Because *they* think it's about everybody *else*. And five minutes later, they're up on stage, saying, 'Damn! Can I start over?'"

My little monologue earns a chuckle, but I can tell Hamster's anxious about something. His gaze shifts to the end of the bar, where a squad of gray-haired men are gathered around Mt. Rainier.

"What's going on?" I ask.

He curls a lip. "My distribution system appears to be on the fritz."

"Yikes! You may have to deliver drinks by hand."

"Perish the thought. You think the singers will come to the bar for their drinks?"

"Sure. I'll make an announcement. I don't know, Hamster. You sure this thing isn't an Amtrak?"

"Ouch! Thou doth smacketh me with barbs of truth. If those Union Pacific freights would just give us a right-of-way once in a while. Can't tell you how much of my soul I sent down the chipper telling some passenger 'This hardly *ever* happens.'"

"Seems to me that bored, frustrated passengers might naturally turn to drink."

"Paid for this restaurant," he says. "But I still hate lying to people."

I feel a quiet presence behind me, accompanied by the smell of old-style after-shave. It's a trio of codgers. One is wearing an engineer cap. I'm trying not to laugh.

"Bad news," says the tallest. He's a rangy retired-officer type, owner of a bushy moustache straight out of a horse opera. "It's definitely the transformer. Now, you know what we told you when we put this in, Ham. Y'got an enormous system here, with an unusually powerful transformer. You need to keep a backup at all times."

Hamster covers his face. "Oh, God. If I give you another pitcher of beer, could you please not say 'I told you so'?"

Moustache-man smiles. "I'll try – but I was really looking forward to that."

"How long to find another?"

He inevitably rubs his 'stache as a thinking device. "Tell you what. I got a pretty free weekend. I'd bet I could get you two by Monday."

"Two? But we only need..."

"Two," says Moustache.

Hamster laughs and gives a military salute. "Two it is. Thanks, George."

"No prob, Cap'n."

That's enough engineering for me. I'm off to deal with my own equipment. This being Thursday, I'm expecting a humble crowd, but of course I'm entirely wrong. Within the first hour, I've got two birthday parties (thirtysomething and fiftysomething, respectively), a small battalion of mom's-night-outers (one of them dancing rather naughtily for the engineers on an AC/DC song), and a dozen college karaokeans bent on a future with *American Idol.* The personnel management is like a *New York Times* crossword. I've got forty-eight singers, and I'm running out of business card holders, farming the extras to a windowsill behind my station.

Somewhere in the chaos I notice Kevin the Cop, wearing a tropical shirt that is anything but Octoberish. He's got the skin for it, though – and, in fact, is looking rather fetching all over. He drops "Suavamente" for "La Bamba" – the first time I've heard it sung by someone who actually knows Spanish. Then he flashes a grin and returns to his friends.

It is often at moments like this, when I'm clamped in a non-stop rush, that my thoughts come through with alarming clarity. They have to – murkiness takes too much time. I have precisely two ideas on this renewed attraction. One: a month and a half ago, I asked Kevin to back off – and he did. Two: having tapped into such a torrent of sadness on Sunday, it could be that I have opened up my other emotions as well. Like lust. I am stealing this from Shari's hypothesis, the emotional tool belt, use 'em or lose 'em.

After Kevin, I've got yet another singer I've never heard of, but the selection stands out: "The First Time Ever I Saw Your Face," by Roberta Flack. It's a gorgeous song, but excruciatingly slow. The entrances arrive at long, long intervals. I have yet to see someone make it all the way through without coming in early at least once. I line up track five on the disc, right after "Killing Me Softly," and then I reach for the mic.

"We have yet another newcomer! Please welcome Jade."

Jade is quite a sight. She wears a dark, pleated schoolgirl skirt, a blouse of emerald silk with small white specks of Chinese calligraphy, and black pumps with stiletto heels. Her round Caucasian eyes are shadowed in layers of black and green, and her thick jet hair hangs in a long braid down her back. She wears a necklace of black string holding a circle of jade. I seem to remember they call this a blessing disc.

She perches on a stool and crosses her legs, content to wait out the long intro, then closes her eye on the opening phrase and sings almost to herself, tasting the words. This is something I have noticed about performance: if *you* are involved with the song, the audience will be involved with *you*. We don't get Jade's blue eyes until the third long phrase, and even then she doesn't seem overly concerned with us. She's concerned with the first time ever she saw his face. It's a matter of theater – you can feel the fourth wall sealing her off, making it safe for us to watch.

With "Little Girl Blue," she had to win us over – the bachelorettes, the horny men. This time, she has us within seconds. Something about the song, the long reaches of quietude. Church. I'm eating her sustenatos, great fields of tone that carry a drive and a shape, without ever seeming forced. I am *so* envious.

She climbs the last ladder of chromatics and leaves us dangling. Again the bank of silence, broken again by Harry's happy woof – and again, she's headed for a slippery exit. I do something I've never done. I hit the play button on a Joan Osborne song and let Shari figure it out for herself. I am fixed on my target, following Jade out the door like a teeny-bopper chasing a Beatle.

"Hey! Jade! Amber!"

She stops but doesn't turn, holding a pose like a figure in film noir. She's not about to get away – not in those heels – so she turns and faces me with folded arms.

"Yeah?"

I feel breathless, silly.

"You're so... good! You're extraordinary."

She stares at me and blinks her eyes, once.

"You think I need someone like you to tell me that?"

"No... no. But I was just wondering..."

"Why I don't stay? Why the fuck would I stay? To poison my ears with your so-called singers? Or that pile of shit you call a sound system? I'd be better off with a fucking megaphone."

I'm absolutely stunned. She turns to go, then comes back for another volley.

"You're lucky I come at all. You're lucky that I'm *crazy* about singing. But one song is all I can take."

She's gone, clicking across the lot, calves tightening at each step. I follow my feet into the bar, where Shari is asking if God is one of us. I hold my ribs, feeling all the world like I've been punched.

If I were you, I would take the rest of this with a grain of salt, because I am looped. Faced with record numbers of singers, deprived of the assistance of toy locomotives, I have nonetheless managed to slam enough rum and cokes to souse a baseball team. I'm at the bar, trying to snap the lid on my CD case – a project I've been working on for some time now. Hamster appears over my shoulder, humming like a disapproving clergyman.

"I have *never* seen you like this." I brace myself for the sound that follows: "Tch, tch."

"Do my singers suck, Hammy? Does my sound system suck? Do *I* suck?"

He's trying really hard not to laugh.

"What is your problem?" he says. "Everybody loves you, Channy! Your singers worship you. Your sound system is great! Why are you letting one person's opinion drive you into a ditch?"

Now I seem to be standing, slapping my hands on the bar.

"Did you *hear* her? She sings like a fucking angel! She *knows,* Hamster! She knows I'm a big fucking phony with a... with a Salvation Army PA! God I suck so much!"

I get the feeling I'm being very loud. Hamster is laughing now, big baritone peals of laughter. The fucker.

"S'not funny! S'not funny!"

"Is too!" he squeals. "I just... I just didn't know you had this in you, Channy."

"Chan*son,*" I say. "From now on, the fucking name is fucking Chan*son.*"

I take a slug from my glass and get nothing but ice. Hamster takes it, and wraps a big hand around my shoulder. "All right, Chan*son.* Come on, let's go."

"Where?"

"My place. You are certainly *not* driving home."

"I knew it!" I say. "You've been waiting for this chance ever since you hired me, you dirty old lech."

I'm swatting him on the shoulder. He's still laughing. *God* that's annoying.

"You're a very attractive woman, Channy – about five drinks ago. Now, come on. I locked your CDs in the office."

I'm surprised to find myself boarding a small boat. The jiggle of my first step sends a small wave of nausea through my stomach.

"What the hell is this?"

"This," he says, "is the best damn commute in Washington state." He revs the engine and backs away from the dock. "This," he yells, "is Hamster stickin' it to the man!"

Hamster kicks it forward into the wind, looking like a goddamn cigarette ad.

"You know, Hammie?" I shout. "For a second there, you actually sounded like a black man!"

I wake to a gray light seeping through the windows. I am wearing every stitch from the night before, flat-out on a white quilt. I stumble to the blinds and peer through to see the public dock, directly across the harbor. That means we're in the white house with the green trim – the one I've been lusting after for six months. I feel the need to express this thought out loud.

"Shoulda invited myself over sooner."

Yikes. I sound like Stevie Nicks with strep throat. I also have a tongue made of shoe leather, an indescribable amount of thirst and an urgent need to pee. I catch a sliver of porcelain through the door and I head in that direction.

Cupping my hands to drink, I find in the mirror a fruit salad of colors, and turn to discover a jumble of plastic pipes soaking in the tub.

"What the hell?" I croak. I follow another door into the hall, where I find neat lines of similar pipes lining either wall, carefully framed around the door jambs. When I put my eye to a section of baby blue, I find a fuzzy, toothy face staring back, and squeal accordingly.

My boss leans into the far end of the hallway, holding a cup of coffee, wearing a red silk bathrobe like a black Hugh Hefner. It hits me all at once.

"Hamster!" I yell. "Hamster! Hamster!"

He lets out a grand and sheepish smile.

"Yes, damn you: Hamster. You want some coffee?"

Eight

It's been a rough, rough week, but things are beginning to look better. Friday night at Karz was freakishly normal; Saturday morning is freakishly *ab*normal – as in sunny. In Washington, in October, you don't expect this. The logical response is to visit my sand dollars.

I take the trail at the back of the Craigs' lot and follow its snaky curves down to the Y-camp. The sugar maples make a fiery yellow ring around the basketball court. I stop at the free-throw line to wallow in a slice of sunlight.

It's off-season now, but the ranger was nice enough to give me the combination to the boathouse. Ten minutes later, I am shadowing the spine of the inlet, peering through preternaturally clear water to my jumbled colony of dollars.

I'm betting there are lots of folks who don't get to see them in their natural environment, so let me clarify something. Those white things that you find at the beach are skeletons. Imagine the same item with a coating of coarse purple-green fur, and you've got the real live deal.

I am startled landward by the distinctive bark of TV's Lassie, and I look up to find Java, wide-stanced on a boulder, delighted at his discovery. John Craig pops from the trees ten feet behind, at the end of one of those fishing-reel leashes, dressed in sweat pants, a T-shirt and a headband. John treats everything like a workout, and it shows. At seventy, he's in better shape than most people *my* age (and is trying for better, preparing for a reunion of his old Navy squadron).

"Hey!" I shout. I wince at the volume, but then I remember that, for most people, 11 a.m. is not early.

"Oh!" John spies me and waves. "I thought Java was after another seagull."

"Training for VP-21?"

"I ain't goin' for Mister Congeniality!"

"You're going to make those old Navy guys feel bad!"

"Good!"

Java performs a time-step on the boulder and lets out a stutter of half-yelps, overstimulated by all the hollering.

"Hold on a second!" says John. "I'll be right there!"

"You will?"

Dog and master disappear around the corner, and I feel like I've been abandoned – until I find a rowboat tracing the shore, afro silhouette at the prow. John pulls his way to my spot and plants his oar in the water for a brake. Java is stiff on his haunches, a perfect triangle of dog. John grabs an oar by the blade and extends the handle to me.

"Hold on to this. It'll keep us from drifting apart."

"Does Floy know you've got a boat?"

"I don't. This belongs to Jerry Flores, my VP at the homeowners' association. He's got a private dock just around the corner. It's a great upper-body workout."

I roll my eyes. "Yeah yeah. Everything's a workout. Your dog is exceptionally calm."

John lets out a husky laugh. "More like petrified. He lost his balance once and found out just how cold the Puget Sound is."

I've never quite been able to figure it out, but John's face carries trace elements of several multi-ethnic celebrities. The soulful brown eyes belong to Desi Arnaz, the oval face and prominent nose to Bill Cosby, the swept-back widow's peak to Jerry Lee Lewis, the broad forehead to Harry Belafonte. I wonder sometimes if I have just made all this up.

"Is the water heater behaving?" I ask. (This is the latest of many home-ownership challenges.)

"Sadly, no," he says. "I'm having a plumber come out tomorrow. It's pretty old, so it might be time to get a new one, regardless."

"I haven't had a problem at all," I say. "But then, I guess I shower at odd hours."

"You're also downhill from the heater. We're at the point where gravity makes a difference." He looks around and reaches over to ruffle Java's mop-top. "Pretty amazing day we've got going."

"Yeah, it's great," I say, but my thoughts are elsewhere. There's some question I've been meaning to ask John. It escapes my mouth of its own accord.

"John, were there times in your Navy days when you thought you might... die?"

"Hmmm..." He rubs the back of his neck, giving the question a good going-over. "Most of the time, in a crisis situation, you're too busy troubleshooting to fully comprehend the danger. On the other hand, if you had danger, *and* a lot of time to think about it – there's your devil's brew."

"So the hardest part," I say, "is the waiting."

"When we were stationed in Maine, I was sent out on the October Missile Crisis. Flew a P-3 Orion over the Atlantic, looking for Russian subs. The strange part was kissing Floy goodnight, telling her I couldn't tell her anything – when of course she knew exactly what was going on. We were surrounded by it. It all turned out so well, in the end, I think we all forget what a powder keg that was."

"Amen." I'm suddenly more impressed with John, knowing that he was a small part of history.

"Another time, also in Maine, I was in a much more specific danger. We were out on a routine patrol when the entire Eastern Seaboard was socked in by a blizzard. They kept telling me to stay put up there, and I kept watching my fuel gauges get lower and lower. I wasn't scared so much as *intensely* anxious. They finally had to bring us down or we were coming down on parachutes. I had quite a reputation for my landings, for making them as smooth as possible, but I needed some luck on that one, because we were working entirely on instruments. May as well have had Ray Charles flying that thing. But I remember thinking of something my commander told me: 'Life demands every bit of our strength, so we give it. Then it demands more, so we give that, too.' There's no decision up there – you just do what you have to do.

"Well. I didn't mean to go on. But inactivity, loss of control – there's your big scary monsters. When my eyes went bad, and they took away my flight time, that's when I had to call it quits. I can still navigate a rowboat, though."

"Thanks to Ensign Java." I give our friend an awkward slap to the ribcage. Java's still too anxious to move, but his eyes get big at the sound of his name. And by now I've forgotten why I needed to ask that question.

I love being a flapper. I love my grandma's old dress; it's a tight-fitting cocoon, draping down in overlapping tiers, giving me a beautiful, lean silhouette. After that it's a goofy-long string of fake pearls, a pageboy wig from a costume shop, and entirely too much makeup, like Mary Pickford in a silent movie. I picture myself draped over a piano, whispering Gershwin tunes to a roomful of men with slicked-back hair and spats.

Yeah, yeah. Silly. But it's Halloween – I'm allowed. Perhaps this masquerade is just what the doctor ordered. Lord knows, it hasn't been much fun being *me* lately. Let's just hope they don't notice I wore this same dress last year.

My regulars are dressing to type. Harry's a dashing mafioso, pinstripe suit, dark shirt, white tie, rakish fedora. Shari's a Blues Brother: dark shades, black suit, skinny tie, white shirt. Caroleen's a full-on hippie chick: tie-dyed shirt, hiphugger jeans, fringy leather vest and round purple Lennon spectacles. Kevin's a Keystone Kop: high bobbie hat, long coat, gigantically wide belt and a Charlie Chaplin mustache. (Hamster's taken a rare night off for a party in Federal Way. I imagine him dressed as an actual hamster, but I doubt he'd ever do it.)

It's also fun to watch the song selections. I kick things off with "Superstition," Harry does "Spooky," and then (because *somebody* has to) Kevin tries out "Monster Mash." Then Caroleen does "Mama, He's Crazy," which actually sort of fits. A quartet of guys from Pacific Lutheran University kick in with "Werewolves of London," "Thriller" (complete with zombie dance and Vincent Price monologue), "Dead Man's Party" and "Godzilla." It's amazing how many songs fit into the Halloween genre.

Which is why the next seems grossly out of place. I'm also having a hard time making out the name.

"Al? Al Lofus?" I'm surprised to find Harry, Kevin, Shari, Caroleen and Alex heading my way. Harry takes the mic.

"All of us," he says. "We wanted to make a little presentation. We know, Channy, that you've been having sort of a tough time lately, and we thought this might be a good time" - he drops into a Tony Soprano accent – "to let you know exactly what we think of you."

Caroleen snickers. Harry hands the mic to Shari.

"You see," she says, "we just come here three, four times a week, and we're the ones who get to have all the fun – and the whole time you're working. And yes, we know it's your *job*, but you're so good at it – so good at making each one of us feel so special and cared for, and we really appreciate that."

She hands the mic to Kevin. "So we got you a gift," he says. "Something to go with that sexy flapper's outfit. Here."

He pulls an arm from behind his back and offers a long, thin gift box, wrapped in silver foil. I unwrap it and pull out a long black cigarette holder. I clamp it between my teeth like FDR.

"So what you're saying is, I'm in a costume rut."

"It's not a rut when it works," says Harry, all Skye Masterson (what's next, Robert Deniro?). "We got you this, too."

This box is small and square, containing a silver necklace with a treble-clef pendant.

"Oh guys," I say. "It's gorgeous!"

"Now," says Kevin, slapping a nightstick against his palm. "Put on the damn CD so we can sing to ya."

"Yessir!" I reply.

I spend the next five minutes at an elevation far above sea level, soaring over Gig Harbor like a figure in a Chagall painting as my regulars take turns singing "You Are So Beautiful." I study my silver clef, radiant in the stage light, and think, *This must be what a teacher feels like on the last day of school, when her students surprise her with a present.*

Still, the attention is a bit much for me, so I'm almost glad when it's over. We exchange hugs all around and then I pick out "H-E-L-L" by the Squirrel Nut Zippers and slap it on the CD changer.

Our esprit de corps is short-lived. There is a song slip in my lineup that bears the name "Ruby." I have learned to detest gemstones, and I can't believe that she's come back, she who performed such a handy little female castration on me. Why does the world produce such people?

So I dread the passing of singers, I dread how she works her way to the top. I also dread her choice, "I Don't Stand a Ghost of a Chance With You," which is dreadfully clever, and I dread the unwritten KJ code that keeps me from taking a match to her song slip.

When I call her name, she's a flapper. My exact dress, in red. A goofy-long string of black pearls, a black cigarette holder, and, oh gosh, a gold serpentine necklace with a teardrop ruby pendant. The two of us are like a very small production of *Chicago*. I try hard not to notice her – which is easy, because she's ignoring me, taking her usual torch-singer perch on the stool.

The arrangement is lush, orchestral. It's from a collection of standards that don't get too many requests. Very few have the talent to sing them. Ruby closes her eyes and gives voice to the first line as if she's thinking out loud, minor-chord intervals shifting like a thin fog through trees. It makes me wish I were in love.

Something's wrong. She disconnects, manages to finish the second verse but then she folds her hands, takes a huffy breath and levels a stare in my direction.

"What the hell is this? This is *not* the arrangement I asked for. Fucking incompetent. I can't believe..."

Then she stops, because it's hard to talk when someone's slapping your face. And there I am, standing in front of her, screaming a little speech I've been practicing since Thursday.

"If you hate this place so much then WHY DO YOU KEEP COMING BACK!? *No one* treats me like this and *no one* talks shit about my singers. *And,* for you information, I put on exactly the CD that you asked for, because unlike other people I am not an EVIL FUCKING BITCH!"

My performance sets her back a bit. Perhaps she thought the injured lamb was the only act in my repertoire. But I'll give her this much – she recovers quickly.

"It won't be hard to find a better place than this backwoods shithole. Fuck... you... all."

And she makes a grand exit, like she always does. My regulars, who have finally recovered from hearing animal shrieks out of sweet Channy's mouth, give her a round of boos and hisses worthy of a melodrama villain. After she's gone, they break into a rousing applause. It takes quite a while before I realize it's for me. I put on my best Academy Award smile.

"Thank you! Thanks *evah* so much. I love you all, *truly* I do. Now, can we sing some songs? Eric, get your ass up here before I rip you a new one!"

Eric catches the gag and races to the mic. Sliding his choice, "Hard to Handle," into the changer, I consider the damage that a public shouting match can do to an evening of karaoke, and decide to go on with my "bit."

"So," I say. "I suppose you think that just because this is by the Black Crowes, it qualifies as a Halloween song?"

Eric cowers like the Scarecrow before Oz. Bless the boy, he's got stage sense.

"Y-yes, Mistress KJ?"

"See me after class, young man! I've got some erasers you can... bang together."

It gets a laugh – that's enough. I start the song and leave my post, heading to my regulars for some much-needed social affirmation. Shari greets me with a big Oprah hug.

"Honey," she says. "I've never been prouder."

"Thanks. I hope that scares the little witch away. Helluva singer, though."

Shari holds me at a bemused arm's length. "Your musical objectivity knows no bounds."

A half hour later, we're nearing the bottom of the barrel. Harry does "Rock Lobster" just for the *Munsters* organ music, then Sergio, one of the college boys, takes on "Jeremy," that Pearl Jam song about the high school kid who shoots all his classmates.

Followed by a gunshot, which startles Sergio right out of his song. He spins around as a second shot spatters the window with a phlegmy sunburst.

Kevin the Keystone Kop, fully inflated by a half-dozen brewskis, stumbles to his feet to declare the obvious.

"Eggs! Evidently some sort of Halloween…" (wait for it, wait for it) "Prank! This! is a job for a. Constabulary!"

"Yeh!" says Harry, all Sly Stallone. "Do we got wonna dose?"

Kevin's on his way to the door, nighstick at the ready.

"Kevin!" I shout. "Take it easy. It's just kids."

My plea for mercy is answered by a trio of eggs, striking the window in a yolky constellation.

"Give 'em hell, Kevin!"

Kevin dashes outside, suddenly coordinated. We hear shouting, and the scuffling of footsteps. A minute later, in comes Kevin trailing a red flapper in handcuffs. I guess I'm not entirely surprised.

"I have apprehended this prostitute in the parking lot," Kevin announces. (He seems to think he's in a Vaudeville melodrama.) "From her attire, I'd say she was trolling for senior citizens."

I walk over and stand at a safe distance to give my appraisal. Gem-girl is ready to claw and/or bite anything that comes close. It's a good thing we've got a genuine cop holding her back.

"Helly, Ruby." I throw in as much sneer as possible. "If that's your *real* name."

"Let me *fucking* go!" she hisses. "Let me go or I'll call the cops."

Kevin almost buckles laughing. Harry comes up to assess the situation, flipping a silver dollar as he speaks.

"She does have a point. According to habeus corpus subjiciendum polly wolly doodle, we really can't hold her without a charge. But perhaps we could solve the problem by jumping directly to the punishment."

Kevin uses a foot to nudge forward Ruby's grocery bag, which still contains four dozen eggs. "And why not make the punishment fit the crime?"

This is how ten otherwise normal adults find themselves tying Zelda Fitzgerald to a deck railing and lining up a firing squad armed entirely with eggs. It's utterly logical in design – overshots will land harmlessly in the water (though I'm not sure the Russell Foundation would approve). I have given Ruby a certain level of eye protection with the Elvis sideburn sunglasses, and duct-taped her mouth to keep her screams from attracting any non-Keystone cops.

I'm beginning to think that we have wandered into something criminal, or at least barbaric. These thoughts disappear, however, as Kevin kneels at my feet and presents me with a perfect white ovoid.

"First offended, first avenged," he says.

I approach the railing with deliberate steps, running the cool enamel skin across my lips. I stop and hold the egg to her face, savoring the look of anger and anxiety beneath her sunglasses.

"*You*... are a lovely singer, Ruby. As a human being, however, you suck eggs. And that's why we're here."

I tear off Ruby's pageboy wig, revealing short pinned-back hair. I hold the egg at the top of her head, cover it with the wig, and press down on the whole assemblage with a delicious *crack*. Trails of yolk descend her forehead. I smile, walk to the side – well out of range – and I declare "Gentlemen! You may fire when ready!"

What follows is hard to describe. The public execution of a transvestite Elvis, were Elvis's blood composed of a viscous yellow-white fluid. Ruby's body bursts forth in splatter after splatter. After thirty seconds, the flapper dress is caked with goo. I am utterly enjoying myself.

Schadenfreude, however, has its limits. After taking the first barrage with a defiant posture, Ruby curls to one side and slowly sinks to the deck, dangling from her handcuffs. She's sobbing, which is entirely unfair. But alas, I do have a conscience. I take a step into the firing zone and hold up a hand.

"Hold it, guys! That's enough. Harry, can you get me some damp towels?"

Eric the college dramatist complains: "But we've still got a dozen left! What'll we do with 'em?"

Eric's chums immediately savage him with eggs. He runs inside, squealing "Assholes! Assholes!"

Kevin undoes Ruby's cuffs, as Harry returns with a towel. I remove the Elvis glasses and start with Ruby's forehead, making sure that nothing drips into her eyes, which are closed and flooding with tears. I'll be damned, but I'm beginning to feel sorry for her.

"Ruby, Ruby. How can you sing so beautifully and still be such a raving bitch?"

"Try..." she chokes, and stops to sniffle. I hand her a fresh towel so she can wipe her nose. "Try putting yourself in front of every fucking director in New York for eleven fucking years, and being rejected by each and every one. Try doing that when you know *exactly* how good you are."

I peel off the pageboy wig and run a towel across her hair

"Oh yeah?" I say. "Try having your husband put a bullet through his head."

So this is what finally brings it out. A pity contest with a human omelet. We compare tragedies. I win.

Nine

The pivot point of Tacoma's Stadium District is a triangular sliver of park where the avenues of Tacoma and St. Helens meet. Further on, the two roads are connected by what have to be the shortest streets in the city: First St. N and Second St. N, the former of which stretches all of twenty feet. Ruby is cutting figure-eights through all of them, looking for a parking spot. She drives an ancient blue Corolla with a bad carburetor, which forces her to pump the gas whenever we strike an uphill. All the aerobics makes her laugh with embarrassment.

"This is my stealth car," she says. "Looks like shit, but she got me here from New York with nary a hiccup. Once she hits an interstate, she tracks in on seventy and just stays there. Damn! It's the Rotarians, that's why."

A Masonic temple rises over St. Helens Avenue like a concrete King Kong peeking over the hillside. Bland businessmen in bland suits funnel beneath a marquee reading WELCOME TACOMA ROTARY. Ruby cuts a right onto Second, spots a car-size rectangle of dirt and seizes it with piratical zeal. We're soon clip-clopping the sidewalk along window-size wedding portraits as Ruby gives me the neighborhood spiel.

"Call it a sickness, but all these old buildings remind me of New York. Check the crazy church across the street. Presbyterian congregation, Eastern Orthodox spire, Romanesque pillars and good ol' Northwestern brick. I think the architect was a closet Unitarian. And now, on your right, the soulless white high-rise apartment building."

The lobby and front garden are actually pretty inviting, but a glance upward illustrates Ruby's point: flat windowfront fields devoid of ornament. The sidewalk holds something more interesting: a shrine of flowers and candles around a bus stop sign. I think of inquiring, but Ruby's on to the next attraction.

"And this is my stealth apartment building."

It's a squat building of dark bricks, surrounded by a low wrought-iron fence. Ruby leads me into a lobby of mustard walls and floral green carpeting, the kind you might see in an old hotel. We board a flight of stairs that leads to a narrow hallway.

"Would you believe this was built in 1896?"

The hallway comes to a back stairwell. Ruby stops at a door to the right and pulls out her keys.

"This is actually two separate buildings," she says. "That little hall is part of the center section that joins them. *And*, even though my mailing address is St. Helens, technically I live on Broadway, which is perfectly suited to my sick, undying dreams of glory."

This is Ruby's primary shtick, the heart-piercing sentiment delivered in an offhand manner. Perhaps this is therapeutic, perhaps it's just a built-in part of an actor's armor. Whichever, you can still feel the pain behind the words.

We stop in the entryway to remove our coats. Ruby takes off a black cap to reveal her shock of red hair, then takes my hand and leads me into the living room, wearing an expectant, close-lipped expression.

What strikes me is not the room itself but the view framed by the wide center window: the port of Tacoma, lit up like the largest auto sales lot in the universe, a trio of mill stacks billowing steam into the frigid night air. Ruby drinks up my surprise with a satisfied grin.

"Stealth car, stealth apartment – stealth view." She runs a hand along the sill. "All in all, I'm almost invisible. The natives seem wholly unaware of it, but *that* is the most beautiful fucking port in the country. It took me about five seconds to sign the lease."

"You have *got* to have a party up here!" I say, sounding exactly like a gay impresario.

Ruby gives me a sad smile. Sad smile, tragic jokes – she is the middle child, bastard daughter of the comedy and tragedy masks.

"Give me some time to get some friends first," she says. "Perhaps I'll put out a casting call. But hey! Let's have a party for two. Set that puppy on the coffee table, and I'll get some wine."

The "puppy" is a pizza called The Hipster, loaded with trendy toppings: sun-dried tomatoes, feta cheese, capers. Ruby sets out plates, forks, napkins and Pinot Grigio, and we embark on some much-needed consumption. It's our longest stretch of wordlessness in the past two hours (she is a talker with remarkable stamina).

Ruby polishes off her first slice, takes a swallow of pinot and studies me with those unsettling stage-size features.

"Do you think the folks at Karz will ever forgive me?"

"I'm the KJ, Ruby. If *I* forgive you, *they* forgive you."

"You're that powerful, eh?"

"Yes," I reply, and can't help snickering. "Besides, there's nothing the karaoyokels enjoy more than a good old-fashioned soap opera – and you certainly supplied *that*."

Ruby snickers in return. "And I certainly got my comeuppance. Which *was* inevitable, by the way. I was so full of juice, I wasn't going to stop until someone smacked me down good. Picture Ruby standing in line at the Safeway, eleven o'clock, Halloween, holding six dozen eggs. Could my intentions have been any more blatant? And I'll tell ya, if your cop friend hadn't wrassled me away, I would have stood there in that parking lot and chucked all seventy-two."

"It actually worked out well," I say. "You supplied all the necessary ammunition for your own eggs-ecution."

"You're a bad, bad girl," says Ruby.

"Do you know how long I held on to that pun?"

"Well," she says in a mothering voice. "Perhaps you should have buried it somewhere, honey."

Her expression turns abruptly serious. For the first time tonight, I feel like I'm getting the real Ruby.

"There was nothing wrong with that CD at all. I was just picking a fight. And before, when I pulled that apocalyptic bitch session in the parking lot. My God, honey – why didn't you just shoot me?"

"I was in shock. It was so far out of my experience that someone could be that... mean."

The memory brings an awkward silence. I pretend to show some interest in my pizza. Ruby reaches under the coffee table and pulls out a small box.

"Would you like some herb with your meal?"

Her meaning escapes me, but then she takes out a plastic bag and a large ceramic pipe.

"Oh! Yeah, sure."

"Such a relief," she says. "Hauling out the ganja is so fraught with politics."

"Where I grew up, pot was considered about as racy as chewing gum. I'm not a huge fan, but if someone offers a bowl – why not?"

She hands me the pipe and a lighter, and shows me where the carb is. I take a lungful, hold it in, then pass the pipe to Ruby. When I speak, my throat is already scratchy (and there's the reason I'm not a huge fan).

"What's up with that shrine at the bus stop?"

Ruby's conducting a deep inhale, producing little snorting sounds that, in any other context, would be considered quite rude. She turns red and coughs it out.

"Oh God, that. Some guy fell out of his apartment. Ten floors."

The thought of it is like a nail in my chest. All I can do is gasp.

"Can I tell you the story?" she says. "Let me tell it to you, just the way I heard it."

This seems like a curious preface, but what the hell do I care?

"Yeah, sure," I say. "Go for it."

"I was coming home from karaoke – this was Jade, that little bitch. When I pulled up, there were four cop cars, all the lights flashing. They had roped off the entire street in front of the building. As I walked up, there was this one big cop – Asian guy – walking back to his car. He was shaking his head, like something was in there and he was afraid of letting it settle. Over his shoulder, about thirty feet away, I could see a yellow emergency blanket spread out over something on the sidewalk. And I began to make connections.

"When the cop finally noticed me, I felt the need to justify my presence. 'I live next door,' I said. The cop looked at me like he really wasn't seeing me and said, 'I can't tell you anything right now.' And I took that as my cue to disappear.

"I was back two nights later – in fact, on Halloween – when I saw the shrine. There was a Xeroxed photo of this young, young, guy with his girlfriend, and a note that read, *I met you once in the laundry room. You seemed very nice.* I went to the grocery store to buy some flowers – alstroemeria, they were called – and I was setting them down when this big linebacker-looking dude came out from the lobby. It seemed like he was the apartment manager or something, he had that air about him. And this is what he said:

"'It was a freak. That safety glass is just about foolproof, but once in a great while someone hits that single wrong spot at that single wrong angle – and when safety glass goes, I mean it disappears. Gerald was talking on the phone with a friend, maybe sitting on the top of his couch, maybe leaning against the glass. He swings an elbow, hits that single wrong spot and the gravity takes him right out.'

"Linebacker dude came over and and sat on the bus stop bench. He pulled off his baseball cap and scratched his bald head. I think he could picture exactly what was going through my mind: that awful split second when Gerald found himself airborne.

"'There's more,' he said. 'You know that nutcase who pulled out an AK-47 at the Tacoma Mall, shot all those people, then took hostages in the music store?'

"'Sure,' I say.

"'That shooting took place the day after Gerald fell. And that was the very morning that Gerald was supposed to report for his first day of work at that same music store.'"

"No!" I say.

"Exactly what I said," says Ruby. "Our friend Gerald was headed down a dark tunnel, with two trains coming the other direction."

Ruby punctuates her conclusion by taking a luxurious drink of wine. I'm beginning to understand the power of her theatrical skills (Exhibit A, endowing the apartment manager with just the right gruffness of tone to set him apart in the narrative). She smacks her lips, places her glass carefully on the table and shoots me an expectant look.

"So. What do you think?"

"Awful!" I say. "Awful. Horrible."

"Is it the truth?"

"Why... wouldn't it be?"

She ruffles her hair, as if she's wiping the slate clean.

"Let me tell you a second story. Gerald is hopped up on 'shrooms, desperately depressed, surrounded by personal crises. He calls 911, tells them he's going to kill himself. They tell him someone's on the way, but no one comes, so Gerald takes a run at that window and smashes right through. That shrine is not just a shrine – it's a landing spot. Notice the distance from the building. No way he gets there on a dead fall."

I feel like a mouse nibbling on spring-loaded cheese. But a woman's gotta eat.

"Who's your source?"

"Inge, the manager of *my* apartment building – and close friend of Gerald's ex-girlfriend."

I give it a careful study. "Could Gerald have struck the building early in his fall and... bounced?"

"Not likely, but possible. However, that's not the point I'm selling. Notice how these stories cross over on themselves – how the sources seem to flout their own self-interests. The apartment manager confesses the danger of his own windows. Friends of the dead doing nothing to protect his reputation. And the connection with the mall shooting – added for dramatic effect? Useful distraction? Comforting apologia for the hand of fate?

"Private lives being private, I don't think you or I will ever know. See how slippery the truth is? How like a moray eel covered in Vaseline?"

This is much more thought than I had bargained for. I feel the need to move, so I pick up my glass and wander to Ruby's window, which feels much safer than poor Gerald's. Landward from the gray freighters and the blue loading cranes, toward the flatlands of Fife, fifty sawhorses line the highway, blinking their hazard lights in patterns that never seem to sort out.

Ruby knows the question that comes next, but she also knows it's flammable, so she speaks it to the air without turning.

"Are you going to tell me about your husband?"

All I can conjure is a long exhale, but alas, she waits me out.

"That seems to be the reason you were sent my way, Ruby. To leach the poison out of my system. But it's not gonna be easy, and it *is* gonna be messy."

"Start out slowly," she says. "Tell me how you met."

Hazard lights.

Ten
Ruby

When I was an infant, my mother held me by the ankles and dipped me in the river Competence, bestowing upon my person the glow of professionalism. Let's let Ruby handle this. If we put Ruby in charge, then the rest of us can be flakes. It began in preschool, at the end of coloring time. I was the one who gathered all the crayons, and the only ones I missed were those that had been ingested.

Myth number one about being an artist. You can only be creative if you're flaky. Truth is, flaky artists are only flaky because they know they can get away with it. It's very convenient, and it even adds to the aura. As far as the actual artistic product, it makes not one iota of difference – other than pissing off all the artists who have to work with you.

Competence was a trap, but I had no choice. I was a good Jewish girl, progeny of solid-minded intellectuals – the kind of girl who uses *progeny* in a sentence. The kind of girl who takes pride in her competence, who enjoys being a leader, and thus lacks the capacity to see the trap for what it is.

When I went for my theater arts degree at Florida State, I had one minor role in *Lysistrata* and then whammo! the director's chair, ever after. Directing is another trap, because it allows you to be creative and in control at the same time. Even the most detailed of playscripts are just blueprints. Shakespeare's are thumbnail sketches, filled up with perfect words. The director stands before a stage-wide canvas, equipped with a palette of movements, an assortment of brushes she calls *actors,* and has at it. The level of responsibility and respect is intoxicating; you begin to understand why so many generals turn into dictators.

I directed a dozen shows: *Godot, West Side Story, Lear, Earnest, Cat on a Hot Tin Roof, Equus.* By the time I graduated, I had the resume of a 30-year-old man, and magna cum laude, and all that other impressive crap. A month later, I got an interview at a film studio. I got it because of my dad – old college pal, that sort of thing – but when I got the *job,* that was different. Competent daughter of a competent father; the studio guy was hedging his bets, playing the DNA exacta. And he was right, I was so *bloody* competent.

The job was assistant to a casting director. Riding herd on extras, filing head shots – pretty mundane stuff, but every once in a while the casting director, Stacey, would turn to me and say, "So what do you think of our Mr. Davenport? Does he have the right mojo for Second Waiter?" Stacey called me Little Miss Binary, because I always answered yes or no. I had memorized the script, and I knew exactly the paintbrush we were looking for.

Within a year, I began to see my name in the credits of major motion pictures. Movies that were based on best-sellers, with stars that you didn't have to describe as "the guy on that doctor show." The kind of names you were sorely tempted to whip out at cocktail parties – but you never did, because you were too fond of being the consummate professional. I had college classmates who might work their entire lives, might give incredible, heart-rending performances – but who will never find the letters of their names mingling in such lofty constellations.

Three years into my personal Xanadu, my father came out west for a business trip and took me out to dinner. It was a ritzy new Italian place – Stelle, which means "stars." In case you didn't get the translation, there were stars everywhere: floating glass stars in the fountain, star-shaped napkin holders, whole galaxies etched into the plasterwork.

All through the meal, we could hear piano music in the lounge. Afterwards, we walked in to check it out, and found an old-fashioned piano bar – a massive grand piano with a counter around the edge for drinks. Daddy grabbed a couple of seats, ordered two champagne sours, then leaned over and said, "I think if a father buys his daughter dinner, the *least* she can do is sing him a song."

Not that I needed much persuasion. I flipped through the little book on the piano and found the song I sang at my high school graduation party: "It Could Happen To You." Sinatra recorded it. Also Robert Palmer, the rock singer.

So I waited my turn, finished my drink. It was different than karaoke; the singer had to provide the pianist with actual musical info: a key, a tempo. You could tell that some of them had been coming for years, working up their small repertoires. I had spent so much of the previous three years attached to a clipboard, I was actually a little nervous.

When I got up there, though, it was like firing up this alternate circuitry that I'd forgotten was there. I checked in with the pianist – this hip-looking grandfather type, wearing an old tuxedo with burgundy lapels – and asked him to play it slow and moody, so I could stretch out that fetching melody. It's a restless old tune; each line is like a snaky staircase that winds around the next, you never know where you're steppin'.

I didn't expect much from the audience; they were Angelenos, after all, accustomed to world-class talents on every streetcorner. But they began to hush down as I sculpted the first verse – especially the older ones, who probably knew the song but hadn't heard it for years. I, too, was busy with remembering – that sense of attention and connection, the liquid light going out through my mouth, in through my fingertips. All those years ago, before I became a child genius. Heroin has nothing on a good stage buzz.

I got a huge applause, and was surprised when Daddy handed me my coat and led me out to the parking lot.

I laughed. "Are you in a rush, Mr. Cohen?"

"It's always best to beat your applause to the door."

"Ha! I thought *I* was the theater major."

"I use the same principle for business meetings."

A few miles later, as I drove him to his hotel near the airport, he said, "Honey, I still marvel that a product of my DNA can sing a song the way you do."

"I'd almost forgotten I could."

"Which makes me wonder. Are you happy out here? Are you happy doing what you're doing?"

Just then, we were passing one of those monster billboards, the kind you only see in Los Angeles or Times Square. It was for a movie that I had worked on.

"I'm living out a dream, Daddy. I'm in Wonderland."

"But are you Alice?"

His persistence made me laugh. Once Daddy landed on a notion, he was like a labrador with a rawhide chew.

"Mr. Cohen, why do you ask such silly questions?"

"Why are you crying?"

We pulled up to a red light. I put a finger to my cheek, and found that it was wet.

Eleven

It seems impossible that we have told our stories (mine about meeting Harvey in the Signpost Forest), eaten our pizza and still have an evening of karaoke ahead of us, but that's the nature of Northwest Novembers. The darkness stretches on and on, and it's your job to fill it up. We're driving the Narrows Bridge in Ruby's beat-up Toyota, and we're not even running late. I'm hoping Ruby isn't as stoned as I am – but then, I'm such an infrequent toker, it was bound to knock me around a little.

My misty vision makes it easier to marvel at the construction on the New Narrows Bridge. They've extended hanging footbridges from tower to tower so the workers can spin the cables, and strung it with white lights. The result is a luminous foreshadow of the bridge to come, lasered against the dark Sound. And you would never, *ever* get me up there.

It's awfully nice to have my own roadie – much easier to lug the CD cases and set up the PA. I get the feeling, also, that for Ruby this is good therapy – a tiny vaccine of showbiz to fight off the gloom. I grab an extra chair and set it next to my station, just to make it clear that she doesn't have to brave the general assembly.

I'm setting out my business card holders, and Ruby's scouring a songbook, when Shari, Alex and Alex's latest partner – a tempestuous-looking Russian lady in a leather skirt – walk through the door in a cloud of laughter. When they spot Ruby, they don't exactly do the cliché stunned silence, but they do seem to make a subtle adjustment. Shari skips the usual huggy greeting for a friendly wave as they head for their table, just across the dance floor. Ten minutes later, they're joined by Harry and Kevin the Cop, who have lately become quite the duo, and, a minute behind, Caroleen, looking unusually chic in a leopard coat.

I can tell that Ruby is taking careful notes (she is, after all, a student of audiences), and I sense something simmering just beneath the surface. Just as I'm about to tell her something reassuring, she's up, clomping across the dance floor with a determined expression. She stops before my regulars (who are now exhibiting the aforementioned stunned silence), plants a hand on either hip, and turns into Streisand in *Funny Girl.*

"Boy! Do I have egg on *my* face!"

With an opener like that, the ice breaks all over the place. I'm having a hard time tracing the exact discourse, but the hills of verbiage have the shape of excessive mutual apology and good-natured jokes ("You should've seen the look on your face!"). She returns ten minutes later as if nothing has happened and goes back to her songbook.

I pick out a CD for sound check and give Ruby a stage aside: "*You* are a magician."

"No," she sotto voces. "I'm an actress."

When I return to adjust the levels, the *Choo Choo Ch'Boogie* tootles in on its newly revamped track with two eggnog-and-vodkas. And a note.

Don't think I don't know what happens when I'm away. You're grounded! –H

When I look to the bar, Hamster is whittling one index finger with the other, the universal gesture for *Naughty, naughty.*

The evening is odd in several other ways, as well. People keep arriving in groups of three or four, hanging out for one round and then leaving, disappointed at the lack of a crowd. If they had all stayed, we'd *have* a crowd.

Two that do stay are a tall Latin beauty and her thin, very gay guyfriend. She looks like Bizet's *Carmen* as a supermodel, and sings in Spanish, from a Mexican CD I keep around. But she holds the mic away from her mouth like it's a live rattlesnake, and we can't hear a thing. So she's a *shy* Carmen supermodel. Her name is Mariposa, which I believe means "butterfly."

The guy, Jamie, has big black-framed glasses, sort of Buddy Holly as a mad professor. He also has a good upper range, handling some tough Bowie and Prince songs, but then making faces afterward like he really sucked. I've never understood that – it's like some people think it's uncool to think you might actually be good at something.

Mariposa and Jamie are also resoundingly drunk. Between songs, she sits on his lap, and they conduct full-blown makeout sessions. This little sideshow can *not* pass by without comment, so I turn off my mic and lean toward Ruby.

"You watchin' Will and Grace over there?"

"How can I not?" she says.

"Two possibilities," I say. "Either my gay-dar is way off, or they're both suffering lengthy dry spells and trying to keep in practice."

Ruby snorts into her hand. "Perhaps Jamie is... bi-curious?"

I slap her on the arm. "You're bad! Bad I say!" But then I realize we're distracting from Shari's "Me and Bobby McGee," so I try to regain my composure. Anyway, Ruby's next.

"She's doing "Mama Look a Boo-Boo" by Harry Belafonte. Last time she did "Mambo No. 5" by Lou Bega. Our little control freak, who took such care shepherding each note of her first two Gig Harbor sorties, has now decided to try every novelty song she can find. And still, every note out of that mouth is golden. I am pathetically envious.

And then the luau hits. No kidding. In the middle of Ruby's calypso, a long train of youngsters spills into the bar, adorned in grass skirts, leis and aloha shirts. I scamper over to hijack a hula girl.

"What the hell's going on?" I ask.

"Hi," she says, half-crocked. "Luau party! UPS! Neighbors called the cops, so we said screw it! Let's kay-ray-OH-kay! Whoo!"

UPS is the University of Puget Sound, across the Narrows in Tacoma.

"How'd you get here?" I ask.

She opens her sweet, perfectly betoothed mouth and says, "I have no fucking idea!"

"Okay, honey," I say. "Sorry to keep you."

There's only one way to handle a drunken college party. I turn to Hamster at the bar and flash my middle finger, our little joke signal for *Get me a fucking drink!* What arrives on the *Metro*, two singers later, is a big bowl-shaped glass holding a lime-green drink with a stripe of raspberry red syrup. It's mightily delicious. I take a long draught, then turn to find a dozen singers lined up at my station, song slips in hand. The first is "Tiny Bubbles."

After that, I can't tell you. It's like driving a long ramp into a hurricane, and somewhere along the line you forget where you came in. The world is walled off at the bar windows, a swirling sherbet of color and noise, blurred like a slow-shutter photograph. When the bus rolls into the station I am screaming "Rock 'n' Roll" by Led Zeppelin as youthful bodies bump their parts together (so *clever* how this generation has turned simulated sex into choreography). Just as I reach the tough part, I feel a hand gripping my left nether cheek. I turn to find Shari, wearing a Little Mary Sunshine smile.

"Oh!" she says. "Was that you?"

I pat her on the left (upper) cheek and return to my wailing. Zeppelin crunches to a finish, and the room explodes. I call up Kevin for "Suavamente," wait till he gathers the inevitable salsa mob, reach in to squeeze that firm constabulary butt and scuttle away like a cockroach.

I wake up on the floor. I can't move my arms, and I feel something smooth and plasticky against my face. When I open my eyes, the ceiling is a maze of color and slowly moving dots. And a large brown blob with a single white stripe. And a shower of green confetti.

"Hamster?" God. I sound like Tom Waits doing a Louis Armstrong impression.

"Good morning, my little cash cow. This is your bonus for last night."

I'm surrounded by presidents: Washington, Lincoln – Franklin?

"Jesus. What'd I do? Sleep with you?"

He laughs entirely too much. "Now *that* would be funny!"

I go to give him a playful slap, and discover why it is I can't move. I'm wrapped up tight in a sleeping bag.

Hamster grins. "I don't know what major corporations those kids' parents own, but last night we separated them from large chunks of their trust funds. The biggest night in Karz Bar hiss-tow-ree!"

Hamster kisses me on the cheek – for him, an exceptional gesture. He claps his hands together and gives them a robber-baron rub.

"Now! What does my prize employee wish for breakfast? Sausages? I've got kielbasa."

Just the word "kielbasa" makes my stomach gurgle. "Ooh! Can I start with a glass of Sprite? By the way, what was that *evil* drink you gave me last night?"

"Hamstah Hooch. Its exact ingredients shall remain a secret."

"But probably include tequila."

"Probably."

He hops to his feet like a Ukrainian dancer and heads for the kitchen. "Sprite followed by coffee!" he declaims.

I snake my hand up next to my throat and locate a zipper pull.

"Hey!" I croak. "What happened to Ruby?"

Hamster leans into the room with a salacious expression. "Ruby was last seen leaving the bar with Harry Baritone."

"Oh," I say. Ten seconds later, the information arrives at my brain. "Really?!"

Twelve

I'm out on the back deck, but feeling like I'm somewhere else. Snow comes to the Puget Sound only two or three times a year, and last night's was exceptional, painting my evergreen view with a vanilla frost. I sit with my third coffee on a thick-timbered picnic table and imagine myself at a long-ago trip to Tahoe. I'm nestled into the corner of a deck overlooking the intermediate runs, sharing a sourdough bowl with a handsome, dark-eyed devil of a man.

The present calls to me in a jangle of metal, and I know what's coming: a merry flight of chocolate fur and a resounding "Woof!" I can almost parse the letters: W-O-O-F.

Java bursts through the trellised archway and takes a mighty leap onto the deck. He is completely unprepared for the effects of snow on a hard surface. When his paws fail to make purchase, he performs a four-footed Astaire routine and collapses, legs flying out like the poles of a wrecked pup tent as he slides on his belly, drops off the end of the deck and lands with a *whump*! During the entire stunt, he wears an expression that is both puzzled and ridiculously calm – and that's the part that sets me off. When Floy Craig pops her blonde curls around the trellis, she finds me nearly suffocating with laughter.

"What the hell was that?"

"Oh!" I squeak. "Hard to... Can't..."

She wipes off the opposite bench, takes a seat and watches me with much amusement. Then she sees the long swipe leading to Java, who's standing in the yard, shaking himself dry.

"Ah! I can picture it now. He's got the same problem with the tiling in the kitchen. Does that cartoon thing where his feet are just swishing around like a propeller. If we could only get one of these on tape, we could make some serious money. Can you talk now?"

I'm not going to take the chance, so I shake my head.

"I was going to ask you what the hell you're doing out here, but then I saw this view. Must remind you of Alaska." She takes a panoramic scan, then turns back to me and rests her chin on her hand.

"Are you doing better, Channy? Because... you seem like you are."

Floy's caring expression succeeds in disabling my funny bone, but I swallow a couple of times before answering.

"Yes. Yes," I say. "Things are better. There are some things I needed to get out of my system."

"Oh," she says. "Well you know you can talk to me whenever you want, right?"

"Yes, I know. But this one thing, I needed someone a little, I don't know, farther away? It's hard to explain."

Floy looks the slightest bit hurt. *People do love the role of therapist,* I think. But I can see her flipping my answer over in her mind, and her features relax.

"No, I understand. The things people tell me at the hospital... Well there you are! Are you done with your extreme sports?"

Java has found a safe route to the deck and is nudging Floy's hand with his snout, trying to jump-start a petting session. He barely gets a response before he's off again, streaking through the arch at full bark.

"Oh!" I say. "That's probably my friend. I'd better grab Java so she can get out of her car."

"Can you hang on to him?" says Floy. "I'll fetch the leash so I can take him for a walk."

I arrive at the driveway to find Java on his hind legs, front paws planted on the hood of Ruby's Toyota. Ruby's inside, laughing hysterically. She rolls down her window to greet me.

"He looks like this director I knew in New York. Very gay and *very* fierce."

I grab Java by the collar and pull him down. "Java is on a comic roll this morning."

Floy trots out the front door and hooks a leash to Java's collar as I reel off the introductions.

"Floy, Ruby. Ruby, Floy. RubyJavaJavaRuby."

Ruby gets out and waggles a hand over Java's floopy head.

"That covers all the combinations. Nice to meet you, Floy."

"I'll take *this* monster far away," she says, "so you two can have a nice quiet talk."

"Thanks," I say. Ruby and I watch as Java drags her around the bend.

"Well," says Ruby. "Where shall we take our story-swap?"

I can't stand it. She's wearing this long, lovely scarlet coat, and she has all this color in her cheeks, and her eyes are so full of energy. I have so carefully tended this garden, only to give it away to a houseguest.

"Like to freeze on my deck?"

"Hmm," she says, sucking on a fingertip (what's *that* about?). "No offense to your Northwest sensibilities, but I've had enough snow to last a lifetime. All right if we walk somewhere? Keep the blood pumping?"

"Sure." The logical route is the loop trail – the opposite direction from Floy and Java – no artful landmarks, but lots of fir and cedar to hold the snow. "Want me to fill a thermos with coffee?"

"No, that's all right," she says. "Let's walk unfettered." She smiles much too widely.

"Okey-doke. Walk this way."

We take a right at the end of the driveway, follow Water Drive for a block, then duck into the forest at the trailhead, onto a wide path covered in woodsy mulch.

"Pastoral," says Ruby.

"Yeah, it's nice. I could swear someone's been tending it. It seems too neat to be natural. So I never though to ask, but what brought you here, exactly? To the Northwest."

"A geopsychologist would say it's the logical fourth corner: Florida, LA, New York – Washington. However, as a wise woman once said, that would be too neat to be natural. In actuality, I have a brother out here. He's been having some trouble, so I thought some sibling-time was in order. Hey Channy, do you mind that I'm going out with Harry?"

Damn! I hadn't expected her to bring it up first.

"I'm okay," I say, not terribly convincingly. "He's sort of like a big brother, mostly. He's very sweet. He's been through a lot."

"So he says."

In a pathway conversation, you can measure awkward silences in feet. This one takes thirty.

"So what's he... like?" I ask.

Ruby laughs. "Well, *you* know what he's like."

Yikes. "No, I've never slept with Harry."

Ruby stops and looks at me. "Neither have I."

Twenty feet. The pressure gets too much, and I have to laugh at my presumption.

"Oh shit! Should I just shut up now? I think I'll just shut up now."

"No," she says. "I've had too many cautious fucking friendships in my life. You say whatever you feel like, Channy. And I promise you I won't get upset."

Ten feet.

"So what did you guys do?"

"Went to a Shari's in Tacoma. Had a two a.m. breakfast. Don't you love those?"

"Yeah. I do."

"I was pretty toasty."

"Who wasn't?"

"Harry. Or maybe he just holds it well. He drove me home, gave me a courtly goodnight kiss, and then – get this: the next day, *he tows my car home.* Knocks on my door, hands me my car keys – which I didn't even remember giving him. Is this guy for real?"

"Yes," I say. "He is."

"Well, that kind of freakishly anachronistic chivalry demanded a reward so, that night, I took him to this place in Seattle. The Kingfisher. All painted up inside like a Louisiana roadhouse. And there's some kind of unwritten code that only *thee* most gorgeous black people work there – and eat there. It's like a casting call for *Ain't Misbehavin'*. Hamster would fit right in.

"After that, we went to this play about a gay man who falls in love with a shark at the aquarium. And when the gay man is kissing the man who plays the shark, I peek at Harry to check the squirm factor, and he's just laughing his head off, like everyone else. And I'm thinking, Damn! Is this guy for real?"

"Yes," I say. "He is."

Ruby stops for a second, reading my repetition, then shakes it off.

"And again, a goodnight kiss. Well, a long one. Yesterday, he had to work. I'm meeting him tonight at karaoke. I think we're both rather covetous of Channy's Sanatorium for Wayward Singers, so we're circling each other rather carefully. But… well, I don't want to turn you into a double agent, Channy, but I'm feeling a little dizzy. Can you toss me a couple of clues?"

I yank a handful of needles from a Scotch fir and hold them to my nose.

"'Bout a year ago, Harry had his heart drawn and quartered. I think he's okay now. Just…"

I stop, because I don't like the quaver that's working into my voice. But Ruby doesn't miss much.

"Let it fly, girlfriend." She slaps me on the back, like I'm choking on something.

I stop walking, and place a hand on her fuzzy scarlet shoulder.

"Don't go underestimating him just because he's nice."

She looks at me for a second, then turns to walk. As I pull alongside, I swear I can feel the sadness pouring off of her. *It's no wonder she's an actress,* I think. *Her emotions turn on a toggle switch.*

We enter a long, flat stretch of trail beneath a high tunnel of Douglas fir. Fifty feet. When she speaks, it's barely audible.

"Don't worry. That's a lesson I've learned."

Thirteen
Ruby

My endgame was Broadway – or off-Broadway – but I knew I couldn't go there directly. I needed to go to some third place, so I could reinvent myself, rewire my circuitry. The first item on the scrap heap would be that nasty director's omniscience; the first purchase would be a brand new suit of flakiness.

Things began with my old college chum, Shelley, who lived in San Francisco, in the Ocean District. Shelley was a singer-songwriter, trying to figure out how to work the music scene. The day I called, she had just discovered that one of her roommates was moving out. This served to further confirm my instincts – the fates were intervening on my behalf. My production company was between projects, so I really didn't even have to quit – just let them know I wouldn't be around for the next film. Stacey was pretty sad to see me go (all that *competence* out the window), but it's not the general policy of the Dream Machine to step on an aspiration.

I was moved in in a matter of a week. The place was a cool old Arts & Crafts – the living room a dark hardwood plain covered by an enormous Persian rug, several guitars and every percussion instrument known to humankind. I expected Carlos Santana to walk in any second. Maybe Jefferson Airplane. I found an acting conservatory that operated out of Fort Mason, and signed up for a beginner's class. I wanted to go right back to the roots.

The classroom was a dance studio – miles of floor, lots of mirrors, a barre for stretching. The teacher, Mr. Burman, was a playwright-director with a gruff, blue-collar exterior: rumbling voice, big Polish nose, thinning hair. It became readily apparent, however, that he was also kind, and the owner of a guerrilla sense of humor. (His actual humor was brilliant and twisted, a discovery I made at a performance of his satirical skits. In one of them he took the Catholic molestation scandal to its logical extreme: the priests were now *eating* the children.)

On the first night, we started with a few standard warmups – acting games I had done in college – then he gathered us for the night's central activity, something he called "one-minute wanders."

"This is largely for my own evil purposes," he said. "I want to know how your little thespian minds work – what level of raw material we're working with. This here cowboy hat is filled with slips of paper. Each is the beginning of a monologue: 'The last time I went to London, I...' 'I have never been able to tapdance because I...' Your job is to improvise from there – fact, fiction, doesn't matter – for whatever seems like a minute. You are to speak as continuously as possible, and to avoid stall words like um, er, yaknow. The main thing is, don't think too much. Thinking is our enemy. And *I'm* thinking I should begin with this eager young lady in the front, or else she will burst from her shoes. Um... damn! What was your alias?"

(This from the evening icebreaker, a name game.)

"Red slippers," I said.

"Dorothy. No – Ruby!"

I extracted a slip and got *I hate peanut butter because...* And here's what I said:

"I hate peanut butter because I once read that you could put it on the roof of your dog's mouth, and it would take him, like, hours to lick it off? Now, I know this sounds really cruel, but what was even more cruel was the way that our dog Sputter, who was a Shih-Tzu (isn't it fun to say 'Shih-Tzu'? It's like you're swearing but really you're not). Well anyway, that fucking dog would yip and yap and yop all day long, and one day I just got fed up, so I loaded a spatula with peanut butter and spackled the roof of that furball bitch's mouth. It worked so well that she spent the next three days licking, and the problem was, her doggie bed was right next to my human bed? And all night long: licklicklicklicklicklicklicklicklick! Finally I put her outside, and she snuck under the gate, wandered into the road and – sniff! – got run over by a garbage truck. The driver told us he didn't see her until it was too late, and Sputter didn't move a muscle, she was too busy licking the roof of her mouth. And that – sniff! – is why – sniff! – I *hate* peanut butter."

A director's note here: for comic effect, I actually spoke the word "sniff!" instead of actually sniffing. I had the class laughing pretty hard, but they stopped when they saw Mr. Burman glaring at me. I knew exactly what he was up to, however, so I glared right back until he broke.

"There is nothing more *rude,*" he said, "than a student who gets more laughs than her teacher."

And then I got my applause.

The nice thing about going first was that now I could relax and study my classmates. All in all, they were a remarkably quick-witted bunch, and I was feeling more and more certain that San Francisco was exactly the right place for me.

One student who really caught my eye was Eddy (whose alias was "whirlpool"). His monologue wasn't actually all that good, but he was such a *character* to begin with. His face was all sharp angles – sharp chin, generous sharp nose, and small, quick eyes. Very coyote-like. Plus an improbable pile of curly brown hair that reminded me of Lyle Lovett, or a young Bob Dylan. He spoke in a rapid London accent, very clipped and (here we go again) sharp. The rapid speech, in fact, was his prime handicap, forcing his brain to improvise at an untenable pace and dragging "erms" and "ehs" into his monologue (which began, *The last time I played golf with John Travolta...*).

I had no need of seeking him out after class, because I looked up and there he was.

"Hey, that peanut butter. That was fucking brilliant."

"Thanks."

He said "fucking" in that particular British way, verging on "fawking," that made it seem much friendlier.

"And condolences on poor Sputter. Such a loss!"

"Eh!" I said. "She was expendable."

"Oh!" He feigned shock. "Heartless. Say, would you let me buy you a drink and simultaneously interrogate you? I know a fabulous microbrew on Columbus. They have every ale known to mankind."

How could I say no? After taking ten minutes to pick a pear cider from Rhode Island, I sat as Eddy regaled me with the story of his brother's wedding, which ended with the groom swimming across a small pond in nothing but his top hat. The story was terribly long, but never boring – a rare combination.

"No offense, Eddy, but where was all this storytelling talent during your one-minute wander?"

"Oh God yes, I know!" He beat himself on the forehead for full effect. "I was thinking too much – precisely what he told us *not* to do. Halfway through, I was thinking, 'Where the hell is this story going, Eddy?' And that mucked me up even worse. I think that's why I'm taking this class, actually. I need to rid myself of that internal critic, learn to dive out and stretch my boundaries."

"So you're not on the acting track?" I asked.

"Nope. Strictly for funsies. Although I can't figure out what that Bear, Fish, Mosquito nonsense was all about."

"Just silliness, I'm sure. I'd guess almost the entirety of most acting classes is just to give you license to do things you wouldn't *dream* of doing in everyday life. How long did you last?"

"Three seconds," he said, laughing. "I went for the bloody obvious Bear, and a cute little Asian Mosquito gave me the malaria."

(He pronounced it "malari-er," in that peculiar British fashion.)

"Ha! Good thing *I* didn't run into you. I went straight for the fish. But then, I'm a good swimmer."

"Rrowr!" he said, swatting a hand. "Not good enough to avoid my enormous claws!"

As it turned out, Eddy was an inventor. His latest pursuit was a hydrofoil wakeboard that would lift waterskiers above the water.

He spent most of his summer weekends performing test runs on the lakes of the Central Valley (and most of his summer Mondays recovering from the bruises).

The acting class was one of a long series of endeavors that he pursued just for the hell of it. He referred to this as the NUP, or No Ulteriors Program. I found this aspect of his personality most endearing, and vowed that I would pursue a few NUP activities of my own.

He lived in an open space preserve in the Santa Cruz Mountains, forty miles south of The City, in one of a cluster of cabins at the end of a mile-long dirt road. They were originally constructed as a family hideaway for an early Silicon Valley industrialist, and "grandfathered" in after the open space purchase. The road was hell on my shocks, but I came to regard Eddy's place as my own private retreat, whenever my packed schedule of classes and clerical day-job allowed a bit of sunlight.

Eddy maintained his tinker's independence by running a one-man deck-staining business; he billed himself as the Deck Doctor. Once in a while I tagged along, and was always amazed at the places where he did his work: grand rustic palaces that overlooked miles of redwood forest, the Pacific a thin blue promise at the horizon. He invited me to become an employee, but I could see the amazing amount of abuse he piled on that wiry body of his, and I doubted it would gibe with my dance classes.

Once or twice a month, we would shimmy downhill to a bar in Menlo Park, to pursue this new thing called "karaoke." I suppose I could rationalize it as another chance to work on my singing and stage presence, but for Eddy it was pure NUP – particularly because he had not one iota of talent. In the bizarro world of karaoke, however, he probably had more of a following than I did, because he was absolutely fearless. His one sure bet was "Another Brick in the Wall," which matched his accent and chutzpah, but anything with much of a melody sent him into the William Shatner zone, where he was content to declare the lyrics with much enthusiasm and little regard for the music.

All this admiration might sound like the prelude to a romantic venture, but who can figure the roadmaps of chemistry, the crapshoot of two human frames of mind? For one thing, I had no capacity for it. I was determined to treat San Francisco as a way station – to tap a little syrup from her trunk and head to New York in search of pancakes.

Or, it might have been Eddy. I had such affection for him, but compared to my serious-minded endeavors, his pursuits seemed inambitious, almost childlike. Or maybe he was just too bloody nice. Once, when my day-job fell prey to a round of layoffs, I was having a hard time coming up with the rent. When Eddy heard about this, he insisted on giving me a loan. But as he began to think out loud about all the fiduciary machinations he'd have to go through to come up with the cash, I stopped him and said, "Eddy, I have this thing called a father? I think it's time to call him."

Earnest generosity is not necessarily an aphrodisiac. It often makes it seem like the man is trying too hard. I think women prefer a certain level of self-centeredness, because that's a quality we can trust.

In any case, Eddy never made a move, so it was easy to place him in that innocent big-brother category. We were great friends, and we had great fun – so no loss, right?

I did, however, take him up on a couple of pressure-washing assignments, which were really quite enjoyable. Each pass of the spraying wand took an impressive amount of grime out of the wood, which provided a pleasing sense of productivity. At the same time, the constant halo of mist kept the August heat nicely at bay. Soon after, I got some assignments from a temp clerical service, and my little cash crisis was averted.

Come October, my year – and my classes – had come to an end, and I was ready for the Big Apple. I had also managed, through my dear sweet casting director, Stacey, to find a year-long sublet on the Upper West Side. Nicely timed with my departure was a big blowout at Eddy's cabin.

Not that the party was for me. Eddy was up to his elbows with Burning Man, a late-summer festival in the Nevada desert. It was simultaneously a brazen sex party, dustblown survival camp, artistic Carnaval and pagan hippie rite – centered on the immolation of a humongous man-like statue. The network of "burners" was broad and vigorous – almost like a new generation of Deadheads – and they conducted regional gatherings throughout the year. Eddy decided that his cluster of cabins was the perfect destination for one of these, and thus was born Burning Jam, an all-night music party.

With the musician network afforded by roommate Shelley, I was instantly a crucial cog, and happy to contribute before I abandoned the Bay Area. Eddy invited fifty people – three hundred showed up. But burners are great at this stuff; they've been trained by the Nevada desert to bring their own necessities, and to readily adapt to the unexpected. Almost instantaneously, the retired orchard next to the cabins became a campground.

The center of activity was Eddy's deck (the rehabilitation of which was the genesis of his staining biz). Shelley kept the lineup of musicians rolling on- and offstage, owing largely to the use of a "community" drumset and PA system. This was also my first chance to see the end product of all those rehearsals in my living room. Shelley's band, Slippery Sisters, was definitely pursuing a Lisa Loeb/Natalie Merchant vibe, with Shelley on acoustic guitar and spritely vocals. (Half of the Sisters were actually brothers, but no one seemed to care.)

There was no shortage of dancers, in various phases of exotic dress and undress. The invitation had expressly forbidden dour colors, which opened the door for burner standards like the feather boa, candy-colored spandex, dominatrix leather and various illumination devices that kept them from getting run over on dark festival nights. I went for a retro lime-green pantsuit and a pink British garden hat, plus an Irish brooch of amber-colored glass.

As the roster of official bands gave way to an all-out jam, Shelley proclaimed her duties fulfilled and grabbed me by the elbow. We proceeded to Eddy's art-car, a chopped-off Honda Accord outfitted with a boat-like deck and pirate sails. He used it to conduct revelers around Burning Man at parade-float speed, and had fitted it with twin outboard margarita blenders. He had spent the whole afternoon there, dutifully sousing his patrons. I felt sorry for him, working so hard at his own party – but then it was probably the most efficient way to get face-time with each and every guest. I had been to the well thrice already, and Shelley seemed eager to catch up.

Like everyone else who ever met Eddy, she was much impressed, and gave me the kind of glance that said, *So what's he, chopped liver?* We assisted with his blending for an hour, then excused ourselves to drift across to a small barn outfitted as a disco, complete with spinning lights and a '70s-'80s soundtrack. The old floorboards were not exactly conducive to dancing, but the crush of bodies seemed to prevent any falls. Shelley and I used this to our advantage, faking several stumbles so we could land on various hunky males.

We were pretty crocked, to be sure, but not half so gone as this one blonde girl, who was basically being propped up by the crowd. She looked about twenty, with the baby fat that a twenty-year-old can get away with, plus an impressive display of cleavage, threatening to escape the confines of a blouse that she must have purchased when she was twelve. She took plentiful opportunities to rub against neighboring physiques – be they male or female – and ended each song by lifting a fist to the sky and screaming "Fuck yeah!"

Shelley bopped over to me during "Rock the Casbah." "Damn, woman! Have I ever behaved like that in my life?"

I laughed very loudly (because, why the hell not?). "You've come pretty close, Mother Teresa."

She punched my shoulder, very boy-like. "No! I have not!"

"Okay!" I complained. "You have never screamed 'Fuck yeah!' in quite that fashion."

"Damn straight."

"Nor have your tits ever been *close* to that size. Ow! Quit it!"

A few songs later, we wandered outside to find a man and woman dressed like gypsies, spinning illuminated crystals at the ends of strings. Then we noticed a crowd gathering at the music-deck. I tapped on a broad, black-clothed shoulder and got a pirate: fake parrot, hoop earring, eyepatch – a pretty thorough job.

"Ahrr!" he inquired.

"What's going on?" I asked.

"My girlfriend... I mean, me wench, she's got this fantasy about doing a public striptease – so hey, we're here to push the envelope, right?"

"Groovy!" I said, feeling instantly that I had lost my moral compass and was quite happy to be rid of it. Shelley and I sat on a rug over the dirt as a thin Asian girl pranced about between two redwoods. The jammers served up a slow, chewy blues entirely appropriate to the occasion. The pirate, meanwhile, began giving me a neckrub, which might have been his way of releasing sexual tension – but I didn't care, because he was good.

His girlfriend, however, was a dud. She took forever to take off her top and skirt, revealing a set of very unimaginative underthings. Then she sashayed around in her panties and bra for frickin' ever, leaving all the guys waiting for more and not getting it. In both the British and American senses of the word, I was pissed.

"Come on!" I shouted. "I can see this much at the beach! Give us a freakin' nipple!" I gave Shelley a hearty nudge, but she was involved in a liplock with her drummer. (Uh-oh, I thought. There goes *that* band.) Then the pirate abandoned his duties as my personal masseuse to wrap his girlfriend with a blanket. It seemed like a good time for a pee-break.

I climbed the steps to Eddy's cabin and found a long line of women at the bathroom door (I assumed the guys were lined up at redwood trees). Every last one of them was snickering uncontrollably, and I soon understood why. Behind Eddy's bedroom door, two or more someones were going at it like dogs in heat. The moaning and slapping built to a pitch until a successful O was punctuated with a cry of "Fuck yeah!" So the blonde from the barn had finally found her release. The girls in line were performing a kind of knock-kneed Rockettes routine, trying to keep from laughing lest they literally peed their pants. As the line inched forward, I came even with the bedroom door, and I could hear the clipped tenor of her partner: "Fawkin' great, baby."

I can't quite recall my movements after that, but I do remember coming out on the orchard as the moon climbed over the trees, turning the brown California grass to silver pasta. I managed to find Shelley's tent and crawl through the flaps, the air crackling with chips of laughter and conversation. I was deathly intent on sleep, but I heard another pair of lovers – this from the tent next door – and suddenly I couldn't remember how to breathe. I imagined dying alone, surrounded by all this humanity, simply because I had forgotten how to let my body pursue its mindless occupations. But my body raised a coup d'etat. My lungs let go like an untied balloon, and the breath came out, turning to tears, turning to sobs.

I awoke to a street gang of Stellar's jays and a far-off call that I couldn't quite place. It gradually took on human syllables.

"Fuck-a-doodle-doo! Fuck-a-doodle-doo!"

The tent flaps made a papery ruckus, and in popped Eddy's face, bearing a goofed-up smile and bloodshot eyes.

"Hello! I'm the morning cock! Time to wake the fuck up! I've got a shitload of blueberry pancakes for you morning lovelies."

Shelley kept right on snoring, I shook out my hair, which felt like it had been stored for months in a musty attic, and managed to produce a bleary smile.

"You look awfully happy," I said. "Or happily awful. Any blonde, big-titted reason for that?"

"Ah yes, the lovely De-*bor*-ah. Anything but De-boh-*ring.* Recently thrown to the dustbin by her brutish boyfriend, eager to seek vengeance by grabbing the first penis she could find and having her way with it. And imagine my surprise when it turned out to be mine!"

I laughed, and reached up to pat his whiskered cheek.

"Good for you, Eddy. I'll be right out."

"Lovely!" He vanished into the outside world, continuing his duties as town crier. "Fuck-a-doodle-doo! Fuck-a-doodle-fucking-doo!"

I was ready for New York, because I had become an *excellent* actress.

Fourteen

Ruby takes a deep drag and lets it out on a "Phew!"

"That is one nasty smoke, girlfriend!"

I fondle my last box, reviewing the six soldiers lined up inside. "They've been through a lot."

"Where are they from?"

"Iraq." I give a glance around the pier. Halfway down, there's a mid-sized yacht – an old one, lots of lovely wooden trim. The *Scuttlebutt*, Port Angeles. One of the mast lines is draped in white Christmas lights – which is either way too early for the holidays or simply a year-round decoration.

"I can't tell you more than that," I say. "It's part of the story. I usually perform this little ritual *after* karaoke, but I assume you'll be heading out with your boyfriend."

Ruby performs a smoke-take. "Phew! 'Boyfriend'? God, that is *so* high school."

"High school never ends, Ruby."

"You're tellin' me. Check out the theater scene sometime. Well, my goodness!"

She's reacting to the snow, which is falling in wet, wet flakes that seem to melt inches from the ground. It's a bracing sight. Through the thickening flurry I see the flashing crosswalk on Harborview, broadcasting the presence of a tall model with a mane of white hair. But it's really blonde, and it's really Shari. She arrives at the near sidewalk, pauses to look our way, then turns toward Karz.

"How come you never hooked up with one of your singers, Channy? I mean, I understand the grieving process, but sex can be a powerful healing force. How about Kevin the Cop? He's got a thing for you, honey. I can tell by the way he wrestled me into those handcuffs. He was avenging his lady's honor. Hell, I might let him slap those cuffs on me again sometime."

I try my best to take a meaningful, Bogart-style pull on my cigar. (Ruby's so naturally theatrical, she makes you want to play along.)

"Karz has one hell of a gossip distribution network. That would be one whole *mess* of trouble. Nah. I need a non-singer."

"No!" says Ruby (she's one impulse away from holding up a vampire cross). "Singers are the only people with souls. Maybe you just need a singer from somewhere else."

"Maybe." I take my Swisher Sweet to the last bit of tobacco (where it's anything *but* sweet) and toss the wooden tip into the water.

"Is that part of the ritual?" asks Ruby.

"Is now."

She finishes hers and tosses it in. "I'm picturing a salmon with one of those tips in his mouth, tellin' all his friends, 'Try it, man – it'll make you look cool.'"

It's funny, but I'm not laughing.

I'm just about ready to start when Ruby brings up a large cardboard box.

"Is it time for Girl Scout cookies already?"

"Time for fun," she says. "Ya got yer maracas, a cowbell, claves, two extraordinarily chintzy tambourines, and le piece de resistance..."

She extracts a plastic toy guitar, the color of spoiled tangerines. It appears to have strings – tuning pegs, even – but I can't imagine that it produces actual music.

"I'm not sure I get it."

"It's an air guitar!" she says. "Only... without the air. Imagine all the fun our grownup little boys will have with *this*."

Ruby waits for a reaction, but it doesn't seem to be coming.

"What *is* the matter with you, Channy? Showtime! Time to bury your real feelings and pretend you're happy!"

I take the guitar and run a hand over the strings. "Sorry, Ruby. I don't know what it is. Perhaps I have released too many ghosts."

She pats me on the knee. "That's all right. Soon we'll have music."

I adjust one of the pegs and hand it back to her.

"Your G-string was loose."

She smiles. "Straight lines will get you nowhere."

The toys are an enormous hit. But first I'm careful to set some ground rules. No joining in on percussion unless you're invited. I am ever-cognizant of singers' rights, and I've seen what a tambourine can do in the wrong hands.

In a case of utter ethnic stereotype, it turns out that Kevin the Cop and his Puerto Rican hands have the best rhythm. He plays the tam as I sing Melissa Etheridge's "I Want to Come Over" – spare and tasty in the verses, loud and broad in the chorus. It really does add a lively acoustic edge to the prefab sound.

Our supreme guitarist is Harry Baritone – who, as it turns out, used to be in a garage band, so really, that's cheating. Ruby keeps ordering up Led Zeppelin songs just to keep him occupied. When she does "Back in Black" by AC/DC, he's on the floor, on his knees, literally bending over backwards.

"You'll notice," I say, "that although we singers make little mistakes all the time, Harry never misses a *note* on guitar."

Our finale is Harry singing (and pseudo-playing) "Smooth" by Santana, which naturally brings out the entire percussion section: Kevin on cowbell, Shari and Caroleen on tams, me on maracas and Alex on claves. We've got a whole damn band, really, and our noisy finish earns a rousing applause from the Petersons, elderly captain and captain's wife of the *Scuttlebutt*.

Ruby gives me a wink and a smile as she and Harry make for the exit (no doubt about it, those two are having crazy, nasty sex tonight). Hamster brings me a cup of coffee, and I begin the process of sorting song slips into envelopes (a new "archiving" service I have begun for my singers). I'm just about done when I feel a large presence behind me, and turn to find Shari, wearing a friendly but anxious expression.

"Hi," I say.

She kneels next to me, bringing our eyes level, and dives right in.

"The thing is, I thought I was your confidante. Maybe it sounds weird, but shit... it was important to me. And now you're always with Ruby – and it's a little hard to figure out how *that* happened. So now, this evening, you're out there smoking cigars with her on the pier. I guess I'm feeling all, out of the loop. I'm sorry..."

She stands and turns away, embarrassed by her feelings. I'm utterly at a loss – maybe because I had no idea how much it meant to her; maybe because now I'm feeling really stupid.

"God, Shari. I'm sorry; you're absolutely right. I guess it doesn't make much sense – but I'm getting some really shitty stuff out of my system right now, and it's just easier to tell Ruby. You're too close; you're too... nice."

She turns back, her eyes growing damp. "You know you can tell me anything, right?"

"I know I'm *allowed* to tell you anything. And I will, I'm sure. But... I guess this is like psychotherapy on the cheap, and before I go telling anyone besides Ruby, I need to figure it out for myself. Hey, let me buy you a drink. Then we'll go to the pier and smoke a couple more."

She laughs, just a little. "What kind of fool am I? I just talked myself into a ragweed cigar."

"Hey, Ham!" I yell. "Set up my pal Shari with a vodka gimlet."

"Yes, ma'am!" he says.

So here I am, back at the pier. Is this really catharsis, or am I just chasing pneumonia? It's much colder than before, but at least it's not snowing. I light up Shari, then me, and study my little tobacco soldiers, down to a quartet.

"God! I'm such a Needy Nancy," says Shari. "It's all so... high school."

"High school never ends," I say. Being a guru is easy – you just find a few good phrases and keep repeating them. "Anyway, Shari,

I'm glad you told me. Because tonight I have some very special business to attend to, and I can't do it alone."

I reach into my bag and pull out Kai's metallic care package.

"Oh God," says Shari. "It's Pandora's cashbox."

"Yes," I say. "But it's also one object away from empty, so – just keep me from jumping in the water, okay?"

I take a deep breath and push the metal tab, then reach into the lower compartment and extract a jeweler's box, covered in dark blue velvet. I click it open, revealing something shiny and military. I'm scared, so I hand it to Shari, who dangles it in front of her face so she can study it in the far-off light from the waterfront.

"My God, honey. It's a purple heart."

I take another breath and look for the words embossed on the inside of the box: *Kai Sharwa.* I toss my cigar into the water. It lands with a hiss.

Fifteen
Channy

I knew I couldn't go long without a job, so I tooled around Sumner in my truck, which seemed to be grateful to be off the Alcan and back on civilized blacktop. It took a dozen applications and three interviews, but I managed to land a spot as a stock girl at a grocery store called the Red Apple. I have to admit, the work was pretty brutal, especially when it came to the canned goods.

Given my cashiering experience, however, I knew I wouldn't be stocking for long. Within a month, I was moved up to checkout, and life was good. I always liked cashiering. The multi-tasking always keeps things interesting: weigh the produce, take the coupons, swipe the ATM cards ("Cash back with that?") all the while maintaining a conversation with the customer – remembering their names, their habits. Carol Mastere, schoolteacher, buys an unbelievable variety of hair care products. John Varna, guitarist for a wedding band, likes those fruity malt liquor drinks. I took great satisfaction in the idea that part of my job was to engage people.

Harvey was also hard at work – setting up his game room. But I really had no grounds to complain. Whether from his own savings or a generous sendoff from his family, he had cash aplenty, and was nice enough to pay the deposit and first month's rent. He found a used console and TV, hooked up the sound to a stereo from Goodwill, and was off on his adventures. Some days, I would leave for work with Harvey plugged in, jiggling the control stick as he leaned forward on an office chair, and return eight hours later to find him still there. I had no evidence that his butt had ever left the seat.

Perhaps I am naïve in the ways of gaming, but all of his favorites seemed to be ultra-violent. The gore-lust of the post-adolescent male is well-known, but it didn't match up with the mellow young man from the Signpost Forest.

His particular favorite was Katacomb, in which the protagonist prowls an endless network of subterranean chambers – very bleak and industrial – trying to off an army of mutants and cyborgs before they off him. When he shot these critters, they exploded in a detailed quick-flash inventory of everything that had once been on their insides. Harvey's nickname for Katacomb was Kill the Fucks.

His second favorite was Squadron Zero, a situational game in which the protagonist leads his men through constantly shifting World War II scenarios (you could choose from European, North African or Pacific theaters). The game demanded constant split-second decisions about the men and their movements. Wrong choices met with immediate and graphic punishment: hand grenades, strafing runs and mortars that separated men from their limbs with splashy relish. The part that freaked me out the most were the sniper attacks. Private Rodriguez would be resting on a log, calmly discussing a poker game or his girlfriend's latest letter, when a bullet would penetrate his temple and his eyes would go cold, like someone had turned a switch. Once all his men died, the captain received a vivid image of his own demise, his vision blurring out as a wash of blood drifted over the screen.

The game's language was peppered with what you might call the military liturgy: words like freedom, glory, duty, honor. I was always skeptical of such words. WWII seems like one of the few times these words weren't being used largely to cultivate power or line someone's pockets. To Harvey, though, it was a pivotal element of the game. He began his sessions by raising a tiny American flag along the TV antenna – with the help of a small rope-and-pulley attachment – while humming the "Star-Spangled Banner." Then he cranked himself up on two cups of strong black coffee, served lukewarm so he could down them like shots of tequila. After that, he fired up the stereo and played "All Along the Watchtower" – the Hendrix version. He said there was something about the "crackle" of it, the chaotic intensity, that reminded him of a battlefield. As if he'd ever *been* on a battlefield.

Weirdness, yes. Lots of weirdness. But I was duly compensated. For a boy, he was very neat. He began to take an interest in cooking. Whenever I arrived home, he immediately put his game on pause so he could give me a proper greeting. And the sex was outstanding. It was like I had jumped from the bunny slopes to the black diamonds in a single afternoon.

One night, I got home late, about eleven. I was exhausted – it was just before Labor Day, and everybody was stocking up. Harvey, however, was amped, and incorrigible. He kept teasing all my hot spots until my libido rose from the dead. The intercourse was bruisingly physical, and although I hurt a little afterward, it was a friendly pain – like I was soaking in a tub of my own hormones. I reached over and walked my fingers up his sternum.

"Not that I'm complaining, but what the hell got into you tonight?"

He flashed a boyish smile. "I got to level 24 on Squadron Zero. I've never been there before. God! It's so intense! You're constantly a finger-snap away from everything going straight to hell. You have to *decide* on the action and *execute* the action at almost the same moment, or you're dead. What a buzz!"

I had no idea what to say. My great physical pleasure inspired by a video game? I was torn between slapping him silly or telling him, by all means, go play some more! I was sitting on the edge of my bed, puzzling this out, when Harvey knelt behind me and started a neckrub. At this, he was an absolute artist. No one else ever applied enough leverage. He could reach all these places far beneath the skin. But there was the pattern again: absolute weirdness followed by immediate compensation.

"I have other news," he said. "I got a job."

I decided not to look at him; I was afraid I would look too relieved. "Really? Where?"

"That's the killer. It's right across the street – the little center with the pawn shop? On the far side, there's a store that sells video games. And now, *I* sell video games."

Like an alcoholic working in a bar, I thought, but I bolted my smile firmly in place. "That's wonderful!"

"I'm also joining the Army National Guard."

And there I was, puzzled again. "I'm not sure I..."

"My dad used to do it. It's a great deal. One weekend a month, and a two-week training camp once a year. The benefits are great – maybe even some money for college. And it's based at Ft. Lewis, which is, like, twenty miles from here. And as far as the danger, you're only called to duty for floods, riots – the occasional alien invasion. Meanwhile, I get to play with some pretty wicked toys."

"Jesus!" I said. "When you get going, you really get going. Just be *careful* with those toys. I intend to get a *lot* more use out of you."

"I'm sure they'll keep me in line," he said. His neckrub stalled out. "Would you mind if I, um... killed some fucks before bedtime? I'm still pretty wired."

I turned around and gave him a kiss. "Yes, honey. Go kill some fucks."

I rolled over and drifted right to sleep, thinking that this was not the kind of pillow talk that most girls took to dreamland.

Sixteen
Ruby

It's amazing how quickly you can find yourself adopted. But then, I did have a strategy. Before I even finished unpacking, I began hunting down obscure little theater groups, with the object of finagling my way into receptions and cast parties. Which was easy, because I knew the key. There is nothing more life-draining than investing large portions of yourself into a production, only to be faced with some turd at the reception who says, "You know, I'm an actor, too!" And to be forced to be nice to them, because either 1) they're friends with someone in the company, or 2) they actually paid money to see you.

The road to popularity, then, was to engage theater folk without once mentioning your status as a fellow traveler. Also, of course, I was one hot little chick. Garnering invitations from men was a cinch – even gay men, who seemed to invest me with a sort of Judy Garland vibe.

Two weeks after my arrival, I journeyed to this little hole-in-the-wall behind a coffeehouse in the East Village, where they were doing a little-remembered surrealist play from the forties. The plot wound around itself like a suicidal passion vine, but the show was intriguing nonetheless, firing along on rapid patter and brilliant illogic, simultaneously seen and unseen, as if you were watching it under a strobelight. In the end, I couldn't tell you what had just occurred, but I relished having my head screwed with, and my face was warm with laughter.

The director and lead actor was Joe Green, a strapping young man who was playing (depending on which version of the story you were buying into) either an insurance detective or an out-of-work mailman. His features were extremely Italian: Roman ringlets of black hair, thick eyebrows, dark brown eyes and a generous nose with a boxer's break. For all I knew, he could be a wiseguy. But he spoke like a director, bits of Bronx breaking through like fossilized ribs at an archaeological dig.

I cornered him at the reception, which was pretty easy to do. Lacking surplus space, they held it onstage, and Joe had enthroned himself on the central fixture, a turn-of-the-century barber's chair. As we spoke, I commandeered a straight-razor (which turned out to be plastic) and pretended to give him a shave.

"I suppose I should tell you about the name."

"Yeah? What about the name?"

"It's Anglicized."

"From what? Salvatore Frangiatelli?"

"Giuseppe Verdi."

I stopped to even up his sideburns. "Correct me if I'm wrong, but isn't that name already taken?"

"Yeah. And my parents aren't even opera fans. What the hell were they thinkin'? When I entered the thee-uh-tuh, I saw my chance. Stage name: Joe Green."

"Chin up, please. But how'd you get from one to the other?"

Facing ceilingward, he cocked an eyebrow. "You're a smart girl – figure it out. I didn't say 'changed.' I said 'Anglicized.'"

Pretty cocky for a guy with a blade at his throat, I thought. I geared up the brainbox and came up with *Giuseppe. Joseph. Joe. Verdi. Verdant. Green.*

"Holy shit!"

"There you go. Imagine yourself going through life as, I don't know – 'Barbra Streisand.'"

"Okay. I get the picture."

"Because you're a singer, right?"

Uh-oh. "Nope."

"Actor?"

"Nuh-uh."

He laughed.

"Hey!" I said. "You lookin' to get yourself sliced?"

"Sorry. It's just so rare to talk to someone who doesn't have a theater agenda. *And* an actual personality. So what is it that you do?"

"Florist shop."

(Actually, I was *delivering* for a florist shop – pretty reckless, considering I had just hit town, and was constantly getting lost. But the owners were my cousins, and I was – Oh God – *competent.*)

"God! I love florist shops. That wall of fragrance that just smacks you when you walk in the door. So... if I'm getting this right, when it comes to the stage, you are an absolute layperson."

"You got it."

"So tell me about the play tonight. Nothing you've read or heard. Tell me what you *think.*"

I ran the razor along my teeth. "Knock-knock."

Joe blinked. "Oh, um... Who's there?"

"Surrealist."

"Surrealist who?"

"Broccoli."

That got him. He laughed, and I noticed what a great mouth he had. His lips were thick, like they'd been bruised in a fight. *Poor baby, can I kiss it?*

"So. What's your point?"

"Surrealism," I said, "is always just that close to being a joke. One... vegetable... away. So it's all left to architecture, and delivery. Give it a solid structure, find some good actors to play it – it can be fucking brilliant. Lose either one – it melts like cheese in a microwave."

Joe rubbed his freshly shorn (cleft) chin.

"What about tonight?"

I used the razor to tap him on the head. "I'm still here, ain't I? Chatting with the director? If you really need me to spell it out, I loved it, and the best thing about it was you."

He hid his face behind his hands – purely an act, because he was fully aware of how good he was. When he peeked out, I could see that his irises had tiny copper-brown chips that flashed when he moved.

"I need you."

Gulp. "Pardon?"

"I'm workshopping a play. And I have *had* it shoveling the bullshit from the theater-folk with their aesthetic agendas and secret jealousies. I need a fresh set of eyes. What are you doing Friday night?"

I unleashed my most devilish smile. "I'm going to a play reading."

Joe lived nearby, on 8th Street, a block over from St. Mark's Place. I was early, so I strolled the cheesy gift shops, sorting through mod sunglasses and dominatrix dog collars (I got the latter for Eddy, betting that he would get some use out of it). I walked into a forest of Indian restaurants, the air laced with curry and tabla music. A dozen locals had set up an impromptu sidewalk sale, arranging appliances and clothing on straw mats and old quilts.

Finding Joe's address, I opened a wrought-iron gate and descended to his basement apartment. But what a basement! Joe greeted me with a kiss on the cheek (which I took as a promising sign) then led me through a modest hallway of bedrooms to a cavernous living room. You could have a basketball game in there! The furniture was shoved to the walls on all sides, leaving the center to a semi-circle of folding chairs.

"Have a stiff, hard seat," said Joe. "You want a stiff, hard drink with that?"

A thin, attractive man waltzed in (and I mean the waltzing part literally), his blond hair cut so tight to his head that it could have passed for a shower cap.

"Stiff? Hard? Who's using all my favorite adjectives?"

"Oh!" said Joe. "Marlin, come over and meet Ruby. She's the non-acting New Yorker I told you about."

Marlin samba'd over and dropped a hand into mine. His eyes were swimming-pool blue, parasolled by neat platinum brows.

"Frankly, I don't believe you exist," he said. "Cause girlfriend, *every* New Yorker is an actor. It's just that some parts are Equity, and some are not."

"Marlin's my partner," said Joe. My brain was running down the list - business partner, writing partner, tennis partner – when Marlin kissed Joe on the lips. Joe replied with a half-serious chiding.

"Marlin! Ix-nay on the issing-kay at the office-ay."

Marlin grinned in my direction. "I never know when it's a play-space. Or a play-space. You look like a tough chick, Ruby Red. I'm guessin' a Manhattan, straight up?"

"You're guessin' right, Marlin." I tightened the bolts on my stiff, hard smile.

Seven actors showed up to read. I was one of three commoners, along with Joe's banker uncle and Sigrid, a German friend of Marlin's who turned out to be a high-priced call girl. (And that's not acting?) When it came time for critiques, I drew on the trinity I learned in college: tough, clear, kind.

"It's a frickin' hilarious play, Joe. I really like the dark place that so many of the laughs come from – that is a *sweet* trick if you can pull it off. You've also got some amazingly good visual stuff. The thing about the artificial fangs – I'm gonna be giggling about that for months.

"However, I also think you're missing a major opportunity. This yo-yo thing between Mimi and Kizer is far and away the most compelling relationship in the play – but you're pulling your punches, and leaving all the conflict backstage. Imagine the juicy battles those two could have; imagine all the juicy sexual tension it would create. And imagine all the *meat* this would give to your play – which is a comedy, yes, but a comedy with *substance.* Have at it, man! Take off the gloves."

I was right, of course. Joe revisited the whole Mimi-Kizer thing and came up with three new scenes (including one in which Mimi illustrates Kizer's screwed-up behavior using stick figures on a coffeehouse chalkboard). I worried, in fact, that I might have gone too far – that my director skills were bleeding through my carefully painted façade.

I got my answer a month later, two weeks before Christmas, when Joe asked us all back to try out his rewrite. One of his readers – Jackie, biggest flake, smallest talent (a popular combination) – called at the last minute with some fib about a sick roommate.

"Ruby?" said Joe. "Could you read Grady? It's not a big part – you don't have to be good at all. I just *really* need to get a full picture of this rewrite before I get obliterated by the holidays."

"Sure," I said. And felt completely *un*sure.

Grady was the manager of a coffeehouse – twice my size, with a shitkicker pickup and a seven-year-old son. I tried to read her as stiffly as possible. I was afraid that my little flubs might prove too transparent. Regardless, I couldn't help enjoying the play, which had achieved a perfect blend of tension, release and laughter. I felt a certain stepmotherly pride.

Afterward, Marlin rolled out a buffet table of honeybaked ham, sweet potatoes, bread pudding and egg nog. After quite a few drinks and the departure of most of our readers, I met up with Joe at the punch bowl. I had just at that moment decided to begin greeting him with international variations of his name.

"Jose Verde! Jean-Paul Chartreuse! Yusef Spearmintsky!"

He responded by refilling our glasses and raising a toast.

"To you, Ruby," he said. "You lying little bitch."

He said it with a smile, so I guessed I wasn't in *too* much trouble.

"Hmmm. Zee jig eez up?"

"The second you opened your mouth tonight. You're not such a good actor that you can hide the fact that you're a good actor. It was a noble attempt at mediocrity, but you kept getting carried away by the action and turning into Grady – a pretty neat trick, considering. So why all the espionage?"

I gave him my special squint – the one that's meant to project extreme distaste. "I didn't want to be another in the buffalo herd of desperate wannabes. I saw enough of that in LA."

That last part slipped out. Joe's eyes grew wider. "LA? 'Daughter of Movie Mogul Goes Undercover to Conquer Broadway'?"

I cringed. "Casting director."

Joe held the back of his hand to his forehead, very Scarlet O'Hara.

"You are a certifiable grab bag, Ruby. If that's your *real* name."

"Yes it is," I said, laughing. "I'm sorry. But your play, Joe. It's fucking beautiful. It's exactly the kind of thing I came here for."

"Well good," said Joe.

There was a secret context to those two words, but before I could ask, Joe fled the room. He returned with two metallic skewers and a candle.

"Good why?" I asked.

"Good because... I wouldn't want you to get bored if we have an extended run."

"I... what?"

"We open on Valentine's Day. And I want you to play Melissa. Do you know why?"

"No?" I think I was starting to cry.

"Because Melissa is also a lying, deceptive little bitch. But wait! Don't say yes. We have a certain way of doing this. It's kind of gay, but so am I. Take this."

He handed me one of the skewers, which was covered with a substance that looked like tile grout. Joe lit the candle, then directed the tips of the skewers into the flame until they began to shoot out sparks. Then he raised his right hand.

"Do you, Ruby Cohen, vow to play the part of Melissa, in sickness and in health, through good reviews and hatchet-jobs, till closing night do you part?"

I raised my right hand and gazed into Joe's Apollonian features through a film of tears and a shower of golden meteorites.

"I do."

Seventeen

Ruby's not five minutes done with her story when her brother walks into the coffeehouse – a retro-funky place in Tacoma called the Blackwater. Steve looks like a run-down house that someone has painted over in the hope of hiding all the cracks. Neat, shortcut hair, spiffy indigo-new jeans, tightly tucked button-down shirt and bright white sneakers. His features, however, are all shaky around the margins – as if, at any moment, he could be sucked into a wormhole.

I'm cheating, of course. I know from Ruby's frequent references that Steve has had trouble, that he's just now working his way out of it. Even as I'm being introduced, I'm running his face through my interior rap sheet: drugs? petty larceny?

"Hi! It's great to finally meet you. Ruby talks about you a lot."

He unlocks a smile, rising in a wave from left to right. "I hope, um… I hope she's been kind."

"Oh! Always," I say.

"I've never been to karaoke before. I hear it's fun."

"Oh it is!" says Ruby. "Especially with Channy hosting. She's the best."

"I will not sit here and be flattered!" I complain.

"Well fine then!" says Ruby. "Let's go!"

"Fine!" says I.

"Fine!" says Ruby.

We stride out the door, waving to Luna at the counter. Steve trails behind, shaking his shaky head.

"Man! You two are nuts."

It's a rainy, brooding night, and stormclouds bear down on the Narrows, buffeting my pickup. This does not bode well for my tip jar. People only need two reasons for skipping karaoke, and on Thursday they've already got that Friday morning alarm clock.

I delay our start-time by a half hour, hoping to work up a quorum. To operate at a smooth pace, you need at least three singers. This gives each participant one song to take a breather and one song to pick the next song. Steve's not going to be much help. Actually *singing* in front of *people* would likely give him a heart attack, and he's already disappeared twice on smoke breaks. (Ruby says this is his first night out in a while, and it seems to be making him very anxious.)

Fortunately, Harry arrives, still in uniform, grabbing armfuls of Ruby as he enters. Five minutes later, we get a trio of newbies – although they're certainly not new to karaoke. You can tell by the way they scoop up the songbooks and rifle the pages.

Turns out they're also good. The first is John, a tall fortyish white guy who sings R & B ballads with a sirloin-steak baritone. The second is Paul, a bald black guy who's interested in things further up, whipping out some falsetto doo-wop from the fifties. The blonde centerpiece is Kim, an attractive thirty-year-old who navigates Annie Lennox and Melissa Etheridge with a consummately pitched voice – almost as good as Ruby's. She comes up for a little side-bar as Harry works his way through "By the Time I Get to Phoenix."

"It's a little deal I've got with my husband," she says. "In order to avoid The Horror That is Dancing with Your Wife, he takes the kids once a week while I go for a trot with my dirty old men. Once we've worn out our feet, we hunt down a karaoke bar."

"So are John and Paul gay, or just well-mannered?"

Kim bursts out laughing. "They are my caballeros. I gotta watch it, though. Sometimes they get too comfortable, and start making racy comments about the other chicks in the bar."

"Well," I say. "Even when they're well-trained, they're still dogs. So what's with this gorgeous voice of yours?"

Kim looks away, a little knocked aside by my flattery. "Tell you a secret: I actually had a full ride to Julliard. Some scout came to my high school for a choir concert. Like I was a quarterback or something. I was pretty blown away. But they wanted me to sing opera and nothing else. I just wasn't into it. Then I met a guy, had some babies. Old story."

"Sounds like you made the right decision. Ruby's been telling me about life in the performing arts, and it sounds like you'd best be really into it before you enlist."

"I knew it!" says Kim. "I knew she was a pro. She's amazing."

"She's my hero," I say, only half-joking.

"So the Mod Squad and I were thinking, if you guys were into it, maybe we could play a little game. First singer does something by an 'A' artist, second singer does 'B,' and so on."

"Tonight I'll try anything. I'll make an announcement after Harry, um, gets to Phoenix."

Kim smiles and hands me a song slip: "Fernando" by ABBA.

In actual practice, the alphabet game turns out to be quite fun. Except that yours truly gets all the problematic letters. Q, naturally, which almost always calls for Queen – which, in the world of karaoke, means "Bohemian Rhapsody." I'm no fool, however – I get Ruby, Kim and John to help out with the goofy opera parts, while Harry throws down some wicked toy guitar.

A half-hour later comes X, and there's only one choice: some '80s R & B group called Xscape. I vaguely vaguely vaguely recall the song, but it's not like not knowing what the hell I'm doing ever stopped me before, so I claw my way through, tossing out some Whitney Houston embellishments that may or may not be on-key. I'm much relieved to hand the mic to Harry for "Cinnamon Girl" by Neil Young.

Ruby's working her way through "Lawyers, Guns and Money" by Warren Zevon (how does she *know* this stuff?) when I hear the door and the familiar high-pitched laugh that belongs to Kevin the Cop. And another that doesn't.

She is a blonde, in jeans, jacket and a crisp white blouse. She has sly, dreamy eyes that remind me of Lauren Bacall. Something about her entrance has knocked the room off-kilter: troubled brothers, newbie trios, Q's and X's sliding around like ping-pong balls in a Bingo basket. Kevin comes up for his usual hug, and I regain my balance long enough to fill him in on the alphabet game.

"So, if my calculations are correct, you're 'F.' Is your, um, friend gonna sing?"

Kevin smiles, glances at the blonde and launches into a completely unrequested explanation: "I went to a reading for this 'how-to' dating book. Figured I could use all the help I could get. So now I'm dating the author! Diane. She is so funny! I never knew how sexy that was."

Kevin finally notices that I'm still waiting for my answer.

"Oh! No – she's just here to listen. I'll go find some effin' song to sing. Ha!"

And then he's off.

The second time around, we decide that a reprise of Xscape is unnecessary, but the subsequent shuffle lands me on Z. I perform a decent rendering of "Tush" by ZZ Top, and am halfway through loading up my CDs when I remember something I have to check with Ruby. She's still at her table, mooning over Harry. They've decided to sleep in their own beds tonight, so they're extending the evening as long as they can.

"Hi guys. That was fun, wasn't it?"

"Shore was," says Harry. "Next time, we go numerical!"

"Three Dog Night," says Ruby.

"Four Non-Blondes," says Harry.

"10,000 Maniacs," I say. "Where's Steve?"

"Smoke break," says Ruby.

"Your brother's a chimney," I say.

"Yes," says Ruby. "But a *functioning* chimney."

I make a mental note to someday figure out what's going on with that boy.

"So Rubbayat," I say.

"Omar Khayam?"

"I've got a DJ gig for a holiday office party, and I need a soloist to do a couple of the CEO's favorite tunes."

"What're *you*? Braunschweiger?"

"I don't need a singer. I need a *performer*."

Ruby purses her lips in a way that probably drives Harry crazy with lust. "Name the songs."

"'Have Yourself a Merry Little Christmas' and 'Christmas Song.'"

"Sold!" says Ruby, slapping the table. "And I also want to marry the CEO."

"Hey!" says Harry. "I might have picked the same songs."

"My ass! You woulda picked that hip-swingin' lip-curlin' trailer trash you're so in love with."

"I'm sorry," says Harry. "I didn't hear a word after you mentioned your ass."

"We'll discuss my dairy-air tomorrow night, Bubba." She crawls up his chest for a lingering kiss, then she looks back at me and her face winds down like a clock.

"Um… Channy? Could I talk to you outside? It's a feminine matter."

"Oh. Yeah, sure."

Harry, being Harry, has to throw his two cents at our departure.

"Don't tell her any of my secrets!"

I have no idea which one of us he's addressing, but I guess that's part of the joke. We pass Steve just outside the entrance, puffing away, and Ruby says, "Fifteen minutes, hermano mio."

"Grassy-ass," he mumbles.

The rain has passed, leaving the asphalt clean and slick. Ruby takes me to a seawall overlooking the harbor. Our distance from the bar makes me wonder about the radioactivity of her subject matter. She stops and turns, her breath puffing in the cold air.

"Okay. I don't know if my surging hormones are tripping my gyno-radar, but you are transmitting this aurora borealis of sadness that is deeper than Billie Freakin' Holiday."

Little did I know about the hot button lurking beneath my skin, waiting to be pressed in just this fashion.

"Why are guys such dicks? Showing off their catches like they just landed a marlin off the Florida Keys… What the fuck is that?"

Ruby reaches to touch me, and I whack her hand away. I'm poison ivy, I'm cactus – no one should touch me. Then I see a line of blood where I've scratched her wrist.

"Oh! Shit, Ruby. My bracelet."

"It's okay," she says. "It's nothing."

"God, I'm being an idiot. Why am I being an idiot?"

Ruby pulls out a tissue and dabs at her wrist. "I've got a theory," she says.

We stop to watch a small boat chug past, a large gray-bearded man standing at the wheel.

"So," I say. "What's your theory?"

"I'll tell you if you let me touch you."

"Sure," I say, but her caring tone is sending me deeper into my funk. I set my elbows on the seawall and prop my weary head on my hands. Ruby rubs the back of my neck. It feels good.

"A guy likes a woman; a woman likes a guy. He asks her out, but she's too wounded to say yes. Still, she's kinda hoping he'll be there at the hospital entrance when she finally checks out. But she looks out her window one night and finds him at a restaurant across the street, having dinner with some fucking blonde best-seller."

I find my face sinking deeper into my hands. The only way to keep from crying is to continue being a smartass.

"Put another bullet through my heart, why dontcha?"

Ruby laughs, and sings a quiet recitative into my ear. "Isn't that why you gave me the bullets in the first place?"

EIGHTEEN
CHANNY

Moving to a new state, meeting a boy, shacking up. Lots of people do these things, they're downright ordinary – but I couldn't believe they had happened to *me*, and in such a short time. I was also lost in the particulars of the boy – the boy who gloried in slaying imaginary beings, who obsessed over military equipment, who brought me flowers at the least-expected moments and made love more tenderly than I knew a boy could. I pictured myself driving a tractor through the long valley of Harvey – this field with soy beans, that with weeds, tulips followed by brambles, wheat, hard-baked pan. Were all men such checkerboards?

His first weekend away came at the end of August. I woke to a soldier in my doorway, dressed in jungle fatigues. It repelled me; it excited me. I wanted to run in claustrophobic terror. I wanted to adopt a foreign accent and proceed directly to role-playing. Oh, American soldier boy. Save me from the Cossacks!

He grinned rather loopily. "I'm off to the front, baby. Tonight we take Tacoma."

"You look handsome."

"I feel like I'm going to a freakin' costume party."

"You'll be fine." I rolled out of bed and slipped my arms around his waist. "One thing, though. That smartass sense of humor that I so absolutely adore?"

"Yes?"

"You might want to suppress that."

"Yes, ma'am." He gave me a kiss, his breath strong with mouthwash. I would have preferred more Harvey, less Listerine.

"Well! I'm running late. Have a good weekend, darlin'. I've instructed the third division to keep an eye on the place."

He was off before I could ask. I flopped back to bed for a much-deserved sleep-in. At noon, I drifted into the living room to find two hundred green plastic army men lined up on the mantelpiece.

It was a beautiful, beautiful day. The cap of Rainier poked over the ridge like a monster bicuspid. I felt small and lonely – and what was that about? Had I not left Alaska precisely to be alone? Independent? Reckless? I employed this thought to whip myself into action, scrubbing the kitchen and bathroom till they shone, mopping the hardwood floors, beating the rugs, and generally enjoying the free space left by the absence of one sprawling male anatomy.

Still, it was a small house, and I didn't kill half the time that I needed to, so I crossed the street to the bison field, trying for the twenty-third time to tempt them with wads of freshly picked grass. Not that grass was hard to come by, but I was hoping that presentation would count for something. Bessie and Ben moved not an inch from the exact geographical center of the field, and considering the sad history of American-bison relations, I could not blame them.

I was wandering in the direction of the strip mall when I noticed a man shuttling between Kerby's Café and a burgundy SUV, toting various large black objects. He had a thick shank of white hair, and wore large, thick glasses that reminded me of Dr. Steinwitz, my pediatrician in Anchorage.

I had a rather dim view of Kerby's. The patrons were a rough bunch, and they often kept Harvey and me awake, yelling to their buddies across the parking lot. At closing time, a parade of headlights flashed across our windows.

But I was bored, so I crossed the parking lot to investigate.

"Hi! Whatcha loadin' up for?"

He gave me a studied look, absolutely nonplussed.

"Karaoke."

"Oh! Cool."

"Ever try it?"

"Once. At a birthday party. They only had thirty songs, though."

"Ha! We've got seventeen thousand. All on a computer."

"God! Are there seventeen thousand songs in the world?"

"I still get complaints about the ones we don't have. You should sing tonight. We start at nine."

"Oh, well... I'm only eighteen."

"No problem. If you bring those mic stands in, I'll make you my official roadie."

"Wow! Thanks."

"Strictly Coca-Cola, mind you."

His name was J.B., which I later found out stood for James Brown. He was about the whitest-looking man I'd ever seen, so I didn't really see the need for the initials. (One day he met Bobby Vinton at a party and said, "Wow! You're Bobby Vinton." Vinton said, "Well what's it like, meeting Bobby Vinton?" And J.B. said, "I don't know. What's it like meeting James Brown?")

By day, J.B. ran a computer shop, and he took great pleasure in showing me his high-tech karaoke system. He could hunt for a song using a keyword, then play it with a mouse-click. A window to the left kept a running roster of singers, along with the songs they had picked that night – and, for the regulars, every song they had *ever* sung. At the bottom was a list of filler songs that came on whenever a karaoke song was over, and he could also play canned applause – or, at the end of the night, the Warner Brothers' "Th-th-that's all, folks!"

"I actually helped design this," said J.B. "I was in a test group for the software developers, and they used a lot of my suggestions. That's why I like it so much."

"Is he boring you with his technobabble?"

This came from a woman behind me, wearing big glasses just like J.B.'s. She was short and squat, a bundle of curves with a round, pleasant face. And, evidently, a wry sense of humor.

"He's more in love with that program than with me. So who are you?"

"Oh, hi. I'm Channy."

"She's my summer intern," said J.B.

"J.B.! Is she underage? You're gonna get us in trouble."

"Oh, nonsense. I checked her in with Laura. Nothing but Shirley Temples and Roy Rogerses."

"Well, okay. Why don't you sit up here with me, then? I get bored when Mr. Man's making out with his computer."

Her name was Debbie – wife and emcee, which meant she had plenty of time to chat between singer intros. You could tell, also, that she took a lot of pleasure in the characters who populated the bar. There was Diana, the archetypal brassy broad, who sang bawdy country tunes like "You Can Eat Crackers in My Bed." And Cowboy, who wore an old hat covered in patches and pins, and sang nothing but Lynyrd Skynyrd, curled up in the corner with a cordless mic. A plentifully soused blonde named Jolene took great pleasure in singing "Jolene." And skinny, bald Rory kept trying to do '70s rock anthems that were too high for him.

I was really enjoying this – all of it. The way the songs drew instant connections between people. The way the old guy in the beret showed his approval by yelling "Sing that shit!" The feeling of deep history, friendships that had survived decades, perhaps broken apart by crises and fights, but brought back together by the same gravity that created them. And Debbie, who took her husband's recklessness as a license to be my foster mother for the evening.

"So what's the story, Channy? Everybody's got a story."

"I came down from Alaska last month, and... I met a boy."

"Oh! She met a boy. I sure know *that* story."

"It's so... unsettling sometimes. Actually, that's how I ended up here tonight. He's in the Army National Guard, and this was his first weekend away. I was feeling pretty isolated."

"Well! I'm glad you found us. Are you gonna sing something?"

"I don't know. I've never done this for real before."

"Well." She gave my knee a pat. "Here's what I tell all my beginners. Pick a song that you know frontwards and back. The song you know best in the world. It's very important to have a good experience the first time out. Kinda like sex. Omigod! Did I say that?"

The way she put it, my choice was pretty obvious: "Beautiful Day," my graduation song. The only problem was staying on the melody. I kept wandering to the alto harmonies that James had written (James who just then was headed off to meet his death in Minnesota). But Debbie smiled at me like I'd hit one out of the park.

"That was great!" She spoke into my ear as Rory did battle against Bowie's "Space Oddity." "I like those new parts you threw in. Where'd you learn that?"

"Well, it's a long story."

She patted my knee again. "I've got all the time in the world, honey."

Sunday evening, I sat at the kitchen table with a plate of cold pork chops and asparagus, watching the sun slanting over the bison-field in tangerine stripes. I was interrupted by my pickup truck, dragging into the driveway with my own soldier-boy at the wheel. He edged up the walk with a limp and gave me a weak smile, his face smudged here and there with camo makeup. I wrapped him in a hug.

"Hi honey."

"Hi."

"How was it?"

"You remember what you said about my smartass sense of humor?"

"Yes?"

"A hundred pushups."

I couldn't help but giggle.

"Oh! She mocks my injuries."

"Sorry, darlin'. But I did tell you."

"You did. But a hundred pushups tends to drill the point home."

I ran a finger across his dirty, sweaty brow and down his cute nose.

"Poor baby. Take a shower, and I'll heat up this food."

"Thanks."

He slogged off to the bathroom, pausing at the mantelpiece to salute the third division. I felt bad for him, but it felt good to be needed.

Nineteen
Ruby

Three years later, I was still with Joe's troupe, Greenstreet Productions, alternating between big roles and small, fending off anything that smacked of administrative duties. I displayed my kryptonite competence only when it came to knowing my lines, arriving punctually and performing with every cell in my body. I did, however, have an intriguing proposition in my pocket: Joe had invited me to direct one of the shows for the upcoming season. It was tempting but scary, because I knew I'd be good at it and I didn't want anything to come between me and the audience.

It was late summer, down-time before the fall opening. I found a flyer for an artists' collective at a bar around the corner – a place called Savvy's. When I walked in, the mood was positively Beatnik. The garret from Puccini's *Boheme*. Andy Hardy putting on a show in the barn.

I swam through the bar crowd until I reached a wide pit where a funk band was wrapping up "Sex Machine," a skinny black guy in a British cap spazzing a James Brown shuffle across the floor. Then the DJ called up a slam poet, a short, squat guy with a Fiddler-on-the-Roof beard. He jumped into a piece about trying to eliminate the excess food from his pantry, and instead winding up in an eating competition with Death. The rhythm of his words accelerated with a Bolero graduality until they caught fire and burst into a Ginsbergian inventory of comestibles. People were falling out of their chairs, probably on purpose.

By the time he was done, a reggae band had finished setting up, and rolled into a Jimmy Cliff tune. I took the opportunity to saunter up to the balcony, where a trio of painters were doing "live works." A large black woman was pressing broad swipes of acrylic across a canvas, setting up the strata for a seascape. A baby-faced Puerto Rican kid scratched at a charcoal portrait: an old drunk leaning against a bar, wearing a look of utter dejection.

The third guy was older, mid-thirties, tall, a head of thick black hair with apostrophes of gray. He looked like he had never made an awkward movement in his life. He was working on a cartoonish, beatific creature with fan-shaped wings – or petals, I couldn't tell. It stood upon a pedestal-like body, wide as a tree trunk. The background was an intricate network of lines, but looking closely I could see that it was actually composed of faces, their features melting into the mass: an Aztec warrior in profile, an amoeba with misplaced Picasso eyes, a robot alien with a saucer-shaped head.

The man was dipping a terry-cloth rag into a bowl of raw sienna paint, then scrubbing it into one of the petals – or wings. He gave me a quick glance, but kept steadily at his work. For a moment, I felt guilty for distracting him, but of course that's what he was there for. And, to answer stupid questions.

"Whatcha doin'?"

He looked up with eyes so black you could fall right in. "You want the short version or the Encyclopedia Britannica?"

"Um... I'm gonna go for the short."

"We begin with a central figure: the ruby-throated angelflower. A profoundly positive presence. I filled in the background with a coterie of beer-coaster creatures, then sort of macramed them together in order to, in order to... Actually, I have no idea."

"To make them look like a crowd?"

He snapped his fingers very loudly, then stared at them in surprise. "Wow – what's *that* about? But yes! A crowd. Out of which rises the angelflower, like the rare and sudden blossoming of the century plant, erupting from the desert of the hoi polloi.

"I have this thing about complicated backgrounds. I get so attached to a project that I hate to see it end – so all this meticulous stuff helps to extend the work. Right now you've caught me at the final step, which is frankly like a three-year-old with a coloring book. I like to water down my acrylics, then scrub them in. Gives a nice solid block of color – but transparent, so it reveals the flaws in the canvas."

"Why do you want to reveal flaws?"

"I like a surface that's seen some livin'. This one was a dropcloth. Note the little splatters of black at the top of the stem. That was an oil change."

He took another swab at his bowl and worked a corner of the petal, drawing the paint right up to the thick black line at its periphery.

"I can't stand art that's too smooth. If you're not going to reveal the process at all, then why bother? This notion of creating perfect, untouched forms is riven with hubris. What are you doing after the show?"

He said all of this at a shot, and I wasn't entirely certain that I'd been asked a question.

"Um, I don't really know."

"I have to show you something."

I laughed. "Don't think I've never heard *that* one before."

He took my hand and held on tight, as if we were about to shake on a deal.

"What's your name?"

"Ruby."

He smiled. Large, dazzling teeth. "You see?"

"Ruby-throated," I said. "As in fate?"

"As in coincidence – which is better, and tastier. *You* are one of the special ones. You do something creative?"

"So now you're a psychic?"

He laughed. "Ask the right question in the right milieu, and your odds are pretty good."

"Yes," I said. "Actress."

"Ah – of course. Lots of personalities swimming around in there. When you first came up, I thought there was a whole mob watching me. I'll be done at midnight. Can I meet you at the bar?"

"What? I can't watch you?"

"Actually, no. I'd be too distracted. Along with being one of the special ones, you're enormously attractive."

Picture me as an LP on a turntable; my needle has just been yanked away. I tried and failed to fight down a goofy smile.

"Wait a minute," I said. "What's *your* name?"

"Scootie." He shook the hand I'd forgotten he was holding. "And yes, there's a story behind that, too. But I need to get back to my painting."

He let go, and I drifted downstairs. I gave some serious thought to leaving – he was entirely too smooth. But this cool punk band was playing, dressed in big chunks of black and white fabric, and a beer sounded really good.

Two bands and a standup comic later, Scootie appeared over my left shoulder, continuing our previous conversation as if we'd never stopped.

"When I was a baby, I had a middle ear infection. It messed up my sense of balance, and I took to crawling sideways, like a crab. So I got my nickname: 'Scootie'. Have you done any Beckett?"

I fixed him with a look, and attempted to restart the conversation in a more normal fashion. "Hi, Scootie. How ya doin'?"

He blinked. "I'm fine. How are you?"

"Good! *Waiting for Godot.*"

You could see that little tidbit striking a speed-bump in his head – which was exactly my intention.

"Isn't that…?"

"All-female cast," I said. "We thought of calling it *Waiting for Goddess*, but we figured we were pushing our luck as it was."

The bartender raced by, planted a Heinekin in front of Scootie, spoke the words "Jacks and Queens" and kept going.

Scootie eyed the label, said "Ah, Jacks and Queens," and took a drink. "What did you think of it?" he asked.

"Jacks and Queens?"

"Beckett."

I did my best to look thoughtful (I'm sure I did – I had practiced my "thoughtful" look in a mirror many times). "Irrational. Maddening. Plotless. Ridiculous. I *loved* it."

"You ought to love me then."

"Umm... maybe?" Keep it moving, keep it moving. "So where do your figures come from?"

"John Cage."

"Oh. I thought Cage was a musician."

"You thought Da Vinci was a painter. Music was Cage's day job. When the moon came out, he was a philosopher. And the master cartographer of chance operations."

Scootie took a pen from behind his ear and flipped over a beer coaster. Then he drew a long line, vaguely ess-shaped.

"I can't illustrate worth shit. Any time I attempt to pull in something from the real world, it goes through some kind of crippling filter and ends up looking like the work of an unimaginative toddler. So I go backwards."

He drew a straight line through the ess at a slant.

"I keep drawing lines until something makes itself known."

A question mark with no period. Three sides of a square, facing down.

"When I arrive at the point of identity, I finish the job with universal signifiers: eyes, nose, mouth – sometimes ears, or hair."

He gave the question-mark head a pair of almond-shaped eyes, then angled a mouth-line with a small notch for a smirk. The nose was already there, a product of the first two lines. The upside-down square offered a torso; he added long, thin rectangles to imply arms.

"Sometimes they turn out, sometimes not. Sometimes they become ruby-throated angelflowers."

"This one looks French," I said. "That smirk might actually be a cigarette."

Scootie smiled, initialed the coaster *SJ* and handed it to me.

"Here. Might be worth a dollar someday."

He had a loft (of *course* he had a loft). It was pretty bare of furniture, and instead of a rug he had a canvas dropcloth, ten foot square, nailed to the floor. Affixed to the far wall was a canvas, five feet tall, three wide. It appeared to contain a swarm of mosquitoes, but closer inspection revealed words, hundreds of them, written with a black marker. I saw *libretto, 1967,* and *Sutherland.*

"What the hell is going on here?"

"Chance operations," he said. "The human mind craves organization – and that's the problem. I was in a choir once, singing a piece that called for white noise, within a certain range of pitches. Inevitably, we would gravitate toward consonance – toward chords. So we had to spend a half-hour assigning individual pitches to individual singers. There were some who hated that piece, but I thought it was the most beautifully constructed chaos I'd ever heard.

"The thing is, in order to achieve true randomness, you have to set up some ground rules beforehand. In this case, I determined to take the *New Grove Book of Opera* – all 687 pages – and extract the first word from each page. On the canvas, I depended on my natural ability to shuffle, beginning with any available white space and not caring if it ran roughshod over other words. I wanted a virtual windstorm of verbiage. Unbeknownst to you, I have already pencilled in the central figure, and will now bring him into being. Please – sit."

He handed me a cushion, and I sat on the floor, cross-legged. He produced a small housepainting brush, dipped it into a jar of black paint and drew a rough line over the canvas. He began with two lines that started at the top center and extended outward. He drew a vee from one shoulder to another, trailing into a shape that resembled a tie. At either side of the X, he affixed the same almond eyes as his coaster creature, then a wide, flat oval for a mouth, vaguely merry. He stood back for a moment, then dipped the brush, took the tips of the X and extended them to the upper corners. He took a last look, notched a pocket on either side of the tie, then tossed the brush over his shoulder. It landed on the dropcloth with a splat. Then he knelt behind me, gripped my shoulders and said, "So. What is he?"

I took a few moments to study.

"The Creature from the Black Lagoon in a business suit."

"Or a suit for the opera," said Scootie.

"But those antennae...?"

"Yes! That popped in just now."

"Like a cockroach. A giant impresario cockroach, off to the opera."

"Luciano Cucaracchi," he said.

I let out a burst of laughter, like a sneeze. "Okay."

"Hey, I don't make up the names. They just come in on the satellite dish. Now, take off your shoes."

There was my decision point. A girl doesn't take off her shoes just for anyone.

So I did. Scootie disappeared and came back with a pair of square plastic tubs. In one he poured red paint, in the other black.

"It's just like roullette. Pick a color."

I stood up and gave them a study. "Dare I ask why?"

"Ask yourself this question: what color do I want my feet to be for the next week?"

"You're nuts."

"We've established that. Now pick."

"Red. Of course."

"Communist!"

"Vampire!"

"Go ahead. Do the Hokey-Pokey."

I knew if I thought about it, I wouldn't, so I didn't think about it. I don't need to tell you how it felt, because you know how it felt. Scootie pushed a button on his stereo and conjured a waltz – that soprano from *Boheme*, in the café. He rolled his trousers to his knees, planted himself in the black, then left a trail of dance-instruction footprints on his way to the center of the dropcloth. He raised his hands; I stepped forward and took them.

And he could waltz (of course he could waltz). And of course *I* could waltz – I was a performer. We stopped at regular intervals to reload our feet. After that came Sinatra, "Saturday Night is the Loneliest Night of the Week," and we switched to swing. Scootie's lead was perfect, all the signals there in his big hands, twirling me one way, wrapping me the other. At the ending, he dipped me so deeply that, the next morning, I found streaks of red and black in my hair.

Scootie pulled me to my feet, kissed my hands and said, "We're done."

I stood on red tip-toes, kissed him on the neck and said, "Not hardly."

Twenty

The holiday party is a bigger deal than I expected. The company is a small chain of sporting goods stores, and the boss is much like Scrooge's Fezziwig, willing to open up the pocketbook come Christmastime. Only this boss is much better-looking.

I'm all set up at the Tacoma Museum of Glass, inside the "hot shop," where the artisans conduct demonstrations of glassmaking. The furnaces are on a sort of staging area, readily viewable from a bank of stadium-style seats. In between are sturdy metal tables where the hot-shoppers perform their hazardous tricks. Every item in sight is shiny and metallic; it's like being on the inside of a giant industrial refrigerator. The ceiling is remarkably high and conical, designed to funnel nasty vapors toward the ventilators at the top. I was expecting the height to suck out all my sound as well, but the Museum allowed me to plug into their beautiful PA, and the results are astounding.

Our Fezziwig – Scott Jenalyn – has also procured access to the museum galleries. The main gallery is filled with brightly colored forms resembling sea creatures – a style inspired by the hometown hero, Dale Chihuly. The smaller exhibit gallery features the work of a young Russian woman who concocts statues of clear, colorless glass. The figures are dressed in everyday clothing – waitresses, cops, even a group of girls playing basketball – and the verisimilitude is downright unsettling. You feel like you could sit down and have a conversation with one of them, if not for the fear that they might answer back.

The capper to the evening is the mode of transport. After a sumptuous dinner in Gig Harbor, the workers are boarding Uncle Scottie's yacht, crossing the sound and arriving at a dock a hundred yards from the museum entrance. (I'm now considering a career in sporting goods.)

From my DJ table, I can see Ruby, returning from a nervous stroll around the galleries. This seems like such a small gig, but it's been a while since she's had a real audience. I have utter faith that she will be a knockout. And if anything preposterous happens, I'm sure the outfit will more than make up for it. Were it an exhibit, I would title it *No One Says No to Mrs. Claus*: a red fur miniskirt trimmed in leather, a red sequin top that leaves as little to the imagination as possible, and black knee-high boots with stiletto heels. If ever there were an incentive to be on the Naughty List... I might even be worried about her, but I'm sure it's all for show; underneath the brass, Ruby is just another boring monogamist.

"The acoustics in this place really suck," she says. She's descending the wide steps next to the seats, being very careful with her boots. "And I mean that literally."

"Not to worry. I have tapped into the magic forces of the Museum. You just unleash that rapturous voice of yours, and Mama will take care of the rest."

Ruby smiles, like she's putting up a brave front. "It's been a while."

"Oh save it, sister. You know and I know that the music will start and you will click in like you always do. If you freeze up, just flash 'em your tits. You're already halfway there."

"Ha! Use 'em if you got 'em, I always say. Maybe I'll feel better if I go outside and look for the ship. Or not."

She's looking over my shoulder at a strapping middle-aged man, wearing a Santa suit that looks like it was tailored by Armani. Instead of the bushy white beard, his is a well-trimmed silver, to go with a moussed head of same, crow's feet to die for, and eyes of the most oceanic blue. This is our Fezziwig.

"Scott! Hi."

"Ho-ho-how are ya?" he declares, trotting the steps.

"How was the crossing?"

"Brrr! Froze off my mistletoes."

"Some Santa you are. And aren't you supposed to be fat?"

"Not sporting-goods Santa! Sporting-goods Santa likes to work out." He gives Ruby an appreciative look. "And who is this? My fourth wife?"

"Well!" I say. "You certainly dress alike. This is your holiday chanteuse, Ruby."

"Joyeux Noel," says Ruby, and reaches for Scott's hand.

"Ah!" says he. "All the best Mrs. Clauses are Jewish."

"Oy!" says Ruby. "And here I thought I was fully assimilated."

"A Christian icon should never admit this, but I've always had a profound weakness for the Hebrew goddesses." His eyes are threatening to twinkle. "In fact, I married three of them. And sent most of my... income to... three of them."

"Hmm," says Ruby. "This could be the Reverse-Shiksa Syndrome."

Scott lets out a Santa-like roar. "And *that* is why I love them: that rapid-fire wit. Channy promises me great things from you."

"Oh God – more pressure. Where's the rest of your crew?"

"I thought it best that they view the galleries first. I'm thinking spiked egg nog and expensive glass art is a *bad* combination."

"That's why you're the boss," I say.

I've never done a DJ gig before, and it does present some interesting adjustments. In karaoke, the relationship is automatic: they order the song, I play it. DJ'ing involves much more judgement, gauging the mood of a party and picking the music to match.

The employees drift in from the galleries, looking a little imprisoned by their suits and dresses. I'm keeping things on the down-low, a mix of mellow jazz and Christmas tunes. Then I look up to find seven young adults gathered at my table. Their ringleader is a tall, lean white guy with a military haircut.

"You got any Black-Eyed Peas?"

"Oh! Um, sure. I didn't know you were ready to dance."

"We was *born* ready, f'shizzle!"

The white kids shore talk funny these days, I think, and slap on "My Humps." I notice, also, that they are apostles of the latest dancing trend, which focuses all movement on the region of the buttocks. I throw on some Outkast, the Gorillaz, Eminem. A half-hour later, I look up to find an older manager type, looking forlorn.

"Could you play something slow? I'd like to dance with my wife."

"Oh! Um, sure. Very next song."

"Thanks."

I play "Lady in Red," a sneaky reference to Ruby's outfit. And I play slow songs until someone asks for "The Cha-Cha Slide," "The Hustle" and "YMCA," complete with spelling-through-extremities dance moves. Then I insist on "White Christmas" (Bing Crosby being a Tacoma boy), and everybody looks at me like I'm insane.

So with this crowd, at least, DJ'ing is just as much servitude as KJ'ing – but servitude with no clear instructions. It's a relief when we arrive at Ruby's portion of the evening. Scott gives a holiday greeting that's marvelously light on ego and oratorio (I'm beginning to consider the advantages of a May-December relationship), then Ruby takes a crowd of feuding dancers and zaps them into a classroom of teacher's pets. Her "Christmas Song" is a velvet dream, as pitch-perfect as Nat King. She takes a moment to explain how "Have Yourself A Merry Little Christmas" is actually a *sad* song – that Judy Garland in *Meet Me in St. Louis* is singing about being forced to leave her beloved Missouri immediately after the holidays. What's amazing is that no one's even singing along. Even through a fog of nog, our sporting-goods employees seem to understand that what they're watching is *theater*.

During the applause, I hear the past whispering in my ear. It says, "That is one fine damn singer." When I turn to face the past, it's Kai, wearing a grin as white as the snow in Bing Crosby's dreams. So I stand, and give him a huge hug.

"Kai! It's so good to see you! And the question would be, what the *hell* are you doing here?"

"I work for Scott. He's a great boss. Shouldn't you have some music on?"

"Oh. Duh!" I slip on a filler disc of Christmas tunes. Fortunately, the next item on the agenda is a hot-shop demonstration. Two burly men in aprons have extracted long rods from the furnace, capped with honey-like gobs of molten glass. We head upstairs to the lobby, gravitating to a glass Christmas tree that looks more like a bristlecone pine – barren, gnarled limbs hung with figurines in various military uniforms.

"So how are you?" I say. "What's the new job?"

He looks at me and just laughs.

"What? What'd I say?"

"I'm working in the mountaineering department."

So I look at *him* and laugh. "Do you even *have* any experience?"

"I'll tell you what I told Scott during my interview. Wouldn't *you* want to buy your climbing gear from a genuine Sherpa?"

"Rascal!"

"Your pizza from a guy named Luigi? Your Guinness from a guy named O'Reilly? So yea, I played the race card. But I *do* have a sincere interest. First chance I get, I'm scaling Rainier. Take a picture at the top, send it to Mom and Dad. So you're DJ'ing now?"

"First time. I like it, though. And I like the money."

Kai dons a calculating expression. "How did you get here tonight?"

"Ruby. She lives up the hill from here, but she was so amped up, she insisted on being my driver."

"How much gear do you have?"

"Just the stuff on the table – and a couple CD cases. What's up?"

He just smiles, takes my hand and says, "Let's dance."

When we enter, the hot-shop guys are still at it, clamping and bending the glass into something resembling an agave cactus. On the remaining half of the stage, a handful of dancers are waltzing to "Silver Bells," including Scott and Ruby (I imagine Scootie's red paint on her shoes). Kai strikes a posture of invitation, and I notice that *he* is not imprisoned by his suit at all. I take his raised hand, feel his other hand at my waist, and we're off into the crowd. And he can waltz. Of *course* he can waltz.

As a suitably ironic finale, I play "Get Ths Party Started," then proceed directly to my packing, slotting my CDs into their plastic pockets. I'm joined by Kai and a couple of young cohorts.

"Channy, this is Jeremy and Sasha. They will be loading your stuff on the company van and meeting us in Gig Harbor. You, meanwhile, will be joining us for a cruise – that is, if you'd like to."

"Of course!" I say. I direct them to all the proper equipment, then track down Ruby to tell her she can leave without me. Soon I'm descending the wide steps of the museum to the dock, where the *Designated Clipper* is motoring up. Soon enough, we're pulling into Commencement Bay and past the Brown's Point Lighthouse. Though it's absolutely freezing, I can't resist standing on deck, connecting the Seuratian dots of Tacoma's skyline as they fall and shimmy on the dark Puget water. Kai joins me and uses the cold (as I hoped he would) as an excuse to stand close and wrap me with an arm. The moment seems about right.

"Kai, I wanted to thank you for the Purple Heart. It means so much to me. It would have meant so much to Harvey."

"It's not for Harvey," he says, rather abruptly. "The victim of suicide is not the one who commits it, it's the ones he leaves behind. I will miss him, Channy, but I will never forgive him – not for what he did to me, not for what he did to you."

There's something about this statement that seems rehearsed. As if he has had these thoughts many times, and has chiseled them down to these exact words. He must have known that we would eventually run into one another, that I would thank him for the medal. But his tone is unexpectedly intense. It reminds me that Kai, despite his seeming innocence, has witnessed events that I could not possibly imagine.

"Are you all right, Channy?"

I'm not sure if he means at this moment, or generally speaking.

"Yes. I'm fine. And you're very sweet."

The dots of Tacoma disappear into his dark eyes, and his lips – the ones I have thought about more times than I would care to admit – are alighting upon mine. A chamber in the doorlock of my mind clicks in, like the lift of a lyric set carefully into the pocket of a song.

Twenty-one
Channy

I was covering a Sunday shift at the Red Apple, so I wasn't there when Harvey returned from his Guard weekend. Not that I minded. When people asked me, I said he was "having one of his weekends," which was not necessarily a term of affection. Since 9/11, my signpost prince had become increasingly "butch," and it ran strongest on Sundays, when I could still smell the camo makeup on his face.

I had my theories. The Zero Squadron video battles centered on an enemy that was incontrovertibly evil, and drilled the point home with their military liturgies. For a man of Harvey's generation, raised in the murky shadows of Vietnam, the clear-cut moral crusade of WWII must have held a tremendous appeal (and don't think *Star Wars* didn't play right into this).

The modern, educated human is expected to process a thousand gradations of good and evil, but the brain carries a strong survival instinct regarding its own capacity, so it streamlines matters by shuffling some of these issues into the black-and-white, one-or-zero auxiliary drive.

Thus, when a bona fide monster invaded our country and took out a few thousand civilians, Harvey was hard-wired to become a patriot. Osama bin Laden removed all the shadows from Harvey's life, made his joining of the Guard a matter of prescient destiny, and afforded a military mission more justified than anything since Pearl Harbor.

And suddenly, this talk of Saddam Hussein. The Guard was no longer a corps of professional bystanders. If we went to Baghdad – with so many of our career soldiers still in Afghanistan – there was a good chance that Harvey would be among them. I spent a lot of time feeling absolutely terrified. To Harvey, I'm sure it all looked like a big mother lode of glory, the Luke Skywalker fantasy come to life. But he didn't seem to understand that the bullets were real, that their express purpose was to break apart human flesh.

On Sunday evenings, he spoke to me in blunt, government-issue sentences, and moved around on stiff, graceless limbs. He gave no response to humor or affection. I was afraid to hug him, for fear of cutting myself on his sharp edges. But I knew if I was patient, and held out till Monday, things would be okay.

I turned off the freeway and realized I was pressing my left foot against the floorboards, so much that my calf was twitching. When I got to our street, I found a strange, beautiful car in my driveway – gleaming white, with gold trim and sexy, long-torsoed lines, like something from an art-deco mural. A dark-skinned man peered over the roof and smiled at me. Harvey, standing near a headlight, followed his friend's gaze and released a puff of smoke from his mouth.

I parked at the curb and crossed the yard. "Harvey? What are you doing?"

Harvey, still in his desert fatigues, held out a small cigar with a wooden tip.

"Sort of a Clint Eastwood thing. The guys in the Guard are crazy about 'em. Gets you in the proper frame of mind for blowin' up shit."

"And gives you *terrible* breath," said the dark man.

"This is Kai," said Harvey. "He's a Sherpa."

Kai put his hands on his hips like a disgruntled housewife. "Would you stop introducing me like that?"

"Why? I think it's damn interesting. And you can introduce me as Harvey the Cajun. Two of the world's more interesting ethnic groups, y'ask me."

"Hi Kai," I said, wincing at the rhyme.

"Hi Channy. I know plenty about you. In between blowin' up stuff, Harvey talks about nothing but."

I allowed myself a smile. "I'm glad to hear that."

"Oh and sorry for blocking your driveway. I thought I was just doing a drop-off, but my Cajun friend forced a beer on me."

"The post-Guard beer is the sweetest you will ever drink," said Harvey. He punctuated his point with a long drag on his cigar.

I couldn't help noticing the way that Kai's presence had softened up my boyfriend, and I decided that this was a friendship I needed to encourage.

"Would you like to join us for dinner, Kai? I made off with some lovely pork chops from work."

Kai glanced at Harvey. "Long as I'm not… infringing?"

Harvey shook his head. "You kiddin' me? Come on in."

After the meal, Harvey stood from the table. "I don't want to go into details, but I need to go sit for a while. Can you two maintain the high level of discourse?"

I gave him a sideways squint. "I *never* should have gotten you that thesaurus."

"I'll take that as a yes," he said, and disappeared down the hall. I immediately went for the beverage option.

"Can I get you another beer?"

"How 'bout a coffee? I've got a bit of a drive ahead of me."

I went to the kitchen and spoke to Kai over the counter. "Where do you live?"

"Fife," he said. "The flatlands of industry. And cheap apartments."

"Wow! You mean people actually *live* down there?"

He laughed. "I get that a lot."

"You wouldn't know from that car you're driving."

"My parents promised me a new car if I graduated college. I'm guessing they didn't think I'd actually do it. The day before commencement, I'm sitting in front of a place in Ballard that sells coffee and cupcakes when a snow-white retro Thunderbird pulls to the curb right in front of me. Then this impossibly tall and gorgeous blonde gets out, and she's wearing a white sun dress. And I tell her, 'That is the most beautiful car I have ever seen.' And she says, 'Thanks. I just bought it.' And I say 'Oh! How long have you had it?' And she says 'Ten minutes.' So you see I had no choice. I had to have a car just like that one."

I punched the button on the coffeemaker and returned to the table. "You know? Everything in life should happen exactly like that."

"Yes!" said Kai, with surprising enthusiasm. "Life should be one long fairy tale. Was that how it was when you met Harvey?"

"Yeah. A Dickensian waif wandering in a signpost forest. Somewhere between a ragamuffin and a studmuffin."

"More of the latter, probably. He's an amazing soldier."

I glanced down the hallway. "Maybe that's why he's such a butthead when he gets home."

Kai smiled and folded his hands behind his head. "Forty-eight hours of stuff exploding and men freely farting does tend to have that effect."

"Well," I said. "I think you're a good influence, and I'd like you to join us for dinner every Guard Sunday."

"I'd love to. As long as Harvey..."

"Oh the hell with Harvey. This is *my* invitation. You're coming."

We indulged in quiet laughter, which drifted into a silence packed with thoughts.

"Are you going to Iraq?"

Kai blinked his dark eyes. "I think so. We've been told to be ready. Adjusted our training to desert and urban warfare. Learning phrases of Arabic. I don't see any way around it. 9/11 changed all the rules, and we're going to need the manpower."

"It's a scary, scary world," I said. "Let me get you that coffee."

Six months later, at one of those very Guard dinners, Harvey told me about his orders – and then proposed to me. The kneeling, the diamond ring – everything. Kai being there made it all the sweeter.

We were married a week later, at Kerby's. It turned out that J.B. was an ordained minister – and, in fact, that we were his first wedding ceremony. That quiet man always had a way of surprising me. Harvey wore his full dress uniform, as did Kai, acting as best man. After the ceremony, we conducted an elevated rendition of the usual karaoke night. Debbie sang "True Companion" for our first dance, and the regulars sang every sappy love song they could think of. On the hundred-yard walk home, the sky over the ridge turning a robin's-egg blue, I tried once more to feed the bison, but even the formal clothing couldn't charm them.

For the rest of the weekend, we stayed home and made love as if we'd just met. On Monday morning, I drove him to SeaTac airport. I always pictured soldiers flying off together in some huge olive-drab transport, but it seems the modern Army made plentiful use of commercial airlines.

All the way there, we were very quiet, and I began to understand just how tough this was going to be. With the new approach to security, I could ostensibly hang around the airport forever, waving at Harvey every five feet of the inspection line. One goodbye was torturous – seventy-five would kill me.

The Seattle airport has large enclosed walkways from the parking garage to the terminal. Halfway across, watching the streams of traffic below, I stopped.

"Harvey? I can't do this."

He turned and chuckled. "It's too late, honey. We're already married."

"I mean... can I leave you right here? Can we say goodbye here?"

He set down his duffel bag and smiled. "So you only have to do it once?"

Women often have the unreasonable expectation that men should read their minds. But maybe that's because once in a while they actually do, and it's glorious. I attacked Harvey with a kiss.

"Wow," he said. "I'm guessing I was right?"

"Oui, Monsieur Lebeque. Omigod! Do you realize my name is Chanson Lebeque?"

"You sound like one of Pepe LePew's girlfriends."

I should have laughed, but I cried instead. "Harvey, you're going to duck, right? You're going to come back to me, aren't you?"

He placed a hand on my cheek and thumbed away a tear. "It's not really a matter of ducking, but yes, I'm coming back. But I'm also going to do my job, and serve my country. But you *know* I won't do anything stupid, because God damn, look at what I've got to come home to."

He held me at arm's length, as if he were memorizing my face. "We're going to be all right, Mrs. Lebeque."

I held him for a long time, my face pressed into the rough khaki of his jacket, then I slipped a black box out of my pocket and handed it to him. He flipped it open and pulled out a silver lighter.

"A fleur de lis! Now *that's* French. So ma'amselle has decided to support my filthy habit?"

"Everyone's allowed one filthy habit. Especially if they're saving the world for democracy."

"I will hand out Swisher Sweets in the streets of Baghdad, to win hearts and minds."

"That should finish them off."

We shared a relieved laugh, and then we were out of things to say.

"Time for goodbye?" asked Harvey.

I nodded.

"I love you very much, Channy."

"I love you, Harvey. And I want you back."

"Goodbye."

He gave me a kiss, lifted his duffel and left, stopping at the door to give me a last wave. I fought off the urge to shout something, and waved back. Then I turned for the garage, a single married woman, and began the work of passing the months without him.

Twenty-two
Ruby

Scootie's building had one of those old-style freight elevators, and one side of the shaft had windows looking out toward Central Park. When the inside window met up with a shaft window, it created a strobe effect, like a silent-era film. The feature that day was a maple at the edge of the park, going absolutely berserk with scarlets, pumpkins, siennas and mustards. (Scootie was having a distinct effect on my color-vocabulary.)

When I got out, I heard a sound like a reverse heartbeat, like trochaic verse: *thump*-thump, *thump*-thump, *On* the *shores* of *Gitchigoo*my. Making my way down the hall, I realized it was coming from Scootie's loft, and opened the door to find him tossing a violet spheroid against the wall.

"Wednesday *Thursday* Friday!" I shouted.

"Hi," he said, barely missing a beat. "What did you say?"

"WTF!"

Blank stare.

"What the fuck!"

"Right! Here: I demonstrate."

He took a tube of pink acrylic, squeezed a teaspoon of paint onto the tennis ball and fired away. The ball struck the canvas with a splat and bounced on the dropclothed floor. Scootie scooped it up nicely and fired again, then caught it and set it in a dogbowl at his feet. He rose from his stool and stalked my way with gloppy rainbow hands. "Give me a hug!"

"Not on your life, Van Gogh!"

"You love me, you love my art, bebe." He held his hands behind his back and gave me a schoolboy kiss.

"It's like dating a fucking paint monster." I retreated to a clean-looking table, ten feet away. "Okay, mojo man. Give me the game plan."

He stood and made a game-show sweep toward the canvas. "First, I covered the surface with black gesso. Then I took one of my coaster creatures and lined it out in masking tape. Now I'm playing paintball until I get a nice thick coating of rainbow splats and circles. Once it dries, I remove the masking tape, with some assistance from my X-Acto knife, and ba-boom! An eerie black figure, staring out from a Jackson Pollock-Bjorn Borg carnaval."

I followed the tape-strip drowning in tennis strokes and clucked my tongue. "You're a marvel. I don't know five people combined who have as much creative juice as you."

Scootie surveyed his cloud of splats, and I knew exactly what was going on behind those obsidian irises. He was forecasting that perfect moment, that split second when the work took its form, and it was time to set the creature free. But I didn't want him drifting too far, because I intended to steal him away from Mother Art, at least for the evening.

"Hey, boybee – snap to it. Ruby needs a feedin'."

The battle was almost too easy. He took a final snapshot and smiled. "I'll go wash up. Try some of that wine."

He headed for the bathroom as I located the uncorked bottle atop his cabinet. His wines were all obscure and eccentric – I never saw any of them in the stores, and in New York that's saying something. The same quality applied to his curios, books and glassware – all of them looking much more indigenous than anything you would find in an import shop. The wine was an Argentinean Shiraz that fired my tastebuds in a pleasing fashion.

Of course, Scootie was rather exotic and inexplicable himself. I was so pleased with the way that our puzzle pieces fit together (and the way his eternal creativity extended to the bedroom) that

I didn't want to spoil it by probing the vagaries. After a year, we still met only once or twice a week, and had never discussed the exact nature of our relationship. He had also talked me into some adventurous moves regarding my career, and I was feeling a little hung out to dry.

The image of him returning from the bathroom, newly domesticated, slipping into a leather jacket, dashed all of this aside like so many violet tennis balls, and soon we were strolling through chilly twilight to a Malaysian restaurant on Broadway. I dipped my hand over the collar of his jacket to grab a hank of his thick, still-damp hair.

"Yes. The Malaysian iced coffee, some roti canai and the mango chicken. Thanks."

The waiter walked away, and Scootie scoped me with those ebony searchlights, the same way he looked at his paintings. Did I, too, contain a moment of release?

"So what's the matter?" he said.

I rolled my fingers on the table, four beats, pinkie to index.

"Auditions. Mother fucking auditions."

"*Oedipus Rex*?"

"Hilarious! No – *Sweet Charity.* A revival with Molly Ringwald. Big-time stuff."

"Good."

"But I didn't even feel like I existed. That brutally cordial 'Thank you' from some guy you can't see. Imagine someone slapping duct tape all over your person, and then ripping it off, all at once. God, Scootie! What is it about me that doesn't fit? Am I completely delusional? I mean, I'm good, right?"

"Are you nuts?" he said. "You're fucking incredible."

"Not just saying that? Not just the penis talking?"

"No way. Not when it's art."

"So when it's *not* art, you might lie to me."

"Don't be silly. Of *course* I would lie to you."

He was being all cute and funny again, but I was determined to plow on.

"I'm not putting this on you, Scootie..."

"Put it on me if you like. I was only telling you what you really wanted for yourself."

"I know. Now shut up a second, wouldja?"

"Yes ma'am." I enjoyed this about Scootie. I could be a little rough with him, and he with me. It wasn't personal.

"Okay. So I'm just looking at what I had before at Greenstreet, and I know it was big fish, small pond, but the pond was in *Manhattan.* Am I overplaying my hand? Am I screwing myself?"

Our waiter returned with the roti. Scootie tore off a piece, dipped it in peanut sauce and aimed it at me like an instructional pointer.

"Let's get back to the basic question. Where's the heat? What do you *really want*?"

I sighed. "To sing and dance in a musical. Broadway or something close."

"And at Greenstreet?"

"Edgy, fringe-theater drama. No singing, no dancing. Ironically, a gay director named Giuseppe Verdi hates musicals."

"Any realistic career footbridge from one to the other?"

"Not... really."

He took a bite out of his pointer. "So the auditions are bad, and you're suffering. But you're suffering in the right direction. You're suffering for the right reasons."

I tore off a piece and chewed like a recalcitrant cow. "God. You make it sound like childbirth."

"It is."

He didn't give me much choice. Scootie was one big raging package of artistic integrity. He had taken this wacky idiosyncratic work of his and broken into an art world more full of shit than the stables at Churchhill Downs. And once he landed on the other side, the collectors loved him for his personality, his willingness to actually *say something* on the canvas. And his fearless sense of humor. Still, it wasn't easy. I could hear the hiss of my deflating ego, the leak that got louder with each anonymous *Thank you.*

When we got back, I couldn't help myself. I took off my clothes, set them at a safe distance, then moussed a tennis ball with kelly green and gave it a toss. It smacked the canvas with a gooey Medusa's head and came back fast, crawling up my arms and leaving a green circle on my abdomen. I caught a grip and fired it back.

Never one to be surprised, Scootie returned from the kitchen, saw what I was doing and immediately stripped off. Then he unrolled a large canvas, squished out a manicolored delta of acrylics and invited me to lie down.

Just before entry, I told him, "If this sells, I expect forty percent."

Twenty-three

Kai is already family, so there's no need for the usual filters. He even joins me for dinner with the Craigs – the closest thing I've got to meeting the parents – and passes with flying colors. (For John, a deployment in Iraq buys instant acceptance.)

For New Year's, he takes me to a slick restaurant in Seattle's Queen Anne district: candlelight dinner followed by a jazz combo. I took just enough lessons during the retro-swing thing that I manage to keep up with him. I recall what he said about those high school musicals, and it shows – he's a seriously good lead, with a sense of panache and rhythm that you just can't teach.

But then there's sex. I am most definitely ready to end my forced celibacy, but Kai seems hesitant. I can't rush him and I can't blame him; I was, after all, his best friend's wife.

My odds, however, are getting much better. Our sporting goods Fezziwig is rather fond of lending his ski cabin to employees – in fact, sees it as an investment, since it allows his workers to try out the products that they're selling. We are, in fact, completely decked out with demo models from three of Scott's stores, tooling along the Columbian River Gorge in an SUV, headed for Mt. Hood, Oregon.

Our pilot is Conrad, assistant manager at the Olympia store, and a former member of Kai's Guard unit. He's a hybrid of superhero and fratboy – tall, blond, broad-shouldered, square-jawed and boisterous of expression. His girlfriend is Becky, a software engineer bearing no trace of yuppiedom. She seems extraordinarily genuine – which is, I think, a vastly underrated quality. She also projects that rare duality of quiet-but-friendly, which makes you want to tell her things that you wouldn't tell anyone else. She'd make a great psychiatrist.

Our other passengers are Shari and Ruby, and though I'm feeling guilty for hogging the guest list, I've been hoping for just such a chance to bring my two confidantes together. (The original idea was to bring Harry, too, but with the nasty winter weather he's booked up with work.) Shari's a veteran skier who will undoubtedly leave us all in her powder, whereas Ruby's only been twice. I can't imagine her being truly bad at anything, however, so I'm sure she'll find a way to keep up.

We park at a large complex, and find that Scott's cabin is more like an apartment. Given his passion for elegance, I suppose this is a little surprising. The place is nice, though, and reaches for that cabinesque feel with an upstairs loft, replete with loggy furniture and stacks of board games. The living room sports a lovely stone fireplace (fueled by actual wooden logs, stacked on the balcony) and a round, radiant blondewood table.

But the *real* priority, for yours truly, is to track down some privacy, so I duck downstairs and head for the end of the hallway. There I find a master bedroom with a king-size bed. Lest there be claim-jumpers, I flop my suitcase on the center of the bed and hang my ballcap on the outside doorknob. Conrad, toting baggage into the front bedroom, catches me in the act and flashes a knowing grin.

Trying to force the blood back from my face, I return to the living room, which is echoing with sorority chatter. I find Kai coming my way with two glasses of wine, which just about wipes out all of my remaining wishes. After making his delivery, he smiles at something over my head. I turn to find Ruby and Shari leaning over the loft railing like Southern debutantes. Ruby barks like a drill sergeant: "Kai! About face, soldier!"

"Ma'am yes ma'am!" says Kai, and executes a precise military spin.

When I turn back, I find four knockers resting on the railing like flesh-colored water balloons. I respond with a suitably girlish scream.

Ruby and Shari return their shirts to standard civilian position and are about to fill the room with more giggling when they're drowned out by Kai, who has collapsed on the table, crippled by laughter. I scale his body till I'm riding him like a cowgirl, slapping him on the back.

"What? You loony Sherpa – what!?"

Kai has lost the power of speech, but manages to gesture at a mirror on the back wall, which currently holds a portrait of Ruby and Shari's puzzled faces.

We're both pretty knocked out from the drive, so the question of sex isn't really a question. But this is beginning to worry me, because I don't want this thing to grow into some intimidating obstacle. So I play the good girl, put on the Presbyterian flannels, but I indulge in as many snuggles as the law will allow, and I certainly like the feel of the parts against which I am rubbing.

The next day is a slow start, thanks mostly to the strawberry pancakes served up by Shari, which have about the same effect as tranquilizer darts. Still, we rouse ourselves in time for six hours of near-perfect skiing, and turn out to be quite a cohesive unit, despite our differing levels of expertise. Shari's being cautious with her trick knee, so she's slumming in the intermediates – and treating them like her own private NASCAR tracks. On the fifth run, I fire off the chairlift, duck my head, tuck my knees and hit the straightaways like a one-woman bullet train, then shuss into the lift line to find Shari, not even breathing hard, looking like she could have ordered and consumed a caffe borgia during her wait. On the other hand, with her height and her lime green jester's hat, she makes a dandy gathering spot.

Conrad surprises no one by being our usual runner-up, with Becky working hard to keep him in her sights. Ruby's a consistent last, as expected, but her dancer's grace keeps her from falling, even once, so our waits are not long.

Kai and I are the middle children, and an interesting study in contrast. Either one of us could probably reach the bottom more quickly, but we've got other items on our agendas. Kai had lots of lessons as a kid, so he's after style points, carving lovely esses down the flats, navigating the moguls like a schoolboy coloring inside the lines, knees relaxed, legs neatly parallel. I, meanwhile, am after as much low-level air as I can gather, searching the edges for those little ramp-trails and running the tops of the moguls, trusting that I'll find a landing spot on the other side. My legs shoot out every which way, like a dog on ice, as I battle for balance, and I add three festive crash-and-burns to my life list. I'm relating one of these over Conrad's hearty steak dinner as we decompress at the cabin.

"Okay. So I found the snowboarding ramps at the end of the Glen Ridge run?"

"Oh Channy!" says Becky. "You didn't."

"You kiddin' me? I had to. So the first ramp, it felt like I was heading straight up a freakin' wall. But once I cleared the edge, the momentum pulled me forward and I landed smooth as can be, almost as if I knew what I was doing! The next... object... was a deep drop into a fairly innocent-looking scoop-ramp. My takeoff was fine, but sometime in mid-flight I realized that I was about to land in the middle of a *second* scoop-ramp, and I *freaked*. My body went into a flying fetal position, I totally sluffed the second ramp, flew through the air fully sideways, and managed to land on my ass. *Then* I caught an edge, which sent me into a spin, like one of those whirling sparklers that you nail to a fencepost. The landing area was about twenty yards long, iced up from traffic, so I slid and slid and slid until I came to a stop right in front of the lift line, where fifty skiers gave me a rousing ovation."

"Oh!" says Ruby. "That is *harsh*."

"Hey, sistah. Any applause is good applause, right?"

"No. This is not what they mean when they say, 'Break a leg.'"

"However," says Kai. "The next time, she got it perfect."

"You went *back*?" says Shari.

"Oh yeah," says Conrad. "Look who's talking, Dale Earnhardt."

Shari lets out a big whiskey-laugh. "I'm a *big* girl, honey. You just ain't gonna beat certain combinations of mass and gravity."

I take the opening to lift my beer in salute. "To gravity!"

"Without it," says Kai, "skiing would really suck!"

We wrap up the evening with a board game that requires entirely too much mental acumen. I discover that 1) I am quite good at backwards spelling, and 2) I cannot identify a hummed song to save my life (which, given my profession, is downright shameful). Come the last round, as Ruby and I stand on the brink of victory, I mistake "Battle Hymn of the Republic" for "Swanee." I also take this to indicate that I have had enough wine for the evening. Conrad wins the game by properly identifying a dachsund that Becky has fashioned from modeling clay.

The evening is a caravan of laughter, and it floats Kai to my cave of seduction, where I intend to get on with the gettin' on. For a first session, it's remarkably natural. I spend most of my time on top, as I imagined I would, arranging things as I like them. The sense of control is a potent aphrodisiac, and reminds me of my high school passions with the geek boys. Perhaps Kai *is* a geek boy – I'd lay money on it – but he has most definitely graduated. It's this subdermal strata of strength, the power you must have in order to *accede* power. To let the lady be on top. If I'm not careful, I'm going to fall in love with this boy. I feel the surges as he works up to orgasm and stiffens, and I collapse over him, my hair falling to his chest.

"That was beautiful, Kai."

"Yes, it was."

The next morning, things are different. Or perhaps it's just that Kai is in charge of breakfast: omelets with linguisa and caramelized onions. But the feeling of separation is more than culinary. He's not reacting as a lover should. He's expending all his energy on the others, playing the host. I'm thinking, No! Come inside with me. Let's make a separate room, all to ourselves.

On the slopes, he doesn't seem all that concerned with keeping me in his sights, more apt to drift his own way and meet me at the jester's hat. Then he starts taking the lift up with others. Two, three months from now, this would be normal – but not the first morning-after. I want to take last night's warmth and hoard it, drown in it. I catch a lift with Shari, and watch the square of Kai's jacketed shoulder thirty feet in front of us.

"Were you being active last night, young lady?"

"Yes."

Shari chides me with a laugh. "That's all I get?"

"It was our first."

She turns sharply, causing one of her jester tentacles to slap me across the forehead.

"Goddamn, sister. I figured you two were full-blown rabbits by now."

"Such are the assumptions in a horndog karaoke bar."

"Amen. Although I guess you do have some serious stuff to work around."

I'm chewing on the finger of my glove. "Ruby's told you?"

"Um, yeah. Is that all right?"

"Yeah. It's fine. I am just about to the end of my sad, sad story."

"Good."

"So. Do I ask him why he's pulling away already?"

She takes a strand of hair and twirls it around a finger. Everybody's got a thinking device.

"The day-after retreat is common enough – *so* hunter-gatherer – but this matter of boinking your best friend's wife is quite the complication. You can apply all the logic you want, but there's still going to be some guilt. You, however, are the best diplomat I know – Lord knows how you balance all those singerly egos. I'm sure you'll find a subtle, non-threatening way to bring it up. You need to find out if he'll trust you enough to talk about these things."

"Damn!" I say. "You're thorough."

"Those who can't do, give advice. You going left?"

"Yep."

"Groovy. I'm right."

"Have a nice sprint, Jean-Claude."

Shari grins. "Hey, some people get laid, others get to be first down the hill."

"Deal!"

We slide off the chair, and I swoop around the lift tower, looking for Sherpas. Alas, he's already a hundred feet down the hill.

"I don't *think* so," I mutter, pretending I'm Deniro. I shoot down the hill, recalling the field of shallow moguls around the first bend. Kai is going to carve them in loving snake tracks. I'm going straight over the top. And *that's* how I'll catch him.

I'm flying my third mogul, splendidly out of control, when I spot a dark figure, taking a hairpin turn straight into my path. I pivot sideways, hoping to grind my landing, but I catch an edge and topple sideways, taking him out with an NHL-level body check. We explode into the next tier of moguls, our skis locked up, and tumble five-and-a-half more times before we come to a frosty stop. I scrape the powder from my face to find a booted foot inches from my nose, and pray to God it's not mine. Kai groans, and pushes to an elbow to ID his assailant.

"Channy? What the hell?!"

I give a repentant look. "I was trying to catch up, and I got a little... exuberant."

"Exuberant? More like homicidal!"

He sees that I'm not laughing, and he pats my cheek.

"Hey Channy. I'm kidding."

"Oh." I tuck my skis so I can sit up. "I sorta... felt like you were avoiding me."

"Ah, geez!" he says. "I am *so* bad at this. I'm not used to being part of a couple. I guess I was hanging back, waiting for instructions."

I give him a meaningful look. "Why don't you start by helping me up?"

He grabs both my hands and pulls me to my feet.

"And now you can kiss me, in a sweet, schoolboy fashion."

Which he does.

"And the rest of the day, you can pretty much worship my every move."

"Gotcha."

"Well, not really. But just... stay connected with me. If you're off in a corner, playing backgammon with Becky, just look my way once in a while, make eye contact. This is sweet, valuable stuff, these beginnings of things. Spend them wisely. Plus, the first day-after makes us chicks very jumpy and vulnerable. Now – wanna ski?"

"Yeah," he says. "But why don't you go first?"

"Smart boy," I say, and I'm off.

Twenty-Four

Dearest kind gentlemen: Please lower the toilet seat in consideration of our lady patrons.

Life is filled with seemingly arcane items that keep popping into your thoughts, and one of mine is the notice in the bathroom at the Java and Clay. In a world where so many are happy to hammer you over the head with rules and regulations, this little ceramic sign is an oasis of civility. It *invites* men to be courteous, and offers them the chance to feel like Arthurian knights for the simple act of lowering a ring of porcelain. And I would bet that it actually works. It's a chilly Friday in late January, a week after our blessed ski trip, and I am meeting Ruby for another session. The Java and Clay is a particular favorite. The back forty is a full-blown workshop where patrons glaze pre-made vases and platters and pick them up the next day, fully kilned. The front is more like someone's living room, including a large gas fireplace with stone facing. When I come here solo, I end up on a stool before the front window, which affords a vista of Harborview Drive and the Jerisich Dock. The bonus is an occasional bald eagle sighting – once, a mere thirty feet above the sidewalk, as if he were headed to The Tides for a sandwich.

My everything bagel goes off in the toaster just as Ruby pops through the door, looking all Debbie Reynolds in a white jacket and sienna scarf. She's also had her hair bobbed, which multiplies her cuteness sevenfold.

"Girlfriend!" she cries, and we go for a greeting with all the trimmings: wraparound hug, continental cheek-kissing, everything short of high-fives. She fetches a cappuccino, then joins me in matching armchairs before the fire.

"God! I just want to live here. It's so much nicer than my place."

"Tish-tosh!" I try to say with a straight face. "I've been to your place."

"Yes," she rebuts. "But this place is in Gig Harbor."

"Point and... match! The hair is darling. I just want to adopt you."

"Thanks! I wanted it real short for my Mexican cruise."

"Excuse me? I mean, excuse me?"

Ruby bats her lashes, all Betty Boop. "Yay-ess! Harry got a nice fat bonus, so next week our ports of call are Vallarta, Mazatlan and Cabo."

"San Lucas?"

"Yes. We're on a first-name basis."

"Extraordinary! I'm jealous already. Does the ship have karaoke?"

"You have *such* a one-track mind. And yes, they do. It's the first thing I checked." She rubs her hands together, all Cruella DeVille. "A whole new crowd of victims for my siren call!"

I laugh, in a perfectly normal manner, but then I'm drifting, my gaze fixed on the rust-colored hands of the mantelpiece clock. And then Ruby is saying something that fades in and out of my frequency.

"Channy? Are you somewhere in the 253 area code?"

I shake my head around, all Rin-Tin-Tin.

"Um... um... sorry. I'm a little wary of these stories today. Well. Mine, mostly. This might sound silly, but, as we got further and further into our little meetings, I began to believe that, if I told the story exactly right, maybe this time it would turn out... differently."

Ruby takes in my anxiety, folding her hands over her knee. "Would it help if I went first?"

"Would you? Oh! I forgot my bagel. Hold on."

Ruby laughs, all Fran Dreischer. "Jewish food for a Jewish tragedy. Oy gevalt! I'll go visit the restroom."

"Be sure and put the seat down," I say. Disappearing around the corner, Ruby flashes one half of a puzzled expression.

Ruby

I marked my time with Scootie by that maple tree, the one I could see from his elevator. At this time, it was just beginning to bud, which probably meant early March. Which meant we'd been together a year and a half. Everything else was unchanged. We had fabulous, messy sex. We did artsy, creative things together. And I still had no clue as to the true nature of our relationship. We still saw each other only once or twice a week. But I had managed to grow comfortable with this. I began to think of it as the best kind of relationship; the infrequency made our time together that much more valuable. Say this for the female mind: it possesses a virtuosic ability to rationalize.

I was also afraid to mess with the one thing that was going well for me. Same deadend receptionist job. Same invisible turndowns at the auditions. And deep at the core, the same dark dread: that I would pass from the Earth without leaving a single mark on the history of the American musical – that throwing away my roles at the Greenstreet Theater had been a reckless, childish act. And the worst thought of all, that I was just as talented as I thought myself to be – and that the only thing keeping me from success was the failure to find someone who had the eyes and ears to recognize this.

That night, however, Scootie had lined up some excellent consolations. He had arranged for the Italian restaurant across the street to deliver an entire meal to his loft – place settings, silverware, butter dish and all. The fare was Caesar salad followed by seafood fettucine (mussels, clams, crabmeat) in a white cream sauce. Dessert was a canoli on a bed of whipped cream in the shape of a cross. We were sipping ten-year-old tawny port when Scootie's expression took a sudden change.

"I have to stop seeing you."

I laughed, and stopped, and laughed again, but Scootie's expression stayed the same.

"Scootie? Come on, finish the joke. You're making me nervous. I didn't know you could do such a vicious deadpan. You really ought to be a straight-man."

He got up and walked away, holding his port like a worry-stone.

"No joke. No deadpan."

He turned back around, and looked at me intently.

"Ten years ago, I was working at a theater center in California, and I fell in love with one of the trustees, a married woman. After a lot of backs and forths, she divorced, but she found that she didn't want to get married again. She had things that she wanted to do with her life, and she wanted to pursue them freely. She eventually founded a non-profit network for international performing arts groups. I loved her, but I realized that I also had things to pursue, visions bouncing around in my head. I was able to establish my career in New York thanks largely to her generosity.

"Despite our claims to freedom, we are inextricably linked. And when our paths cross, we are automatically a couple. Juliana just wrote to say that her network is transferring its headquarters to New York. So she and I will be back together, and I... will... have to stop seeing you."

When I was a kid in Florida, I used to go boogie-boarding with my brother. I caught this one wave just as it was breaking, and it took hold of me, slamming me into the wash. There was no *me* left, just a bunch of limbs flailing one way and the next with no say-so from Central Command. This was how I felt, sitting before a whipped-cream cross at Scootie's table. But it changed quickly. It became a fever, creeping over my body, hissing out in words that refused to become sentences.

"How... You can... I... Don't..."

I stood from the table. The room shook at me.

"You... mother... fucker!"

I had to destroy something. It didn't take long to find a target. Scootie had been working for a month on a mural with three figures: an evil robot clown in magenta, a shy junior executive in green, and an Easter Island god in gold. I located a dozen jars of paint on a nearby table, opened them up and hurled them at the mural, obliterating the figures in a storm of scarlet, ochre, mars black and cerulean blue. Then I turned to find Scootie calmly watching, arms folded, like a mother waiting out a toddler's tantrum. This pissed me off even more, so I took a jar of lime green and poured it over his head. I'll give him this much: he took it without flinching.

I slapped the paint into his jacket and said, "Fuck you, you fucking pig." Then I grabbed my purse and left. I marched eight blocks in a righteous fury, and didn't start crying until I arrived at my apartment door.

A year later, I received a check for $2,300. It was forty percent of two works: the canvas of our lovemaking, and the three slaughtered figures of our breakup. In the exhibit, the latter was accompanied by a coat rack holding the lime green jacket. If I had any pride, I would have torn that check into a thousand pieces. But I was a brutalized actor in a brutal city, and I was behind on my rent.

"Ruby! That is so *harsh*."

"Hey! That's my word."

"Pssh, yeah. And now I know why."

Ruby looks away nervously, then spoons the last dollop of foam from her cappuccino.

"That's pretty much the end of my story. Don't know *what* we'll talk about now – except perhaps my Mexican cruise."

She's got me laughing again. "You are gonna milk that thing for all it's worth."

"I'm gonna *leche* that thing," she says, then performs an uncanny cow impression – less "moo," more "mrrr."

"But I don't get it," I say. "Didn't you spend about five more years in New York?"

"Five times nothing equals nothing. I kept auditioning. I kept demonstrating my uncanny ability to *not* get parts. I kept doing the day job. I'm an actress, honey – give me credit for not wanting to beat a dead story. In a way, though, those nothing years were the saddest of all. Here I set out to have a scintillating life on Broadway, and I end up with a black hole five years long. It was good to tell you about the other stuff, Channy – and I thank you for listening – but fuck New York. I'm in Tacoma now. And I'm *going* to..."

"Mexico, right. But... So you came out here to take care of your brother?"

"Yes. And I'm oddly grateful about that. The noble mission of saving David – fully funded by my relatives, I might add – gave me a way out of town without having to admit to abject failure. And it's such a relief! From now on, I do not chase the dreams that don't chase me. Give me the *real* stuff."

I can't help myself. I stand up and give Ruby a kiss on the cheek. "Congrats, sistah. You just graduated."

"No more school? Righteous!"

"I'm gettin' a cookie. You want one?"

"Yeah," she says. "One of those pink sugar cookies. I'm feeling juvenile."

We sit for a few minutes in silence, grinding our Valentine's hearts into sweet sugar smoke. And I know that it's time to get to the bad stuff.

Channy

Harvey began sending emails as soon as he arrived – which surprised me. I thought he'd be too busy, but it turned out that a lot of his duty was spent waiting around. And writing, in stripped-down language, of the casual terrors of Iraq.

First day on patrol, spotted a couple Iraquis approaching the checkpoint. We have orders to shoot anyone who passes the periphery without properly identifying themselves. Everybody's pretty jumpy from all the IEDs (that's Improvised Explosive Devices). I had this one tall guy in my sights – to be specific, I had the red laser dot on his heart. He looked down and saw the dot, *and was smart enough, and calm enough, to turn so I could see his contractor's badge. I have no idea what he was doing out there, but I'm sure glad I didn't have to shoot him.*

"Whatcha readin' there, Channy?"

Debbie snuck up behind me at the pool table, holding a huge glass of Coke.

"Oh, hi. Letters from the front. Wow, listen to that: 'Letters from the front.'"

"Is he doing all right?"

"Harvey's hard to figure out. He's either terribly excited or terribly afraid. Me, I'm just terribly terrified, and I have *way* too much time to imagine all the grotesque possibilities. And being alone has never felt so lonely."

Debbie rested a hand on my shoulder and studied me through her thick glasses. "You know, that brings me to an interesting subject. J.B. and I have been asked to do a couple nights a week at this Mexican restaurant in Lakewood, and frankly neither one of us has the energy for it. However, now that we've made the transition to a fully computerized system, we've got enough old-fashioned CDs and surplus equipment to send someone else to Lakewood. Namely, you."

The idea was pure gold, and I knew it. "Really? You're sure?"

"Sure. We would ask, like, thirty percent for using the equipment."

"God, Debbie. That is *so* perfect. You don't know how perfect that is. When do I start?"

"Next Thursday, if you like."

I hugged her so tightly I thought I might hurt her. "Oh, Debbie! I like I like I like. Save me from myself."

"You got it, kiddo."

Had to clean up after a car bombing in a village square. Pretty horrible stuff. A Humvee unit was out on "hearts and minds" duty – go out and wave to the natives while you're wondering which one of them is going to kill you. Found a Lt. Cooper who bled to death, both arms blown off at the elbow. Ten feet away, I found a bottle of bubble-blowing liquid. They were blowing bubbles out the window, something for the kids. The bomb also took out his three comrades, and 14 villagers.

La Palma restaurant had a decidedly funky location, tucked into the corner of a ginormous shopping center parking lot, next to a transit center with a dozen bus stops. The lounge was funky, too: Aztec legends depicted in black velvet paintings, and a great old bar with ceramic tile arches. The room was long and narrow, and I was exiled to the far end, a stage divided from the main area by a low wall with a tile counter. I was afraid that my customers would feel like they were singing from a cage.

That is, if I *had* any customers. My major concern was that no one would show up at all, that I would have to fill four hours all by myself. I waited half an hour just to make sure I wasn't pushing things, then I sang a sound check: "Hallelujah" by Leonard Cohen. When I returned to the soundboard, I found an actual song slip. The singer was Shane, a big guy with an Irish complexion and dyed blond hair. I'd seen him earlier, working on a book of drawings in the corner, and frankly hadn't expected much. As it turned out, he was quite the Dean Martin buff, and he worked through half the list – "Ain't That a Kick in the Head," "Everybody Loves Somebody," "An Evening in Roma" – as I tried to keep up with him with the songs I'd sung at Kerby's. A couple of the barflies finally got soused enough to give it a shot, and we forced the bartender, Paul, to try "La Bamba" despite the small impediment of zero singing talent. By the end of the night, I had five new friends and some assurance that I did not entirely suck at this job.

The next night, I had a rotation of ten. The manager of the restaurant seemed happy.

You might think from all these exciting tales that life here is constantly involving, but believe me, it ain't. We spend most of our days in excruciating boredom, and we are definitely not free to just go for a walk in the countryside. Killing off time has become an art form unto itself. Thank God for video games. No Zero Squadron, but I'm beginning to realize what a big fat lie that game is, anyway.

However. Be careful what you wish for. The insurgents like to keep us on our toes by lobbing random mortars into our compound. Captain Lukafour was at the mess last week, looking in the fridge for a soda, and the next second he's a pile of charred meat.

Sorry. I don't mean to be crude. But it's hard. My commander, Bucksy (have I told you about him? He is absolutely the best), he told me after the attack, "You wait, Harv. Tomorrow morning, there'll be two dead Iraquis outside the fence. I don't know how it happens, but it does."

Sure enough, I'm on guard duty the next morning, and there's a couple extra body bags ready for transport. Couple of guys walk up, give the bags a kick and say, "Wake up, motherfucker!" Pretty cold, but I gotta admit, it made me laugh.

I began to develop a group of regulars, and the manager, Cesar, asked me if I wanted to make it three nights instead of two. With Harvey's combat pay coming in, I decided to use my karaoke money to buy the CDs and equipment from Debbie and J.B. It felt good, finding a job I enjoyed so much, and a way to hedge our bets.

It was morning, early September. The valley was groggy with overcast. I had just rolled out and put on some coffee when the doorbell rang. I opened the door to a young man in full Army dress. He was tall, with a chin so sharp and closely shaven that it seemed more like a weapon. I was just fuzzy enough that I had no idea what he was doing there.

"Hello?"

"Morning, ma'am. Are you Mrs. Chanson Lebeque?"

I was struck by the way he pronounced my first name in the correct French fashion. "I... well, yes."

"Ma'am? Could I come in for a moment?"

"Um, yes, okay. Would you like some coffee?"

He stood in the living room, almost at attention, as I went to the kitchen and filled a mug. A shaft of frosty light cut through from the kitchen window, settling on one half of the soldier's face. In that one blue eye, behind all the military polish, I could see just a hint of fear.

My legs gave way, and I clung to the edge of the counter. My soldier was there in a flash, propping me up, helping me to the couch. A minute later, as the clarity began to return, I looked into his young, young face and offered a one-word question: "How?"

"Sergeant Lebeque died of an apparent suicide. They discovered his body next to a river behind the base, in a grove of eucalyptus trees. He was killed by one of his own bullets, discharged by his own rifle. He was reported to have been distraught over the death of his commanding officer."

Later that morning, I wandered over to the Kerby's parking lot, gathered two fistfuls of grass and stood at the fence for an hour, pleading with Ben and Bessie to come to me. When I felt a hand on my shoulder, I turned and buried my face into someone's chest. I remember the smell of his leather jacket. When I finally looked up, it was Rob, the owner of Kerby's, who had come to open the bar.

Harvey's bullets were designed to pierce tank armor. I was strongly advised not to view the body. I signed a release for his cremation, and attended a burial at the cemetery at Ft. Lewis. That afternoon, I gave notice on the house, and placed Harvey's belongings in a storage unit. Debbie and J.B. wrote off the last few payments on the karaoke equipment. Two days later, I was loaded up, headed for the Tacoma Narrows Bridge. The transition was so seamless, it made me question my pronouns. Had I been hedging *our* bets? Or hedging *my* bets?

I have noticed Ruby's tears, but I was struggling to stick to my story, like a marathoner closing in on the finish line. When I return my focus to our little fireside, I find her holding a soggy wad of Kleenex and trailing streams of mascara. I feel like I've been a sadist, intentionally inflicting pain on her, and I kneel at the foot of her chair to beg forgiveness.

"I'm so sorry, Ruby."

"*You're* sorry," she sniffles. "You're sorry. Jesus. I knew it was coming all along, and yet... I'm destroyed. This image of you in the living room with that poor Army kid. Channy! How can you stand it?"

"But Ruby..."

"And me! Me with my petty bohemian dump stories. Boo-hoo for Ruby, she lost her *boy*friend. I am *such* a dork!"

"It's all the same... stuff, Ruby. It's all grief and loss. It's not a competition."

She manages a laugh. "It was on Halloween."

"That was different," I say. "You were being a flaming bitch. Did I ever thank you for that?"

"Not that I remember."

"Thank you, Ruby, for being a flaming bitch."

She manages to laugh and cry at the same time. "My standard fee is forty percent." She pulls out a fresh tissue and rubs it all over her face, like she's erasing a chalkboard. Frankly, I don't know what to do with her.

"Want a latte?"

Ruby peers above her Kleenex with wide eyes. "Mocha?"

I stand up and muss her cutesy hair. "Mocha it is."

I have officially proclaimed my widowhood, and I'm feeling like Ruby did about her euthanized career – relieved, liberated, and determined that my next dream had better behave itself. I sip at a cappuccino and feel the waves of heat from the fireplace as Ruby slurps her mocha. She wipes her mouth, touches up her lipstick, and gives me a grateful smile.

"Do we have time for dinner?" she asks. "Let me buy you dinner."

"Sure. Mexican?"

I gather my jacket and purse, Ruby deposits her sob-wad in the trash, and we head outside, where it's already dark.

"I hope you don't mind," she says, "but I invited David to karaoke."

"Why would I mind?"

"Oh, there could be reasons," she says, and flips her hair in the manner of a young Shirley MacLaine.

As a matter of fact, there *is* something awry about David. He isn't smoking. At all. And then he turns in a song slip: "Unchain My Heart," the Joe Cocker version. Fortunately, I've got some time to adjust to this new reality. All my regulars are here, as well as a few newcomers, and we have a rotation that is downright robust. It could be that everyone has finally recovered from the holidays, and decided it's okay to get on with regular life.

I'm about to get things rolling when I'm approached by a tall, stout man with gentle silver trimmings. He bears the expression of a schoolboy about to request a hall pass.

"Hi. Our book only had one song slip. Do you have a stash up here?"

"Sure." I pull a dozen from my shelf. "Here. What do you sing?"

He smiles, almost shyly. "Oh, I don't. I mean, not here. I'm an opera coach. I'm here with my partner, Russ, who sings Elton John, Neil Diamond, those kind of things."

"Does he sing opera?"

This brings another sort of smile, close-mouthed, sly. "Won't even *go* to the opera."

"A gay man who doesn't like opera?"

"I know! Another perfectly good stereotype, shot to hell. My name's Cordell, by the way."

A few singers in, it's readily apparent what Cordell sees in Russ. He is a quiet man, in every way – moves quietly, stands quietly – but once the lyric screen comes on he's in his element, giving a thoughtful, polished reading of Neil Diamond's "The Story of My Life."

The boyfriend – *my* boyfriend – is sitting in the deep corner, next to the jukebox. I've been adding up the high school musicals, the way he dances, the lovely tenor resonance of his speaking voice, and hoping he might turn out to be a singer, but so far he's given no indication. Tonight, he seems content to sit and admire, and to be prepared should I sneak his way for a kiss.

But it's back to work for the heartstricken. After Ruby knocks us out with "Diamonds Are a Girl's Best Friend," up comes little brother, looking disheveled despite his neatly combed coif and brand-new ultrasuede shirt. When the piano breaks in, he reels out one arm and it begins to shake. Then he raises the other arm like a revival preacher, sings the first line in a throaty rasp, cranks his neck hard against one shoulder and rolls his eyes back in his head.

This is all making me nervous, but then I catch Ruby wearing a mischievous grin, and it comes to me. David is having no epileptic fit, he's simply doing an excellent Joe Cocker impression. He also has a great voice – which, considering his gene pool, should be no surprise at all. After screaming the last note, he receives an uproarious applause and exits the stage, back to his shy, off-kilter self.

Still, something's amiss. As Shari claws her way through "Piece of My Heart," the ice cubes of déjà vu are tobogganing my spine. David's playful freakout seems weirdly familiar. It only gets worse when Kai appears at my side, wearing a look of intense awareness that is wholly out of context.

"Keep an eye on that dude," he says. "Something very unstable about him."

I turn my face to sneak a kiss – which is all that I truly care about at this moment – and find myself watching Kai's butt, traveling away from me. Not an unpleasant sight, but not what I had in mind. *Wednesday Thursday Friday!*

The snub continues when I sing "Not Too Much to Ask" by Mary-Chapin Carpenter – a wise, tender love song meant expressly for my boyfriend's ears. When I turn to aim the crucial line at Kai's table, Kai is staring at *David,* and wearing an expression like a guard dog on the point. What is this? Is this National Guard Sunday?

Fortunately, David heads outside for a smoke (finally!), which scatters the tension – although I'm likely the only person who knows the tension's there. In any case, at least I'm able to finish my goddamn song, and get my goddamn applause (although I'm feeling pretty goddamn surly about it). When Russ sings "Your Song," and Cordell gives him an adoring gaze, I'm feeling more than a little jealous.

Ruby gets me back on track when she does a Sinatra arrangement of "Let's Fall in Love," complete with the old-fashioned Broadway intro. Then the *Coast Starlight* (a tribute to Hamster's previous career) rolls in with a snifter of brandy – an unusual choice, but heaven on the throat. It's also got a note, which reads, simply, *Everything OK?* Which means that I'm not the only one picking up on the strange vibe.

With all this subterranean hullabaloo, I am savoring my secret knowledge of David's next selection. I am forever astonished at the ability of certain rock guitarists to develop their own instantly recognizable sound, and this one is a prime example: "Whole Lotta Rosie" by AC/DC, featuring the thumbprint vinegar explosions of Angus Young. The buzz of my small arena is immediate. Fortunately for everyone, David opts for the better part of valor, staying on the low octave instead of attempting the savage upward leap of the heavily drugged Bon Scott.

Then comes the solo, and I'm beginning to catch on to David's game. He prefers to mimic people who have a proclivity for spazzing out. All in a sweep, he grabs our toy guitar and hustles to the dance floor, striking each imaginary note as he matches Angus's waggling, tremorous gait, lacking only a foot less height and the shorts-and-tie schoolboy uniform to complete the illusion. Karz is rustling with appreciation, and it escalates when David falls to his knees for a finishing back-bend. Then he has to get up and relocate the microphone so he can get on with the vocals. He ends the song by retrieving the guitar and delivering Angus's final fussilade like he's raking the crowd with gunfire.

Bedlam. Absolute bedlam. In what is supposed to be a non-competitive forum, there are times when a particular singer is master of the evening, and David has already won tonight's crown. He exposes an actual symmetrical grin and departs the stage. Ruby greets him with a hug, and I sense that there's something more in David's performance than singing, antics and fake guitar. It's kind of a coming-out party.

"Shari," I say. "Get up here and calm these people down."

"Oh thanks," says Shari. "What'm I? Boring?"

"Oh, you know what I mean." I punch the button on "You Can Sleep While I Drive" by Melissa Etheridge, and Shari responds with her predictable excellence. Alex hits the floor with his latest partner, an astonishing Latina with raven hair down to her waist, and they manage to turn an acoustic ballad into a tango. I always wonder if Alex is getting any sex out of these excursions. I hope so. But then, perhaps it's the nature of those who *are* having sex to be generous in their carnal wishes for others. I look around for *my* partner, and can't seem to find him. Then the *Starlight* pulls in again with a one-word note: *Sidebar,* which means I need to report to Hamster for a conference. I wait until I've got Harry going with "Devil Woman" by Marty Robbins, then head for a stool next to our mini-Rainier, where the boss is blending a strawberry margarita. He speaks in his inside voice.

"I'm a little worried about your boyfriend."

"Kai? What for?"

Hamster tugs at his soul patch (a recent project). "During David's little guitar-god act – very entertaining, by the way – Kai came over here like the watchman on the *Titanic* and insisted that I call the cops. I laughed, of course, and I said, 'Come on, he doesn't sing *that* bad.' And Kai said, 'But can't you see? He's about to blow a gasket – there's no telling what he might do. No one ever catches this shit until it's too late.' And he was completely serious. I told him if he really wanted to report a crime that had not yet happened, he was free to go outside and make use of the pay phone. I don't think he did, but now he's out in the parking lot, pacing back and forth like he's on fucking guard duty."

For your average citizen, the use of the f-word is no big deal (especially in a bar), but for genteel Hamster, it's a signifier of greater-than-usual anxiety. At the moment, however, I can do nothing, because Harry has reached his ending, and the applause is tugging at my leash. I catch the briefest glimpse of Kai, pacing the perimeter of his T-bird, huffing a loop of vapored breaths, then I get Caroleen started on her ever-apt standby, "Mama, He's Crazy."

At this point, I'm getting a little pissed off. It's a busy night, dammit, and mama's gotta pay the rent. Psycho boyfriend will just have to wait. So I take solace in the rising green tide of my tip jar, and try my damnedest not to look out the window. Meanwhile, David's next turn is rapidly approaching.

On the other hand, I'm rather looking forward to David's turn, because it's "Once in a Lifetime" by the Talking Heads. He delivers an impressive take on David Byrne's radioactive vocal style, and then begins to incorporate the wacked-out choreography from the concert film: the repeated forehead-smack, the construction-site arm-crank, the long-armed snake-wave from right hand to left. He even evokes the Paul Bunyan-size suit by draping his corduroy sportcoat over his head. He's winning ever more brownie points from the congregation, who begin to clap as he performs a Devo-style pogo across the dance floor. His journey comes to an abrupt halt, however, when he arrives at a strange obstacle.

It's Kai. He's standing utterly rigid, like a man trying to explode himself from the inside out. His arms are out and down, an inverted vee, his back bolt-stiff, and I can see the veins in his forehead. He is two feet from David, staring so intently you would think he was attempting telekinesis. David is frozen, afraid to look away. The song fades out, and silence seeps into the room like a cold tide. Kai raises one arm in a threatening manner, but then he seems to snap out of it. He looks around the room, all of us plastered in our places like a snapshot, then discovers his own right hand held in a fist over his head, and suddenly he's off for the door in a quick-march. I rush to the window to see him jump into his T-bird and squeal from the lot.

It's a hard sell, but I decide to pretend that nothing has happened, and I line up "Black Horse and a Cherry Tree" for Shari. The rest of the night is a long, musical blur.

Ruby does me the great favor of seeing her brother off (apparently, he also drives!) and waiting till I've loaded up my CDs before coming to my truck for the post-op.

"What the hell *was* that?"

"Wish I had the least idea," I say. "You got a smoke?"

"You smoke?"

"I do now."

She pulls out a couple of her "recreational" cigarettes and lights us up. I try my best to look like a veteran.

"I realize that David makes people nervous," she says. "But I've never seen him turn someone into a statue. Any luck with the cell phone?"

I take a deep, poisonous drag and let it out with my words. "Nothing but voicemail. He's not answering, Ruby. What the *fuck*?"

"Don't get upset now. I'm sure there's a..."

"I'm *not* upset. I'm pissed off!"

I am a one-woman meteorology course, smoldering like a volcano even as I watch the plains of water beneath our vantage point and feel like I'm under the surface, dying of hypothermia. But reason arrives like the good cop and talks me back down. There are no answers here, no legitimate evidence. So perhaps it's time to change the starting point.

"Roo-bee?"

"Yes'm?"

"Do I know your brother from somewhere?"

She leans against the seawall and sends out a stream of smoke. "The boy does cause a ruckus everywhere he goes. The night they finally arrested him, in fact, was right here in Gig Harbor."

"Really?"

"And, let's see... what else? Oh yeah, in his homeless days, he had a friend who worked in the merchandising department of the Seattle Supersonics. Whenever they traded a player, he'd give some of the replica jerseys to David."

I toss my cigarette and take Ruby by the shoulders. "Super!"

Ruby looks at me with great puzzlement. "Yes, it was... very nice of him."

TWENTY-FIVE

Judging by the things I've read, the part of a dream that we remember is the part that comes right before we wake up. That way, it's still fresh on our short-term memories, like words spelled out in flour that have not yet blown away on the wind.

If you picture my dream-world as a stage, the left half is a small apartment in which everything – furniture, draperies, appliances – has been fashioned from a pure, snow-white material. The right half is an identical apartment in which everything is pure black. (That bastard Scootie would call it mars black.) There is no wall between these two apartments, but there is a sort of clear, fluid plane of separation. Viewed from either side, this plane resembles the surface of a swimming pool.

The residents of these apartments are horses – a white horse in the black apartment, a black horse in the white. Both horses are made of polished stone, and both wear expressions of utter neutrality. Their sole occupation seems to be to stare at each other, and despite the blank expressions you can feel hostility rolling from the stage like heat from a furnace.

When I wake, my eyes are fixed on a pencil-thick hole in the ceiling, previously occupied by a hook for hanging plants. Cottage cheese texturing spreads to all sides in a sparkly moonfield flecked with mica.

And immediately, I have my answer. On a chessboard, the figure of a horse represents a knight. Knights in adjacent squares can do nothing to capture each other, since their moves are limited to a combination of one and two squares (for instance, two forward, one to the side). For these two, however, the stony, hateful faceoff has become their all-consuming occupation, so they've decided to set up permanent apartments.

My epiphany arrives with the sound of panting. I look up to find an actual horse, sitting on its haunches in the center of my room.

"Java?"

Java comes to my bedside and spatulas his long snout under my hand.

"Young dog! What the hell are you doing here?"

"Jah-vah!"

This is a muted call, coming through the hole in my ceiling. It sounds a lot like Floy. I take my phone from my nightstand, hit #1 on my speed dial and get Floy's puzzled response.

"Java?"

"Hi. I don't know if there's a drip in my ceiling, but there seems to be a big poodle in the middle of my floor."

"Oh, that's hilarious!" says Floy. "But how the heck did he get there?"

"Doggy dumbwaiter? Extra-terrestrials?"

"I'm so sorry, Channy! I'll come down and get him. If that's okay?"

"Yeah," I say. "That's fine."

A minute later, there's a rap on my French doors, and Java rushes over to inspect. I slip on my robe and undo the lock.

"Hi!" says Floy. I'm surprised to find her in her nursing uniform. Java pokes his head through the doorway, and she gives him a playful bop. "You goof! How did you get down here? Have you invented teletransportation?"

"Going to work?" I ask.

"Just got back."

"You are *kidding* me."

The ol' Sunday morning six to ten. We call it Hell Shift. This morning, however, we delivered triplets."

"Wow! That's gotta be rare."

"Only the second for me, and that's forty years of maternity."

"Damn."

Something else is on Floy's mind, but she's not coming out with it. We sprawl into one of those awkward silences where the only option is to play the housepet card. I scratch Java on the neck and say, "So how do we get him to reveal his secret passage?"

Floy runs a finger under her frosty-blonde bangs and rightfully ignores my question.

"Is there anything the matter, Channy?"

"No, everything's fine. Since John fixed the garbage disposal, I..."

"No, no. Not the apartment. I mean, with you." She laughs, a nervous piece of birdsong. "I don't know, all that time around the birth canal seems to have endowed me with gyno-radar, and you seem sort of... flat lately. Like you're really not here. Boy trouble?"

The housepet card is gone, so I hallucinate a piece of lint on my sleeve and pick at it.

"Hard to have boy trouble when ya got no boy."

Floy's expression is immediately swamped with disappointment. "You broke up with Kai?"

"Well, I'm not... sure. It was weird – like, off-the-charts weird. And my pal Ruby's off on a cruise, so I haven't had a chance to... Well, you know, sometimes you really can't process something until you tell a friend about it."

"Pancakes," says Floy.

In my fuzzy state, I take this as a synonym for "Pshaw!" or "Nonsense!"

"No, really, I..."

"No!" says Floy, snorting into her hand. "Why don't you shower up, and I'll make some gooseberry pancakes. John's off to Bremerton to use the gym, so we'll have a nice unhindered session of gyno-psychology.

"Floy, I... Yes! I'll be up in fifteen minutes."

The Craigs' living room is bright and playful, a canvas of beige carpeting and ivory tiles underpinning shelves and windowsills of beach objects: driftwood, seashells, a vase filled with frosted glass. They spend a lot of weekends cruising the Oregon coast, hunting new pieces for Floy's *assemblage.* The item that always gets my attention is a brass pendulum that swings over a shallow pit filled with sand. When you pull it to one side and let go, it inscribes a Celtic flower of close-knit lines, drawing closer to the center with each small dose of gravity.

"Ah!" says Floy. "You found our favorite toy. Java managed to topple that over once. We had to search every shop in Northwest Oregon to find the right kind of sand for it."

"He's a rambunctious critter," I say.

"Too long-limbed for his own good."

Java cocks his head, which in this case means, I have no idea what you're talking about, but at least you're paying attention to me. When I turn back to the table, Floy has loaded me up with a steaming stack of pancakes, spotted here and there with igneous burstings of gooseberry.

"Oh Floy! I can't tell you how many different parts of my body appreciate this."

Floy runs a gob of butter along her cakes like she's waxing a surfboard. "Ha-HA! What makes you think I'm doing this for *you*?" She cuts out a triangle and forks it into her mouth. "Mmph! Oh! So how did karaoke go last night?"

"Well. Much as I appreciate all the care and concern being tossed my way, the whole fleeing-boyfriend thing was *way* too public, and I guess I'm feeling the scorch of the microscope."

"Yes, my family does that to me all the time. Which is endearing, when it isn't utterly annoying. So how did this little spectacle come about?"

It takes me a whole stack of pancakes to fill her in. She follows with great interest – this, after all, being the woman who lives beneath her floor. But I forget some of the things I *haven't* told her.

"...so I can't figure out if this is coming from a run-of-the-mill relationship thing, or a post-traumatic thing – or if it has something to do with Harvey's suicide."

Floy holds up a hand. "Wait a minute. Who's Harvey?"

"My husband. Kai's best friend. Who died in Iraq."

Floy's expression freezes into place.

"Oh God," I say. "Oh God. I never told you this."

Floy reaches a hand to mine on the tabletop. Her fingers are shaking.

"Channy! So *that's*... All this time. God, I'm so sorry."

I've had almost a year and a half to deal with Harvey's death. For Floy, he has just appeared and then died within a paragraph.

"It's just that... Well, I wasn't able to talk about it for the longest time. The last few months, I finally found someone – Ruby – to listen to the whole miserable story. And now – God, look at me, blurting out suicides over breakfast. I'm so sorry."

Floy seems to recover a bit, but her eyes are still damp.

"I don't mean to be dramatic, honey. But you don't know how many times I've imagined this kind of thing with John. There was this one night, terribly late, when he got a call, rushed into his flight suit and headed off – and he couldn't tell me what it was. We all *knew* what it was – it was the October Missile Crisis, and John was flying a P-3 Orion over the Atlantic to look for Russian subs – but I played along, kissed him goodbye, wished him luck. And then spent the night torturing myself with every possible scenario, up to and including nuclear holocaust. At daybreak, he woke me on the couch, still in uniform, and the feeling of relief was so overwhelming that I went a little delirious. I think I cried for an hour straight."

"Floy, I'm so sor..."

"Stop apologizing!" She's crying now. "God, honey. I just wish I could have been there to help you."

"But Floy – you were."

These are the words that send her into speechlessness. She holds up a hand, excusing herself, and goes to the kitchen for a cup of coffee. She takes a long time to stir the sugar and cream, and then returns to the table, ready to deliver her summation.

"You need to find Kai. You cannot afford to let this hang. He probably needs to get some therapy. And *you* need to figure out if you're up for this kind of drama. You've already had enough for someone three times your age."

It almost seems like I'm getting a homework assignment from a stern-but-caring teacher. So I say, "Yes, ma'am." And I get back to my pancakes.

Twenty-Six

I have a powerful fetish for the rosetta figures etched into lattes by Northwest baristas. My knowledge of the process is limited to stolen counterside glances, but here's my understanding of the basic steps: you lay down two shots of espresso, suffuse them with milk foam to create a dirty sienna canvas, and then pour a narrow stream of hot milk in a zig-zag weave, creating a ski trail of white that is then seamed into a rough symmetricality by a quick pour down the center. The result is an ivory sword fern, often with branches into the teens. And then you get to destroy the poor thing (philistine!) by drinking it.

I'm lying to you. None of this is important. I am seated in a corner of the Caffe Vita in downtown Olympia, and I am stalling. After staring at my ten-limbed rosetta for ten minutes, I move on to a chessboard balanced on the windowsill. The knights are staring at each other. I turn them so they're back-to-back, pacing off a duel.

"Hello. Is there a guy named Kong in the mountaineering department?"

"Oh, you mean Kai. He's not in today. Would you like someone else from that department?"

"Um, no. It has to be Kai."

"Steve's back there. Steve knows everything about..."

"Nope. Has to be Kai. He's a Sherpa, you know..."

The man laughed. "I swear, that guy has more groupies than the Foo Fighters. Well, listen. He'll be in tomorrow afternoon, um..." – sound of shuffling papers – "noon to six. So call back then, I guess."

"Thanks. Thank you."

"No prob."

That's how I found him. Apparently, he transferred from Tacoma to Olympia as a way of staying out of my sights. As if I were some kind of threat. It's three-thirty-five, and I'm running a mental preview of every possible confrontation, like an improv group doing the same sketch over and over in different theatrical styles. Tennessee Williams. Shakespeare. Gilbert & Sullivan. None of them has the tiniest relationship to reality.

The weather has decided to directly contradict my mood. The air is laced with a brilliant lemon-sorbet sharpness. A bevy of college students, clothed in the latest thrift-store fashions, are cavorting on the sidewalk, taking in the UV rays like they're spoonfuls of caviar. My foamy rosetta has completed its elevator ride to the bottom of my cup. It's go time. I dig out the last bit of foam with my finger and lick it off, and then I fight off years of parental training and leave my cup and saucer on the table for somebody else to pick up.

The sidewalk rolls away before me. I cross the intersection and pass the old State Theater. On the far side, an old-fashioned storefront space plays host to Jenalyn Sports, the windows covered in red banners declaring fifty percent off cleats. Lest I lose my nerve, I keep right on, through the double glass doors, past the cashiers, gun counter, baseball gloves, and then I look up to find spools of rope in fluorescent colors. Kai, my ghost, is demonstrating a locking carabiner for a tall man in a business suit.

"See, you lock that in, pull it tight just to double-check, and there's no way in the world that..."

He stops when he sees me, and our eyes lock in for a long time. Those dark irises are hard to read. I imagine him bolting like a frightened buck, three giant leaps into the stockroom.

"Excuse me a moment, would you?" He leaves the businessman with a dozen carabiners and comes to take my hands.

"Hi. I've got a lunch break right after this customer. Can I buy you a latte?"

There's no reason to say no. And I'm back at Caffe Vita, deflating another rosetta. Kai is five times more calm than he should be.

"I'm sorry, Channy. I'm sorry for the way I took off like that. And I'm sorry I haven't called you. I've been meaning to, but the more I put it off, the harder it gets to pick up that phone."

"You can always talk to me, Kai. I've been through everything. Nothing's going to kill me."

He glances outside at the college kids, as if he's looking for spies.

"The thing is, after that weirdness at the bar, I had to talk to my therapist. Army guy. Sal. Unbelievably cool dude. The thing is, I can't see you anymore."

I'm not surprised, but it sounds a little too much like Scootie's breakup with Ruby. I'm imagining what a bottle of crème de menthe Torani syrup would look like, emptied over Kai's head.

"I know he's... gone, Channy. I know he shouldn't play into this. But he does. He was my best friend. I let him down. I should have seen it coming. The sight of you will always remind me of what happened, of how I failed. There is a real, concrete limit to how much I can recover from that, of how far I can get back to normal. It's just not realistic to carry around this living reminder of..."

He runs out of words, but I get the idea. I'm the reminder. I am Kai's souvenir from Iraq. He buys a little time by taking a drink from his latte, then sets down his cup as a marker.

"I can't do it. I can't see you any more. I'm sorry."

I'm fairly sick of my emotions playing dogpile with me, so I'm holding firmly to my rational demeanor. I glance at the chessboard and find that someone has turned the knights back around. I speak at them so I don't have to look at Kai.

"I think you and I are missing out on something pretty great, and frankly I'm pissed off at Harvey for taking *this* away from me, too. I think he's done enough fucking damage. But there's no way I'm going to talk you into anything. I can't begin to imagine the things you've gone through, the things you might have seen. But Kai, I do want you to consider one other thing. We were friends before all of this, and I know it might take you a while to straighten things out, but if you come out on the other end, I'd like to think we can be friends again. You don't even have to call, just... show up at Karz some night."

He waits for more, but that's all I've got. I watch a skateboarder with dreadlocks grinding a curb. I'm feeling suddenly exhausted, and I can't understand why this man cares about my dead husband more than I do.

"Kai? Could you just... go? I'm not up to all the niceties."

He's gentleman enough to not say another word. He seems to think it's a good idea to take my hand from the table and give it a squeeze, and I'm too tired not to let him. And then he's gone, the front door swinging in his wake. I stare at my caffeine rosetta for a long, long time. When I get around to my next sip, I'm surprised to find that it's cold.

"Okay, this might seem a little odd, but please don't turn around. I need you to play a little game with me. I'm going to leave the coffeehouse and take a right down the sidewalk. I'd like you to count to twenty and follow me, but I want you to stay a block behind me until we get to the Harbor Walk."

The voice is coming over my left shoulder. At first, I suspect ventriloquism. But I am a dedicated follower of instructions, so I face forward until I see the back of a tall man with a blond buzz-cut, headed for the door. Everyone is so eager to leave me. Rousting the molecules in my brain, I realize that this is Conrad, captain of our ski squad, manager of the Olympia branch of Jenalyn Sports.

Spy games. Why not? I have absolutely nothing better to do. I head outside and look around to find him on the far corner, looking casual, waiting to confirm that I'm "tailing" him. I'm fully invested now, so I make no signal before starting down the sidewalk, working up a backstory as I go. Recently divorced mom with a free hour, looking for the downtown spa with the great handmade soaps. Keeping an occasional eye on Conrad turns out to be pretty easy, because he's taking a straight shot down Fourth, crossing a bridge in front of the loopy capital-city fountain then heading for a grocery store next to the marina. He takes a sudden right and stops two blocks later on a wide path constructed of clean, baked-out timbers. This must be the Harbor Walk; I know this because I am a brilliant detective, and also because I can read the words on the large, gray municipal sign that says *Harbor Walk.*

I join Conrad at a railing overlooking the water. Our near horizon is a field of ship's masts that reminds me, for the most transparent of reasons, of a signpost forest. Even now, when I am ready to change my mailing address to End of Her Rope, WA, I cannot resist an attempt at humor.

"The ship sails at midnight."

"The albatross is a mighty bird," he recites back. Conrad is a helpful playmate. He gives me a chuckle. "Didn't mean to go all James Bond on your ass, but Kai's pretty fragile right now, and it's a real bitch these days finding replacement Sherpas."

"What? He'll think we're having an affair? As of about a half hour ago, it doesn't really fucking matter." The f-word feels good on my teeth, and my heart is frosty with abandon. Hell, I would take Conrad right now; it would be a nice, vengeful screw. But Conrad is shaking his head.

"Oh, man. I was hoping he would hold off on that. But that's Kai – he's got this overwhelming affection for a clean slate."

Conrad is still talking in code, but I guess I knew from the espionage that this would take a while.

"We got the word yesterday: they've started the investigation. We're all pretty jumpy. Kai thought that this might all pass over, that life would go on. Tough warrior, that one. Not me. I always knew the shit would come down, and here it is, every gory fucking chapter, ready to fall. I think he also thought that we were doing this to protect *you,* but it's better you hear it from me than some anchorman. Oh Jesus, now I'm just freaking you out. Why don't I just shut up and tell you the fucking story?"

Conrad

Harvey was out on patrol with Bucksy – I'm sure Harvey mentioned him. Man's man, soldier's soldier. Gave his orders straight out, undiluted, but you never felt like you were being jacked around, because he'd always paint the whole picture: reasons, danger, overall strategy. I mean, it's the Army – when it comes down to it, you just do what you're told. But Bucksy figured if he took the time to explain things, he could get ten percent more out of each of his men – and in combat, ten percent is life minus death.

Physically, he had your attention anyway. Six-five, 250, built like a freakin' linebacker. And you know what he did as a civilian? Hairstylist. Fuckin' hairstylist. I always had a hard time mashing that together as a concept. I imagine he didn't get too many complaints about his work.

I used to call him "Captain Glue," because I'll tell you, it is an absolute pile of shit over there, and all the flies buzzing around that pile of shit have explosives strapped to their chests. You're trying to save those people from their own damn selves, and they'd just as soon blow you to pieces as make you coffee. We had a lot of soldiers who were in danger of just plain losin' it, but Bucksy had that magic way of knowing who needed a kick in the ass, who needed a dirty joke, who needed a good old-fashioned verbal takedown and who needed to be left alone. Bullseye, every time.

Conrad turns from the railing and looks at me, as if he wants me to *get* this next part, not as some colorful abstraction but as a physical object, something you can hold and feel.

Bucksy's dead. Worse than dead. He was blown into two discrete pieces. Made me think of the Black Dahlia. I go to horror movies now and I laugh. They have no fucking idea.

It was your husband who drove that Humvee over that explosive. It was also your husband who escaped with a couple of scratches on his right elbow. Goddamnedest thing I've ever seen. Not that I actually saw it. I only saw the remains.

We were destroyed, useless. We spent the day either crying like babies or punching holes in the walls. All except Harvey. Harvey spent the day sitting straight-backed on his bunk, staring into space. He had this huge bottle of water, and every few minutes he would take a swig, and then go back to staring. It seemed like some kind of internal strategy session, like he was working something out. I cannot conceive of the visual information that must have registered on his brain that day, or what happens when something like that starts tunneling around in your head. I'm thinking there also had to be guilt. Nothing rational – there wasn't a damn thing he could have done about it. But maybe the irrational kind is harder, because you have to keep wrestling with it. Especially when you're the one who got away scot-free.

We didn't have much time for grieving. We were desperately short on personnel, the new division wasn't due for two weeks, and the insurgents in the village were getting bolder. There were rumors about an attack on the local mosque. So there we were, two days later, walking around like zombies, a squadron that had literally had its head cut off. The command came down to me, but I felt like Harvey would have been better suited. I was off my nut. I envisioned an IED under my every step, and you just can't operate that way.

We had a lead through one of our translators that a house in the northern sector might be serving as a hideout for insurgents. I was still setting up my men around the perimeter when Harvey bolted past me and busted through the front door. Really threw me. For all I knew he had just barged in on a room full of armed terrorists; he could be gunned down any second. But then I heard him inside, yelling things in Arabic. Stay down. Hands behind your head. That sort of thing. Then I heard a shot, so I told Kai to cover me as I went in after Harvey. From the entryway, I had only a narrow slice of vision into the main room. There were men, maybe thirty of them, all ages, kneeling on prayer mats. This made sense – they were avoiding the mosque, because of the rumors. But what the hell was Harvey doing?

Then I saw their faces. They were terrified, breathing hard. There was another shot, and the sound of a body falling to the floor. A man who was kneeling near the opening tried to stand and run. Another shot. He fell into the hallway in front of me, a hole in his neck. It was then that I realized what was happening.

"Lebeque!" I shouted. "It's Conrad! Listen to me! It's the wrong house! These are not insurgents!"

Harvey's response was belligerent but strangely calm. "The hell they're not! If ya hadn't noticed, Dixon, these people are not too particular about who they kill. Well, neither am I! What about you, pal? Kill any Americans today? Did ya kill my friend? Huh?"

Another shot. Another body.

"Sergeant! You must cease firing! That's an order!"

I leaned into the opening to see him raising the muzzle of his rifle to the head of an old man. He looked at me and said, "I only take orders from Bucksy, and Bucksy's gone. This ain't no fucking Zero Squadron. Zero Squadron has rules. No rules in this fucking country. Alice in fucking Wonderland out here."

He fired. The old man slumped forward.

My teachers had told me how a military mind operates in extreme situations, but this was the first time I really felt it. My thoughts were dividing, half of them scattered and shocked, the other half remarkably calm and rational. The calm half noticed that Harvey was being methodical. He was working his way down the line, front row first. The next was a young boy, maybe nine, ten years old, and this meant that I was about to come to a crisis point. I wasn't going to let him kill that kid.

It was then that Kai stepped into the back of the room.

"Harvey," he said. "You can't do this."

"I can do this all day long," said Harvey. "Motherfuckers blew my friend in half. In half! *This* is a pleasure."

"Fuck them!" said Kai. "It's not about them. I'm with you. But if you can stop right now, we can get you out of here, cover our tracks and everything's fine, okay? You get a couple kills, get your payback, couple more weeks you go back to the States, back to Channy, everything's fine. But you gotta stop right now, Harve. It won't work unless you stop right now."

Harvey stood there for a second, staring at the back of that little boy's head, and he seemed to calm down. *Thank God,* I thought. *He's talked him out of it.*

"No," he said, and raised his rifle to the boy's head. Another shot, and Harvey fell to the floor.

When I looked back toward Kai, I had this weird idea that he had just turned himself into a statue, his rifle still on his shoulder, his eyes getting bigger and bigger. I walked slowly toward him and spoke in my calmest military voice.

"Soldier, hand me your weapon."

I took it from him and continued giving orders. I didn't want him to think about what had just happened. I was afraid of what he might do to himself. I put a hand on his shoulder and shook him a little to get his attention. His face was just wide open with fear.

"Soldier! Go outside right now. Get O'Reilly and Benson." Then I lowered my voice. "Kai, you are not to say a word about this. Let me handle it."

I guess if I had to justify what I did next, I would say that your husband *did* commit suicide. He gave Kai no choice, and I'm sorry, but every time Kai has a week like this one, I wish Harvey *had* killed himself. We carried the body back to the base and reported that Harvey had gotten separated from the squad, that we found him in that eucalyptus grove. The story made sense; it was an American bullet, Harvey's weapon had been fired – his feelings about Bucksy were well-known. Any cursory forensics investigation would have proven us all a bunch of liars, but we were counting on chaos, and we won – no one had the luxury of looking into it any further. And, thank God, those Iraquis were evidently too scared to report the killings.

I got a call yesterday from CID, and I agreed to tell them the whole story. Politically speaking, they'll probably have to release this to the press. And... well, especially with you and Kai being... a couple, I figured I better tell you. I'm very sorry about all of this. I can't tell you how many times I've gone over that day in my head and tried to figure out something I could have done to prevent it. But reliving it, it's all pretty fucking useless.

I'm feeling grateful for the way the human body operates, the way everything numbs up, because otherwise this would kill me. I stare at the masts, bobbing in the wind like a leafless forest. Then I feel Conrad's hand around my shoulder.

"What can I do for you, Channy? Are you gonna be okay – I mean, right now? You want to call someone? Could I drive you home? It's no problem – I'm the boss."

I'm surprised at the clarity of my own voice. "No. That's okay. I've got a place to go. A thinking place."

He nudges my face toward his and gives me a teacherly scrutiny.

"Nothing foolish?"

"Nothing foolish," I say. "I don't operate that way. Besides, I've got a job tonight."

"You sure you're up to it?"

I realize I never knew his last name before, and I feel the need to speak it. "This is what you do, Sergeant Dixon. You keep going."

"Good girl."

"And you – you keep a watch on Kai."

"Always," he says. "That's my job."

The week we moved into Sumner, I found a box of books in the basement with a note from the previous tenant: *Sorry! Didn't have enough room for this in the van – thought you might like something to read.*

At the top was a book of Northwest hiking trails. I opened it to the bookmark and found a listing circled with a highlighter: the Nisqually Delta Bird Sanctuary. I had a profound itch to explore our new region, and this certainly fit into the category of Sign from God.

That Saturday, we had a lot of chores to catch up on – we were still hunting up shower curtains and a microwave oven – so by the time we found the sanctuary parking lot the sun was getting low in the west. We walked straight into it, down a wide gravel path bordered by tall wetland grasses the color of dried bamboo.

"Look," I said. I gestured above us, where the swallows were swirling from one field to the next, a haphazard, aerial tennis match. But Harvey's gaze was fixed on the long trail. Always the distance with this one. I had to take him by the shoulders and nearly put him into a headlock to get him to look. When he saw the swallows, though, I could feel his muscles relax.

"Absolutely stunning," he said.

Harvey the human dichotomy. He was a tough climb, but there was something about the challenge of the ascent that made the view that much sweeter when you got to the top. But. This could be the last kind memory I have of him. Because he snapped. Because he killed people. To *that* dichotomy, there is no bright side.

I am back in that very spot, the swallows of yesteryear weaving circles above me. The tall grasses are now a milky green. The sun is low in the west, but setting much further south.

He stood right here. The hands that massaged my neck at the end of a long day were used to separate five innocent men from their lives. There are no birds in this sanctuary, and the sky is brewing up a football team of icy-looking clouds.

I watch my steps carefully, as if I will be asked to describe them in a deposition. I have begun yet another process – that of deciding if my so-called life partner was inherently evil, or just inherently weak. A violent streak waiting for an invitation, or an average man too harshly squeezed by mortality and frustration. Are we all just one exploded comrade from taking lives? I picture Hamster bisected by an orange burst, and try to channel my reaction.

I am angry at Harvey, I am terribly sorry for him. I will love him forever, I will never ever forgive him. And I am most sorry for myself, who will have to live with these fucking what-ifs for the rest of my life, who will never have a joy that is not cut in half by the sulfuric acid percolating from my memory banks.

Somewhere in there, I should have some anger for Kai. The man killed my husband. Justifiably, yes, nobly, yes – but there ought to be *something.* Instead I find only sorrow, so deep I can't get my hands around it. I don't know if I will ever have the strength to be his lover, to handle these explosive chemicals he carries around in his brain, but I want to hold him and say, *You did the right thing. You did what your own humanity demanded of you.* The beauty of friendship is its forfeitability, and Harvey gave up Kai's the instant he pulled that trigger.

Oh, God. The world is too gray, too empty of wings and song. I crave a bald eagle, a blue heron, some shocking stroke of color to empty my thoughts for the smallest second, but all I have are workaday seagulls rioting over the marsh. I am grateful for my job, which even on the dreariest of days carries the possibility of beauty: a bent note from a blues guitar, a cascade of horns, the apple-ish bite of a hi-hat at the end of a phrase.

I turn and look back at the parking lot. I have covered, at most, a city block. I can still read the numbers on my license plate. It's time to go to that job.

The evening is utterly rote. I'm not even certain who's here but I sense that it's a healthy crowd. I sit next to the pond as a familiar face rises to the surface, sings a song and then sinks back down. I do a lot of smiling and nodding.

But the songs stay with me. "Name," "You Make Me Feel Brand New," "The Sweater Song," "It's All Right With Me," "Beyond the Sea," "Smooth," "Chasing Cars," "Tender When I Want to Be," "What Is This Thing Called Love?" The words drift in and out like a dream before dawn. I try to piece them together, looking for some clue on how a life is supposed to be lived. It's not simply that nothing makes sense to me, it's that I am now beyond sense.

There is a word in karaoke that I've never seen anywhere else: "Outro." It's basically a made-up antonym of "intro." It comes up on the lyric screen to let you know that the singing's over, but the music's going to go on a little longer. You're free to stay at the mic and wait it out, but you're also free to leave. Either way, the music goes on without you.

"Channy?"

Big blonde hair, like Joan Osborne in that "One of Us" video. I think this is Shari.

"Hi."

"I think you've got the wrong track, honey. It's track twelve."

"Oh. Sorry." Smile, nod – nudge the track to twelve. An acoustic guitar comes in like a rowboat in gentle water. It's called "Fade Into You" by a group called Mazzy Star. This must be one of Shari's CDs, because the song is sad and otherworldly, and if I had ever heard it I would remember it. Shari's whiskey voice could squeeze tears from "The Hokey-Pokey," and now she's throwing in this drowsy Patsy Cline lift that grabs at the fraying ends of my heartstrings. I am able to hit the escape valve just in time, and I turn to face my little squad of business card holders. Busywork. Busywork. Ah, that's better – a wide gravel path full of trivia.

The end of the night comes quickly, and before I'm even aware that I've begun, I am piling my last CD case into the truck. It could be that I can sneak away quietly and continue ceasing to exist.

But then there's my paycheck, and the rent that's coming due, so I trudge back in. Hamster is leaning against the bar in a rascally fashion as he nurses an Irish coffee. He's a sipper; that's how he keeps from becoming a drunk in a trade that breeds them by the millions. He lends me a rakish smile, a little bit higher on the right, the one he uses on his bevy of barfly Mrs. Robinsons.

"Hey dollface. Good night tonight."

"Yes." I smile and nod, but I can hear how flat my voice is. "Can I get my check?"

"Sure." He reaches into the cash register and pulls out a brown envelope. "Here ya go."

"Thanks." I start for the door, feeling suddenly panicky.

"Channy? Are you okay? You seem a little..."

Oh God. That tone of courtly concern, it's much too fatherly, avuncular, the vice principal, the elder psychologist, the softball coach, and it's precisely this quality that seizes the frayed ends of my heartstrings – the ones that hold up the marionette – and snips them right off. I sink to my knees and it all comes pouring out of me, a sobbing so deep that it sounds like some large, gray animal at the zoo. I'm melting into the freshly mopped ammonia-smelling floor, and then I'm aloft on a cloud of musky, old-fashioned cologne, Hamster's day-old beard scratching my cheek. I land on the cold vinyl of a bar booth, where my strange new song just keeps spilling and spilling out.

In the great Northwest, gray is our color of choice, the raincloud our team mascot. Precipitation is such a dominant presence that we have invented a term for its temporary cessation: sunbreak. This morning is my sunbreak, ten minutes of slick beauty during which I have forgotten whatever it was that was plaguing me.

I follow the sunbreak across the room, where it lands on three fuzzy balls making their way along tubes of yellow, red and green. I quickly designate the lightswitch as their finish line and place my money on red. The second I do so, my steed is off, as if someone has turned a faucet and shot him forward on a rush of water. He reaches the switch and disappears around the corner, leaving his rivals to choke on his primary-colored dust.

Victory! Followed quickly by consciousness. I'm at Hamster's. I'm at Hamster's because...

Damn.

Sunbreak over. But it's followed by a slowly spreading smile that smells like coffee. I take a steaming mug that says, *It Must Be Love (either that or this coffee is really strong!).*

"Thanks, boss."

"I forget how you like it," he says.

The first sip goes right to my head, sweeping aside the autumn leaves, prodding me into untoward flirtation.

"I like my coffee like I like my employers," I say. "Hot and black."

That sends us both into titters, and I notice that Hamster is fully groomed and dressed: jeans, tennis shoes, golf shirt. Apparently, I have slept in. He leans an elbow against the doorjamb and gives me an appraising look.

"You know, you've really got to cut this out. You're ruining both sides of my reputation."

I've got to latch onto something, and this seems like a solid opening.

"Well now right there! See? Yet another of your enigmatic pronouncements. What the hell do you mean, 'both sides'? And what the hell is your last name?"

"Don't you read your paychecks?"

"Have you *seen* your signature lately? It's a freakin' Jackson Pollock."

Hamster cups a hand around his chin, considering how much of himself to divulge.

"Jenner. Hamilton Beauregard Jenner."

"You have *got* to be kidding me!" I am pounding the top of my sleeping bag in disbelief.

"As for the other bit of information, that is a great big fat secret that can only be traded for a secret of similar proportions. Such as, perhaps, whatever it was that liquified you all over my floor last night."

I take an overlong sip that scalds my tongue. I rub a finger along the hot-spot.

"Well. It's a whopper. But seeing how that bitch Ruby has absconded to Mexico, I guess I gotta tell *someone*."

He beckons me down the hall. "Join me in my breakfast nook."

I smile. "Said the spider to the fly."

Hamster's nook is a key lime pie of white tiles and yellow trim, with a small blondewood table, white chairs and a bay window that looks across the harbor to Karz. I picture him here each morning, nibbling a piece of toast, hamster-like, as he ponders his greatest possession. I sit down and launch into my work, spitting out the whole miniseries, chunk by grisly chunk. My conclusion turns Hamilton Beauregard Jenner into a Catholic.

"Jesus Mary Joseph and Richard Nixon," he says. "Channy! You should be in a mental ward by now. Certainly not doling out pop music in Gig Harbor. Are you seeing someone?"

"Well I just... broke up yes-..."

"Seeing a *therapist,* sweetheart. It's fine telling a friend, but eventually you need a professional. This is some grade-A shit."

I keep forcing my genteel boss to swear, which only adds to my feelings of guilt.

"You got someone in mind?"

He takes a bite from his scone – his first bite, such was his fascination with my story – and smiles.

"How about mine?"

I roll out a finger like I'm laying a tiny carpet. "Which you're seeing for...?"

He proffers a pinkie. I recognize this from childhood. It's a pledge of secrecy. I hook my pink pinkie around his mocha pinkie and we pull them away like we're unplugging a bathtub.

"Just for clarity," he says, "absolute confidentiality."

"Absolutely."

"Your boss prefers men. And he got most of those stock tips during late-night rendezvous on Amtrak."

"Scandalous! So… why the closet?"

"Different times, honey. I didn't need *both* races on my ass. So to speak. My youngers speak to me of rainbows, and Pride movements, but it's just not my bag. Besides, I take great pleasure in the cash of all those Gig Harbor housewives who come to my bar to indulge their Harry Belafonte fantasies."

I laugh out loud, which feels strange and lovely. "I was thinking Nat King Cole."

Hamster lets out a sandpapery Belafonte laugh (I'll be damned) and says "Nat King Cole! I'll be damned."

I stand from my chair, so touched by this long-delayed confidence that I must have an embrace.

"Mr. Jenner – Harry, Nat – give me a big, gay hug."

"I will," he says, and does. Wrapped in Hammie's muscular limbs, I feel that perhaps the world will stop beating on me, at least for the duration of a sunbreak. A trio of cormorants slides by the window.

Twenty-Seven

I'm back on the chessboard, but now the black and white squares are grassy fields on a hillside. One field grows white grass, the other grows black. They are neatly separated by a barbed wire fence. I am astride a white horse on the black field, bouncing along like the token cowgirl in a John Wayne movie (I'm picturing Ava Gardner). My steed is a mountain of smooth muscle, beautifully rideable. I spur him to a gallop and steer us toward a hedge, relishing the hiccup of gravity as we clear the crest.

On the far side, we come upon the fence, composed of pure silver. Across from us, at the center of the white field, stands a black horse. At first sight of us he charges, lips flaring. He's about to hit the fence when a shot rings out. His legs buckle and he falls, sliding to a stop directly in front of us. This frightens the white horse, who bucks wildly, tossing me to the ground. When I gather my bearings, I am lying on my side, face to face with the black horse. As I watch, his red eyes fade away and the rest of him melts, turning the white field to black.

And then somebody barks. And I wake up next to a dead hand. It's mine. I fell asleep in an odd position, and my left arm has gone completely numb. I use my still-living right hand to nudge it out of my way, then peer across the room to see the numbers *5:54* and a fuzzy pyramid of pooch.

"Java! How the *fuck* are you doing this?"

I am secretly happy to see him; in the face of such an obvious dream (where were the evil mimes? the radioactive pickles?), I am hungry for mystery. Java trots to my side, slips his snout under my hand, and I give him a thorough scalp massage. He is my favorite plush toy, and he knows it.

Then I notice the trail of muddy footprints he's left on my white carpeting. At first I'm angry, but then I realize he's just given up his secret. I creak to my feet and follow his tracks into the kitchen; they end at the sink. The cabinet door is unlatched. When I pull it open, I discover that my pipes now come with a backyard view. Evidently, John installed a hatch providing easier access to the plumbing, but neglected to close it when he fixed my garbage disposal last week. As if to demonstrate, Java ducks under the pipes and bounds into the yard, then turns to give me one of his Lassie-barks.

"Yeah-yeah. I get the idea."

I reach for the rope tied to the hatch and pull it shut. But now I'm a little sad, because I have once again wiped my life clean of enigmas – I, who used to have so many. I also realize that I am *not* getting back to sleep, so I head for the shower.

My seven a.m. landscape is cold and foggy – no surprise there – so I grab a big black jacket that I haven't used for a while. As I slide into my truck, I feel a lump in my breast pocket and reach in to discover a lone Swisher Sweet. This should probably be a disconcerting event, but it's not. Lately, I've had this black-pit feeling of being Harvey's accomplice – I did, after all, marry the murdering son-of-a-bitch – and the chance to perform an act of penance is quite welcome. And penance it will be – this thing looks like a core sample from the Mojave Desert.

I actually consider the long drive to Port Townsend, but ritual is hard to break, so I follow my ruts to Gig Harbor. I park at the Jerisich Dock, start my cigar with the fleur-de-lis lighter and trudge waterward, puffing like a freight train. The taste is truly awful, and I wonder if this is how great Catholic martyrs are born.

A stripe of candy red extends from the end of the pier like a windsock, and some crazyperson is sitting in the middle of it. Faint Morse code blips into my brain: *This would be a kayak. Kye-ack.*

As I draw closer, the crazyperson removes his knit cap to reveal a mop of hair that matches the boat. Some loony kayaking rocker teen with dyed hair. He spots me and calls out in a high voice.

"Christ! Are you smoking that thing on purpose?"

And I'm running, scanning the water for black horses and evil mimes, my sneakers slapping the planks. I've been waiting so long to speak these syllables that they come out in sing-song.

"Roo-bee!"

I skid to a halt. Ruby is laughing her head off.

"Well don't kill yourself!"

I'm helpless. I can't get to her without sending us both into the drink. All I can do is repeat my recitative.

"RoobeeRoobeeRoobee!"

She claps her hands together. "And *your* name is Channy!"

I'm all discombobulated, so I stuff the cigar in my mouth and take a huge drag that sends me into a fit of coughing.

"Heh! What the… hemm! What the hell are you doing in that thing?"

"Why, I'm kayaking, honey. It's a noun *and* a verb."

"But you're in Mexico!"

"You're right. I'm in Mexico." She gives me a wide smile. "Someone's lost track of her mental calendar."

"Entirely possible. Would you get your big luscious ass out of there so I can molest you?"

"Best offer I've had in six hours. I'll meet you at that little landing next to the ramp."

"Gotcha." I walk the length of the pier as Ruby paddles beside me. She's much better at this than I would have guessed, pivoting the paddle from one side to the other with nary a hitch. She rolls onto the landing, pulls up the kayak, and then I charge, yanking her to her feet for a huge hug. I can feel the icy water from her wetsuit as it penetrates my blue jeans. I'm also crying.

"Jesus, Channy. Are you all right?"

"I just missed you, you crazy bitch."

She lets out a theater laugh – Beatrice in *Much Ado About Nothing*. "You're getting *so* codependent. What'll I do with you?"

I rediscover the cigar in my hand (nice thing about Swishers, they'd stay lit through Hurricane Katrina) and I take a final drag, pulling the spark all the way down to the tip and hurling it into the water. *Amen.*

"You'll let me buy you some fresh-baked bread at Susanne's."

"Ay, lass. Now you're talkin'."

Ruby deposits her wetsuit in the trunk of her car, ties her kayak to the roof rack, and ducks into the bakery restroom to swap her shorts for a dry pair of jeans. I, meanwhile, obtain a loaf of Dutch crunch, warm from the oven, and a serrated knife. Ruby spreads a wad of butter on her first slice and watches with greedy eyes as it melts into the surface.

"This is pure genius," she says.

I take a bite and adopt a rapturous expression. "I'm a carbohydrate Einstein. So. Mexico? Mexico?"

Ruby grins like a kid in front of a birthday cake.

"I have *such* a story for you! But first: appetizers. We went kayaking in Mazatlan, at this little island across from the big hotels. When we reached the tip of the island, we hit open ocean, and these long swells came in to lift us and then gently set us back down. As we were paddling back, this Mexican supermodel came strolling along the beach topless, with the most perfect set of gazongas I have ever set eyes on. Poor Harry was having a stroke trying not to look. I told him, 'Honey, *I'm* going to stare at her, so go ahead already!' As you may have guessed, I got totally hooked on the kayaking. We got in pretty late last night, but I was so jacked up I woke up at five, stole Harry's kayak, and you know the rest."

"And may I say, you look amazingly at home with that paddle."

She laughs. "Perhaps in a previous life I was an Aleut."

"I went to school with an Aleut."

Ruby takes a huge bite of bread; it takes her a while to chew it down.

"Excuse my piggishness. Apparently I've worked up an appetite. So! Puerto Vallarta. We caught a bus to a ranchero, where we embarked on a rather advanced hike over these hills – sort of the beginnings of the Sierra Madre. The humidity was stunning; I felt like a human sponge being wrung out. We ended up at this little riverside park, where they had tile tubs fed by natural springs and an enormous iguana who stared at us from the crotch of a tree like a surly green security guard. We forded the river and discovered thousands of pastel butterflies, solid squares of pink, yellow, blue and white sunning themselves on the far bank. Our guide walked right into them, and they rose in a cloud, like backwards confetti.

"By the time we got to Cabo, we were a little worn out, so we took a boat into the waterfront for some low-impact shopping. We were immediately set upon by peddlers, so we sought refuge in this pirate bar, where this *loco* waiter brought us our drinks balanced on his head. He was good!"

"How was the food on the ship?"

"Oh!" she says. "Oh! I can't even start. When I got to the final bite of our final meal, I held it up to Harry and said, 'From now on, everything I eat will taste like shit.' Tell you what, though. I saved copies of every single menu. Why don't I bring them, next time we get together, and I'll give you a detailed narration of each meal."

With this, she takes another bite of bread, sips at her coffee and leans back in her chair. Her expression is one of utter contentment, like a woman who has fallen profoundly into love. But she seems in no hurry to explain.

"What?" I demand. "What?"

She closes her eyes, then opens them slowly. "I don't know what I like best: the event itself, or the chance to tell *you* about it."

"Yeah yeah. I'm flattered, I'm touched, yada yada. Now *out* with it!"

She smiles yet again, and indulges in one last pause before taking the plunge.

Ruby

Everything on the ship had an artistic theme, and the karaoke took place in the Starry Night Lounge, before an enormous wallpaper re-creation of its title work. As you might have guessed, Harry and I went there every night. He had the chance to sic his well-drilled repertoire on a whole new crowd of swooning females, and

I had the chance to explore an impressive selection of standards and showtunes. I developed an immediate following among the seniors, who enjoyed swinging and fox-trotting to my songs.

At the end of our first evening, our Australian hostess Lani asked me if I was going to try out for the Legends concert. For the next four evenings, passengers would come to the Starry Night and sing a song by a legendary performer. If the audience decided you were the best at that song, you would appear as that performer in a Vegas-style show before 1,500 of your fellow passengers.

I actually thought of opting out. The contest was obviously aimed at amateurs, and it wouldn't be entirely fair for me to participate. That thought lasted about half a second. If my ship was gonna have a show, *I* was gonna be in it.

One problem: none of the female roles were from jazz or Broadway. I halfway thought of cross-dressing as Sinatra, but I chickened out. So began my journey through the popular music of the late 20th century.

The first night was Aretha, and the song was "Respect." I assumed it was about the singing, and I thought I pretty much nailed it. But then, out comes this perky young Filipina, and she's got *choreography*, for God's sake. So much choreography, in fact, that she's dropping notes right and left. No one seems to notice, and I'm out.

The next night is Madonna, "Like A Virgin." I grew up on that song – hell, I think I lost my virginity to that song. But I've learned my lesson, so I throw in a couple of sexy moves when I can. *However.* The next contestant is this sexy Italian kindergarten teacher from Long Island, and she throws in the kind of moves that *no* kindergarten teacher should *ever* know. At one point, she pulls out a classic Madonna maneuver, lying with her back on the stage while she's singing. So! Am I going to get the part? No way.

My third chance is Gloria Estefan, "The Rhythm is Gonna Get You." I can *totally* pull off Gloria – I grew up in Florida, after all – and I prep myself with some salsa and rhumba moves before adjourning to the Starry Night. But *then*...

The rowdiest pack on the ship is this alumni group from Indiana University. They're easy to spot, because they all wear red, all the time – massing down the fiesta deck, crowding the blackjack tables, doing the frug in the Warhol Club. In the swimming pools, they wear red bathing suits. Nice people, but loud, and the constant red-ness gives off an unsettling Nazi vibe.

I sing a couple of tropical warmups – "Jamaican Farewell," "Girl from Ipanema" – but at nine, when the contest begins, there's a rumbling like someone just lifted the gate at Pamplona. The wide front doors swing open and in rolls the Red Sea, filling every available nook. As you might expect, they're here for a cause: a 50-year-old with dried-out smoker's skin and frizzy hair with traces of several different red dye jobs. She actually seems quite nice, and she throws in some decent Cuban dance moves, but her voice is a creaky, smoked-out mess. Doesn't matter. When the Red Sea explodes, she's a winner.

I can't be the good loser this time. I wait till the next singer takes the mic, then give Harry's hand a squeeze and we make for the back exit. We're halfway through the Internet café when a door opens, and out pops our KJ.

"Lani! How'd you...?"

"Every ship's got its secret passageways," she says. "Look. *That* sort of shit" – she nods back toward the club – "is a truly unfortunate part of my job. It happens at least once a cruise. But I want you to know, I know exactly how good you are, and I know this stuff is *all* beneath your talent, but I can't stand the thought of you not being in that show, and I *really* want you to come back tomorrow night."

"I'm... thanks, Lani. But I don't even know the song."

She hands me a rectangular object wrapped in wires. It's an IPod. "You will, if you listen to that. We usually only give these to the winners, so they can practice for the show. But screw the rules! We're in international waters, right?"

"Oh Lani, I..."

"Oh Lani nothing! Do your homework, young lady. Whoops! Song's over. Bye."

She's back through the door and I'm left floating in flattery. We retreat to the arcade, where Harry and I work out our frustrations on a combination jukebox/electronic drum set (mostly Led Zeppelin) then on to the Matisse jazz lounge for martinis. When we get back to our cabin, I find a mysterious package on my bed. It's a DVD of the Legends concert from a previous cruise. Somebody *really* wants me to get this part.

Which is Britney Spears – "Hit Me Baby One More Time." I never liked it much, but the next morning, when I strapped on the IPod and tried it out, I was surprised to find out how well it suited me. Britney has this deep, low pocket that she slides into, and it seemed to wrap around my voice like a form-fitting dress. After it scratched a few grooves into my synapses, I tried out the DVD and studied the moves of the ship's dancers. (I ignored their Britney, who was Aunt-Zelda-sings-at-your-wedding awful.) If I could work a little of the choreography into my audition, it would give me a nice edge. I pushed our bed to the cabin wall and put myself through some paces. It was pretty sexy stuff; I caught Harry peeking from the bathroom as he shaved.

The costume was a cinch. I picked out a short pleated skirt (intended for some imaginary night of dancing), shiny black shoes that might pass for patent leather, and white knee-high stockings. Then I stole Harry's white dress shirt and tied it above my bare midriff. Voila! The classic parochial slut, and we were off to the bar.

Little do I know, I have become a cause celebre. The regulars are pretty cheesed off about the Red Sea incident, and impressed that I am now risking four-time loserdom. A group of Japanese tourists has migrated to the front row for the sole purpose of cheering me on. I am the 1980 U.S. hockey team, the 1969 Jets. When I begin with Peggy Lee's "Fever" (designed to work up my "sexy"), the crowd lets out a practice uproar.

Come audition time, I'm up first, and I guess I'm better than I expected. I have wisely inserted my dance moves into the generous spaces between the vocal lines, so I can concentrate on one task at a time. Rolling into the ending, I strike a pose at each of four beats, raking a hand along my skirt and over my hair as I arch my back. The place goes nuts.

But then, out comes my competition, and I have every right to be nervous. If you didn't tell me otherwise, I'd say it *is* Britney, this

19-year-old chicklet with legs up to Canada, an utterly fantastic ass, nice rack, big Hollywood lips and a head of hair that rains down in thick ribbons of blondeness. She's a fucking shampoo commercial. The music begins, she vamps to the front of the stage and out comes this voice like an LP played with a concrete needle.

Game over, right? Don't bet on it. Because Britney II has an entourage of fratboys, and it's almost as if she's offered a night of carnal pleasures to whoever yells the loudest. On the first vote, in fact, the ovations are too close to call. But this only serves to piss off my fans even more. A short, bespectacled man jumps in front of his Japanese peers to cheerlead, and when Lani's hand pops open over my head I am blown backward by the loudest, scariest sound I've heard since a Navy air show on Whidbey Island. I am deafened, I am adored, and even a pack of horny fratboys cannot match it. Lani brings the mic to her mouth, declares "I think it's Ruby!" and my fans burst forth in a fugue of coyote yips. My life-long dream of playing Britney Spears has come to pass.

By now you're probably wondering about my talented boyfriend. Unlike me, Harry was no slut for every passing star. He wanted only to be the King. Even though the part of Elvis was the final male audition, making this an all-or-nothing attempt, he would consider no other. As it turned out, his loyalty was richly rewarded – because nobody else tried out. Harry was summarily crowned, and asked to sing "Hound Dog" as proof of his prowess. He was excellent, of course, but I gave him a whack on the butt nonetheless, for the gross inequity of our respective situations.

We spent the next day kayaking – and perhaps that's another reason I got so attached to it. We paddled within the glow of victory, and I could barely hear the sounds of frigate birds, motorboats or waves on rocks with "Hit Me Baby One More Time" playing interminably through my head (without, I might add, the assistance of an IPod). That afternoon, I discovered what a small, magnified community is a cruise ship, and how quickly word of my travails had spread. My biggest fans were the seniors, who relished the fact that someone who sang *their* songs could beat a teenybopper at her own generation's music. Strangers would shout to me in the corridors – "Hey Britney!" "Karaoke girl!" "Go get 'em, Ruby!" – and whenever we came upon my Japanese posse, they weren't happy until I hugged each and every one of them. That night's dinner was a formal-dress affair, and when I entered the hall in my jade-green sequin gown, they *applauded* me. It felt like some wacky Fred Astaire musical, and I ate it up like crème brulee.

You might expect Harry to be taken aback by all of this, perhaps even a little jealous – he was Elvis, after all. But Harry was precisely the opposite, confident enough in his own talent to understand that my four-part battle had become something extraordinary. He had a permanent goofy grin plastered to his mug, and he never tired of telling everybody that he was sleeping with Britney Spears. I think he was also proud that everybody else was finding out about his talented girlfriend, and excited that he would finally get to see me in my element. It didn't hurt when the Japanese contingent would bow down in mock worship and chant "Ellll-vis! Ellll-vis!"

The show was actually pretty easy. They had done it cruise after cruise for God knows how long, and had it carefully programmed for shaky amateurs. After donning our costumes (available in three different sizes), we adjourned to the "green room," which was really just a small landing next to this metallic, Navy-looking stairwell. Harry's Elvis costume – the white Vegas jumpsuit – seemed to turn him into the class cutup, and he went around punching holes in the tension. He turned to Melanie, in her early-Madonna see-through dress, and said, "I hate to mention this, honey, but *we can see your underwear!*" I also remember our lead showgirl, Holly – she of the perfect six-foot body – using the stairway rails to stretch in ways that would probably send the rest of us to the hospital.

Playing the youngest of the icons, I had to wait an interminable amount of time before my escort, a lovely gay dancer named Geoffrey, came to whisk me away. We braced ourselves beside the entrance, elbows coupled, listening for the cue in Britney's intro (I believe it was the word "vixen"), and then he gives me a tug and leads me to a star at center stage. My job is to sing the song without straying from that star, lest I trip up one of the schoolgirls in my "posse," but of course I'm after brownie points. Britney II and her fratboys have every right to be suspicious about the way the same moves I used in my audition are matching up with those of the dancers. The audience just knows, instinctively, that something about my performance is "tighter" than the others. I jolt into that same four-pose ending and freeze with my troupe, taking a loofah shower in the sound of 3,000 hands. It is indescribably sweet.

Geoffrey comes to fetch me back, and we stand in the wings as Harry does his stuff. He definitely has the best production values in the show: the classic *2001: Space Odyssey* intro, followed by a verse of "Hound Dog," followed by "Jailhouse Rock" with a half-dozen twirling babes in Ray-bans and Capri pants. He throws in a couple of leg-waggles and sings his usual excellence, eliding one forgotten phrase with what he calls the Elvis Mumble.

Holly Perfectbody comes to lead him off, and then comes a surprisingly touching elegy: a spotlight on an empty stool as we listen to clips of Sinatra talking about his life. Michael, a journalist from Seattle, comes out in a tux and short-brimmed fedora to sing "My Way" in a voice eerily similar to the original. As the orchestra wells up, the rest of the legends return, and our escorts walk us through a simple choreography. We take our final bows (more loofah, pass the shampoo) and run up the aisle to a nearby lounge for photos. I was tugged away by Harry, who continued talking like Elvis as he kissed away a major portion of my makeup.

"Hey Priscilla, wanna celebrate?"

"And what do you call what you just did?"

"That's just preliminaries, bebe."

"Well first we'd better return these getups."

He ran a hand under the hem of my plaid skirt. "Sure they wouldn't let you keep this just a little longer?"

I had no choice but to squeak like a Mouseketeer. "Mr. Presley! You bad, bad man. I'm gonna tell Colonel Parker on you."

"I'm pretty sure he'd be on my side. Meet me in the Mattress Lounge?"

"That's Matisse, you pedophile."

"Pee-doh… Whassat?"

"Jerry Lee Lewis."

"Oh! Uh-uh-huh."

Harry held my shoulders, keeping me still with those blue eyes, and spoke like Harry again.

"Seriously, Ruby. You were incredible up there. I never dreamed you were that good."

I kissed him thoroughly and sent him off to the men's dressing room with a slap to the hindquarters. He gave me a pistolshot with his fingers, said, "Thankyou. Thankyouvermuch," and joined James Brown in a march backstage.

Between chit-chatting with Aretha and Gloria (silently forgiving them for beating me), receiving my compliments from Geoffrey ("I had you picked out as a pro from square one") and swapping back into my civilian clothes, I was the last one out of the dressing room. When I came back out on stage, the theater was profoundly empty. I have a superstition that goes, Any time you see a mark, hit it, so I ambled up to the star and buried its east and west points under my pumps. A burst of short-term memory washes over me, but it flutters away like a riverbank of butterflies and I arrive at a wall of sadness, as if my veins have all gone indigo. A surge of gravity yanks me seaward, but I fight it, pressing down on that star and turning my legs into treetrunks, letting the tears do what they may.

"Everything OK?"

You could forgive me for thinking it's God – a gruff, booming baritone emanating from stage left. I twist from my star to discover a large man in a double-breasted navy suit. He seems to be in his mid-fifties, balding, with a thick salt-and-pepper beard, but he exudes a virile energy – executive bouncer, high-class Mafioso.

"Stage blues," he says. "You've hit an emotional peak, and now the moment's gone. It's all downhill from here – but at least it's a tall hill."

I perform a few eye rubs to clean the slate.

"No offense, but who the hell are you?"

He lets out a guffaw on a single note, like the ones produced by opera singers during party scenes. "Haw! I'm Albert Camarelli, and I'm quite a fan. You are a marvelous singer."

"Thank you, Mr. Camarelli."

"Please. You can call me Al."

"Al." I take a second to scan the empty seats, trying to put a name to my symptoms. "But you're wrong, Al. I'm familiar with stage blues. I'm a... professional. And I'm wondering why I had to work so *fucking* hard to get this stupid, shitty little part."

"There are no small parts, just..."

"Oh save it, Al!" And here I am, crying again. Al comes over and places a hand on my shoulder.

"I'm sorry. Shouldn't throw cliches at a pro. Would you like to take a walk with me on deck? Just for a few minutes?"

This seems a little forward, but Al's aura emanates benevolence.

"You should know," I say, "I'm already taken."

He smiles. "Everybody knows that. You and Elvis are the golden couple. He's pretty good, too. Nowhere near as good as you."

"I wouldn't say that."

"Honey, there's jazz and then there's the easy stuff. *You're* a jazz singer."

I turn and do a little squeegee job on my face.

"You've heard me sing jazz?"

"All week."

"And I'm a jazz singer?"

"Most definitely."

"Okay, Al. Let's go for a walk."

I take a last, doleful look at my star before following Al up the aisle. The elevator opens on the forward pool area, populated by a few late-night drinkers and a chain-smoking teen in a Ramones T-shirt.

"Britney! You are *hot,* honey."

"Thanks," I say.

We walk a few feet more and Al says, "Feels good, doesn't it?"

I flash him a secret grin. "A teenage boy just called me 'hot,' Al. What do *you* think?"

"Haw! Mind if I puff a stogie? It's a Cuban, so it's now or never."

"Nah. Go ahead."

Al turns away from the breeze, cups his hand and lights up. I wander toward the railing, eyeing the low strip of Baja California, a handful of lights popping from the darkness. Al joins me, proffering his prize.

"Care for a puff?"

"Sure." I twirl the tip in my mouth and take a drag. The smoke carries a rich coffee edge, plus something unexpectedly sweet, like a good port.

"That is lovely," I say.

"You've done this before."

"I've got a friend who smokes Swisher Sweets."

"Egad! On purpose?" He takes it back, tips the ash into a designated container (installed after balcony passengers down below found themselves being attacked by flurries of gray snow), then works the end into an orange glow.

"So! Ruby. Would you play some word association with me?"

"Sure, doc."

"Gershwin."

"But Not For Me."

"Straighten Up and Fly Right."

"Nat King Cole. The trio years."

"Vocalese."

"Take a famous instrumental solo and apply lyrics to it. Created by Lambert, Hendricks and the incomparable Ross."

"Lush Life."

"Ooh! Billy Eckstine. Smokey stuff."

Al stops and turns because he thinks he's got a meaty one.

"Mack the Knife."

"Merry little tune about a serial killer. Kurt Weill, for The Threepenny Opera with Bertolt Brecht. They told him the show needed a prologue to explain the main character; on the way home, he heard a trolley playing that familiar three-note motif: doo doo *doo doo.* Famously recorded by Louis, Ella, Frank and of course Bobby D. Weill also wrote Moon of Alabama, recorded by the Doors, and September Song."

"Um, uh..." Al is running out of steam. "A Small Hotel?"

"Rodgers and Hart. Al? Are we playing Jeopardy?"

He comes to some kind of decision and snaps his fingers. "No. You're *it,* Ruby."

"So we're playing tag? Yaknow, I've really got to meet Elvis in the Matisse..."

"No!" We've arrived at the aft swimming pool. He waves me into a chair. "Just two more minutes, I swear."

I take a seat as Al heads for the bar. He takes out a key and opens a cabinet, then returns with two glasses and a bottle of champagne.

"Al! You're gonna get in trouble."

He gives me a wink. "It's all right. I've got connections." He pops the cork, fills us up and raises a toast. "May you never have to sing Britney Spears ever again."

"You devil! You have come up with something I cannot refuse to drink to."

Al sits down and arranges his legs until he's comfortable, then he leans forward and laces his fingers.

"I've been watching you all week, Ruby. It takes a real connoisseur to know how good you are, and I knew it after three seconds. I spent the rest of the week making sure that I wasn't hallucinating. You have this ability with a song, to mold it, craft it like a fine sculptor – and God forbid, have a little fun with it. What you don't have is this godawful need to flatten out the tone and sap out all the warmth."

"Like Diana Krall?" I ask.

He laughs. "As in, makes my skin Krall. No. You have this marvelous old-fashioned sensibility that never, ever should have gone out of style. Actual vibrato, actual phrasing – call it torch singing, or vocal acting. The seniors appreciate it, because they grew up with it, but only two people on this fucking ship understand precisely what makes it work, and they're both sitting at this table."

I smile and take another sip of Al's very good champagne. "You know, Al? As long as you're not some highly articulate stalker, I could get to like you."

"Haw! That's good, because you might be seeing a lot of me."

"Um… Okay. Why?"

"I'm the vice president of this cruise line, Ruby. I'm also the entertainment director. We get a lot of older passengers on our Alaskan cruises – people who still know and love the great songs. For that and my own purely selfish reasons, I've decided to set up an old-fashioned jazz club, just like the ones you would see in one of those old Astaire movies, and fit it out with a small orchestra and a singer. And I want *you* to be the singer."

That's about the time I lose it. I slam the table with both hands and yell "No!" spilling half my coffee and alarming the couple at the next table.

"Yes!" says Ruby. "I start next month."

"That is incredible! That is... Oh! Oh Ruby!" I circle the table to give her a hug, and then I grab a handful of napkins to sop up my coffee. It's amazing how quickly my thoughts revert to my own selfish needs.

"But... Does this mean you're leaving?"

"Not at all. The cruises are out of Seattle. A week on/week off kind of thing."

I feel a little dizzy, awash with joy. It's true – empathy is a workable drug. But I've got one more doubt.

"Is this... Is this enough for you?"

Ruby tents her fingers. "I believe the quote was, I will no longer chase a dream that doesn't chase me. Well honey, this particular dream stalked me for a week and then toasted me with champagne and Cuban cigars! And I think by now I've got a handle on my basic needs. I need to stand in front of people and sing to them. If it's on a cruise ship, an entire country away from Times Square, then so be it!"

We both relax into our chairs, chewing our perfect bread. Ruby lets out little aspirations of wonder left over from the Mexican Pacific. Then she snaps to and raps her knuckles on the table.

"Oh, Channy. Me me me! I completely forgot – did you hear anything about Kai?"

Don't think I'm not tempted. I have huge, carnivorous creatures crawling inside of me, and if I don't expose them to the light of day they will eat me alive. But I am not about to rain on such a spectacular parade.

"Nope," I say. "Haven't heard a thing."

Twenty-Eight

"Don't like the weather? Wait five minutes!"

It's a tiresome joke, no one really thinks it's funny, but today – St. Patrick's Day – it has done gone literal. I begin the long crawl up Soundview in a thick fog, pass through a brief hailstorm, and a minute later am sitting at a sunny intersection as dainty crystals of snow land and melt on my windshield.

I am headed for the library, which has become my morning destination since Harvey's story went public. I scour the blogs and websites for revelations, and though the many analyses of Harvey's massacre certainly interest me, I am mostly after glimpses of Conrad and Kai. There is talk of coverup and courtmartial, and pundits trying to squeeze it into their side of the debate: symptom of an unworkable cause or simply the everyday price of a noble war? I am selfish – I could care less whether it lands on the black field or the white field. I want the assurance that my bad taste in men will not cost one more soldier one more day of precious life. And whether or not it's convenient, whether or not it's wise, it's clear that I am in love with Kai.

Today I strike gold: a video of Kai, Conrad and their lawyers getting out of a car. They're heading for some impressive building surrounded by evergreen ridges. Around here that could be anywhere, but I'm guessing the military courthouse at Ft. Lewis. Their expressions are neutral – I'm sure they've been coached on this – but Kai spots someone in the crowd and lets out the smallest of smiles. I track the video back and forth, looking for the moment with the most teeth, and send it off to the printer. This is a treasure worth a week of surfing, an image of the Kai I knew, the Kai I want back. I slide him into a plastic sleeve, and I'm off to Susanne's for Dutch crunch bread.

By the time I get my bread it's sunny. I sit outside despite the cold, if only to harvest some UVs. I realize that I'm also looking for a sign – and I am not generally a sign-seeker. But what if I actually *get* one? What then? A murder of crows flies overhead – Kai and Conrad get the chair? A bald eagle buzzes the bakery and snatches my Dutch crunch – freedom for both?

The bird I end up with is a teenage chickie with a blonde plume, pulling up in a silver monstrosity of SUV. She parachutes down and is headed for the bakery door when she spots something and stops. A wiry skaterdude with a helmet of black hair is pushing up the sidewalk (no small feat – he's on quite a hill). He spots Blondie and does that wondrous thing that teenagers do – leaps from his board to race toward his female target and lift her into a hug worthy of an amusement park ride, the both of them exclaiming superlatives all the while. After a third spin, he sets her back on terra firma, looks downhill and discovers that his board has rolled two blocks, taken a left into a driveway and is now headed for the marina.

He does precisely the right thing: gives a surprised smile, exclaims "Dude!" and stays exactly where he is, laughing his head off. Because the board is going to do what the board is going to do, and *that* is simply the cost of true love.

Word of our celebration has traveled the capillaries of Puget Sound's karaoke culture and brought back some interesting visitors. Floy and John Craig step into Karz for perhaps the first time in their lives. Sheila has come, and I am relieved to see that she has brought some tall dark man-candy so she can leave Harry the hell alone. It's not unusual that Alex has come, except that he has come without a dance partner, which is downright unheard-of.

We've even got a fellow professional – Erica, a KJ from California, and her husband Paul.

Ruby interrupts my prep-work to take me to her booth, where I meet the half-mythological Albert Camarelli, wearing a wild silk shirt of African siennas and reds, and Michael, the guy who sang Sinatra on the cruise. David's there, too, and I can't resist leaning over to whisper "Hi, Super." He gives me a wink and says, "Shh! You want to get me thrown out?"

After a few more small touches (tightening a troublesome speaker stand), the time seems right, so I perch behind my soundboard and begin the ceremony.

"All right, all right. Settle down, people! As you all probably know, a couple of our irregulars went on a cruise recently and made public spectacles of themselves, and we're here to assuage their superhuman egos so they'll just get over it and leave us the hell alone."

My decision to do this as a roast was not without some trepidation, so I'm relieved when my opening gets a laugh (much helped by Shari, who is the best laugher on the West Coast).

"Thanks to our lovely host, Hamster – who got his name from the rodents that he uses to power these goddamn annoying model trains – we have hooked the big screen up to a DVD player, so that we may all witness for ourselves the crime that was perpetrated on fifteen hundred innocent passengers last month. Hammy!"

Hamster hits a button and we're in at Ruby's intro. I should have a pretty good idea of what we're about to see, but it's all much more glamorous than I expected: the lights, the skill of the dancers (the *bodies* of the dancers!), even the camerawork, which includes a double-image fade from a stage shot to a closeup. As for Ruby, she's so good that it makes me uncomfortable. It's hard to picture someone you know laying it all out on a stage like that. That's for rock stars, actors, ballerinas – people who are only half-real to begin with.

With Harry, it's different. No quantum leap, just sorta what you would expect if you took this guy we all knew, gave him a cool white jumpsuit and stuck him on a big stage. I'm probably more impressed by the girls in the Capri pants, a six-pack of pure Day-Glo cutesy sex doing the pony behind him.

We keep the DVD rolling through Michael's "My Way" and the variety-show finale, and I'm back to my MC duties.

"Fortunately for us, Harry and Ruby didn't do their usual job of alienating everybody they meet" – Man! I hope I'm not overdoing this – "and they invited their Sinatra, Michael, to come down from Seattle. Michael?"

Michael looks like he wants to say something, so I hold off on the music.

"This was really a pleasure, I can't tell you," he says. "Getting to play my hero, meeting such talented and friendly people. The funny thing is, I really *hate* 'My Way.' It's butchered on a regular basis by middle-aged men the world over, and it's so antithetical to the swinging, playful style that typifies so much of Frank's music. That said, here's a song that I much prefer."

It's "Witchcraft," and I can quickly hear what Ruby was talking about. Michael's voice has a distinct Sinatra timbre that you simply have to be born with; the beverage equivalent would be a Guinness ale – a creamy, stout glass of black-brown baritone. He's also got the loosey-goosey sense of pitch and phrasing, making casually late entrances and scooping up to the notes on the chorus.

"I'm sure you've heard this before," I tell him, "but you really do sound like him. It's *eerie*." Breath. "Speaking of eerie, our next singer is Harry." I wait a beat for the laugh (I think I'm getting the hang of this!). "Harry *used* to be a tow-truck driver, but lately he's been spotted in electronics stores, shooting out entire aisles of TV sets, and hitting up pharmacies for what he likes to call 'leftovers.' You've seen the Thin Elvis, the Fat Elvis. I give you the Paunchy Elvis – Gig Harbor's own Harry Schmidt!"

I switch on "It's Now or Never" and Harry runs onstage, in a mockup of that skin-tight black leather bodysuit from Elvis's comeback TV special. I mean to say, it's like he's wearing a coat of black paint. He's also got big silver motorcycle sunglasses with portholes coming down the sides and a wig of jet-black hair with long sideburns.

After a quick "Thankyou," he's into the song. It takes me till midway through the first verse to realize that something's amiss. Either the Elvis mumble is sloppier than usual or Harry's singing in Italian! Lest there be any doubt, he finishes by mumbling "Grotsy, Millygrotsy," then performs a karate kick before returning to his table.

"Damn you, Harry!" I say. "Here I am, trying to be insulting, and you go and do something impressive. In case you're wondering, 'It's Now or Never' is based on the traditional Neapolitan song 'O Sole Mio,' and Harry just sang it in the original Italian."

Harry waits for just the right moment to answer with a classic Presleyan "Uh-uh-huh," which wins a well-deserved laugh.

I lose my place, and Shari begins the traditional chant of "Dead air! Dead air!" The room joins in, and I have to wave them all down.

"Back, you animals! Hyaw! Geez – the pressure! Forgive the hesitation, but I realize that I'm going to have to give up the roast entirely because I'm about to get all sentimental on your ass."

The room quiets down, and everybody's sneaking peeks at Ruby. She's dolled up in her Irish green dress, the one she wore for her dining-hall applause.

"Even in the beginning, when we didn't think terribly much of her attitude," (laugh beat, one... two...) "we knew that Ruby had extraordinary talent, talent that could not be contained by our humble bar. After a few months in her company, I can tell you that she's also an extraordinary friend. There were times when I simply could not have made it without her. Now..."

I have to stop for a breath. I feel the emotion rising in my voice, and I am determined to get this out straight.

"Huh-hem! Now, after suffering the slings and arrows of outrageous Broadway, our little girl will spend her evenings under the Northern Lights, trolling the Great American Songbook for thousands of lucky passengers. Would you please strike together your appendages for our own... Ruby! Cohen!"

Our modest assembly erupts like a squad of Japanese tourists as Ruby takes the stage and gives me a hug. She whispers "Ready?" and I give her a squeeze of affirmation. I'm sure she would have preferred to surprise me, but I *am* the KJ, so I at least have to know what song she's singing.

She takes the mic as if she's accepting a bouquet of roses.

"It's all true," she says. "I will soon be continuing my pursuit of the great musical beasts of America: the prong-horned Porter, the duck-billed Gershwin, the white-tailed Ellington. But before I embark on that glorious safari, I'd like to pay tribute to my roots, and the talented young lady who got me here. Alex!"

Alex dashes out in a black tango outfit, Zorro minus the accessories, and, much to the amazement of all, unzips Ruby's dress. She steps out to reveal cherry red vinyl pants and bra, then completes the ensemble by reaching behind my speaker for a jacket of the same material.

As she zips it up, I hit play, and I recall this same outfit from Britney's second music video. The song, however, is "Toxic," which rises from a snaky vamp that I just adore.

Ruby sings from a largely static position – a pose here, a pelvic dip there – but once they hit the instrumental she and Alex perform one of those whirling interweaves where you lose track of which limbs are whose. Ruby breaks out and kicks a leg up over Alex's shoulder, he slides her trailing foot across the floor like a paintbrush, then spins her away so she can repeat the chorus. Alex disappears for a few measures, then slides across on his knees, assuming a position like a human table as Ruby places a cherry-red boot atop his back. As she hits the final note, she pushes down and Alex sprawls out on the floor.

He remains in this position as the place simply goes haywire, then rolls onto his side and flashes a big grin. I know an impending dance party when I see one, so I slap on "Play That Funky Music" and watch as my patrons fill the floor.

Late in the evening, Erica from California comes up to sing "The Rose," and invites me and Shari to sing harmonies. I use a low harmony that I learned from Kevin the Cop (who has been strangely absent of late), and Shari takes the upper, launching herself into a gospel descant before the quiet finish. I'm exchanging sisterly hugs with both of them when Al comes up to ask if he can say something.

"Of course, Al. *You're* my hero."

Al turns to address the room. You can tell he's done this many times before.

"Hi. My name's Albert Camarelli, but starting next week you can refer to me as Ruby's Boss."

This brings automatic applause, which Al damn well knew it would before he said it.

"If you'll forgive the pun, I want to thank you for 'harboring' such a wonderful talent and sending her my way. It's my understanding that our Elvis met Ruby on these very grounds – and it was Harry, of course, who took her on that fateful cruise. As a reward, we've invited him to join Ruby on one free cruise per year. As long as he behaves himself, that is. As it turns out, however, our Ruby drives a hard bargain, so I would like to offer an additional free cruise – one time only, mind you – to your charming talent director, Channy."

My reaction is pure and lovely shock. I find myself kissing Al on the cheek and meeting Ruby for a helicopter hug, both of us screaming unintelligible syllables of delight. I make my way slowly back to the mic.

"I'm so embarrassed! Thank you so much, Al. That is incredibly sweet of you. Now, to save us all from utter chaos, let's get Ruby up here to sing."

Ruby drifts our way like a large disembodied smile and takes the mic.

"I think by now you realize that we've spent most of an Irish holiday celebrating a Mexican cruise. And with a name like Ruby O'Cohen, I feel it's up to me to set this matter right, so I would now like to sing the song that will be utterly massacred tonight by Celts and non-Celts the world 'round."

She pauses, like she's trying to piece something together.

"I also think that there is an unacknowledged... presence in the room tonight. If you've read the papers lately, you know that Channy has been having a rough time of it, and although she is not as apt as I am to blurt out her feelings, I know for a fact that she needs you people and your angelic voices as much as you might need her. And I want to thank you, on her behalf."

She looks my way, and I recover myself long enough to press the play button. In comes a fiddle, an Irish flute, and already I know that this music will perforate my heart. Perhaps we forget this amidst all the green beer and hullabaloo, but "Danny Boy" is a song sung to a child who is leaving for foreign lands, and the singer knows that he will never see him again.

I'm shrinking into the shadows behind my soundboard, ready for the melody to swallow me alive, when I feel a hand on mine. It's Alex, and he's pulling me onto the dance floor. His hands are divine instruments, as if there are beautiful movements inscribed on my palms, and all he has to do is touch this button, and that, and I am sweeping across the floor like Cyd Charisse. Toward the finish, as our Irish ancestor names his mourning like a shepherd calling his flock, we join hands, loop them around each other's necks and walk slowly in a circle, gazing at each other like dancers at an Irish wake. I'd never realized how beautiful his eyes were.

An hour later, I'm all packed up, conducting a post-party review with Shari, who's radiating excitement.

"Channy, I swear this is one of the best nights of my life. I am surrounded by extraordinary people, and… it's helped me make a decision. I saw an ad in the paper for a band that needs a female blues singer, and I'm gonna try out!"

"Omigod, Shari! I can so totally see you in a blues band. You'll be like a really tall, Viking Janis Joplin."

"Ha! Huge Sister and the Holding Company. Well, anyways, thanks for the hundred and fifty-third time already, and I'll let you know what happens. Bye! Enjoy that cruise!"

"Definitely!"

Ruby and Alex come strolling across the lot like a two-person laugh train.

"One beat off on that little stompdown, honey, and pop goes the vertebra."

"Now, now. I was gentle."

"You two!" I cut in. "Absolutely scandalous. Sexiest fucking thing I've ever seen."

Alex gives me an embarrassed grin. "I've been looking for a way to stretch my boundaries."

"That leg-shoulder thing scared the hell out of me," says Ruby. "I wasn't sure vinyl could stretch like that."

Harry rumbles up in his tow truck. "Hey, woman! Are we gonna get outta here by daybreak?"

"Whoops!" says Ruby. "We're kayaking the Vaughn Inlet tomorrow. Thanks, Channy. It was a swell homecoming."

She stands on Harry's running board, blows us a kiss and vaults to the seat. Alex and I watch the taillights ascending Pioneer like twin red stars.

"Well," he says. "I'd better..."

I grab his arm. I'm not sure why. "Alex, could I... could you stay just a minute?"

"Sure," he says. "Anything."

If he had said anything but *anything*, I might have lost my nerve. I rub my hand toward his elbow, looking for buttons.

"I think you know that... I'm a pretty fucked-up individual right now, and this is probably a one-time offer, but... could you please take me to your place?"

For once, my instincts are absolutely correct. The Alex who knows the buttons on my palms also knows the buttons everywhere else. I am spring-loaded with anxiety, and by the time Alex is finished with mouth, fingers and penis, I'm a five-time lottery winner, pleasurably destroyed, lying on his bed as the moon paints a skunk-stripe over the Sound. As it turns out, Alex lives in one of those pricey homes on Soundview, the ones I was passing this morning along my weather buffet. You could put a miniature golf course on his front lawn. I'm lying on my stomach, flagrantly naked; Alex runs a hand over my buttocks, as if they belong to a priceless Greek statue. I have decided that I merit just such treatment.

"I feel like I've discovered your secret, Alex. All those women, like a goddamn doctoral program."

"I wouldn't go too far with that," he says. "It's mostly about the dancing. But the dancing sometimes sets off triggers. Maybe a fifth of the time. What I like most is how surprised they are. It's easy to overlook a guy like me."

"Not when you dance."

It's odd when a man you've just had animal sex with gives you a *shy* look.

"Thanks. You know, the words to 'Danny Boy' were written in iambic pentameter. The song's in four, but the contrast gives it this lovely meandering quality. You can't just go hopping and skipping to it."

I can hear the song as he speaks, and recall its meaning.

"I'm still in love with him."

"I almost hate to ask," says Alex, "but... who?"

"Kai."

"Oh. That I knew. And, believe it or not, when you said 'one-time offer,' I took you at your word."

My gaze drifts to a charcoal sketch on the wall, Fred Astaire in coat and tails.

"So it's... okay?"

He runs a finger along the valley of my spine – a gesture that almost answers my question.

"It's not just okay, Channy. It's marvelous. For years – decades, actually – I waited for that life-long love affair, denying anything that didn't have the potential to meet that lofty standard. What foolishness. Some time or other, it finally happened, I finally figured out where I fit into the equation. I am Mr. In-Between, the guy who dresses the wounds and sends the women on their way. But meanwhile, I get to enjoy them, and feast on their lovely bodies, and the very brevity of these affairs affords a variety matched by few men that I know. I am one *hell* of a lucky guy."

I smile. "Nothing but A-pluses here, fella."

He slaps me affectionately on a butt-cheek. "That's what a man likes to hear. Another satisfied customer."

We laugh the laughter of the sexually spent. A minute later, I put on my clothes, give Alex a big smooch on the mouth, and show myself to the door.

True to the day, the weather has changed. I cross the lawn in an envelope of mist, leaving dewy footprints on the grass. As I near the streetlight next to my car, I discover a thousand tiny splinters of light. It's freezing fog, just the kind that one might find in a signpost forest.

I believe it now: Harvey is dead.

Twenty-nine

It's a brilliant mid-April Tuesday. Waiting at the light over Highway 16, I can see Mt. Rainier as if it's a pop-up in a gigantic children's book. I notice another mountain in the distance past its southern shoulder, and realize that I have never seen this mountain before. That's how clear it is. I take a mental note to look it up when I get to the library.

Exiting my truck in the library parking lot always gives me an olfactory thrill, until I remember that the cedar smell comes from the neighboring lot, where a dozen trees have been cut down for a new office building. Across the street, an entire forest has disappeared for the sake of some ginormous retail outlet. Such is the steady encroachment of success – and the new Narrows Bridge taking form next to the old one, promising to bring more commuters from Seattle and Tacoma. I suppose I should be excited for the greening of my tip jar, but I am beginning to mourn the old, modest Gig Harbor like a 70-year-old bench-sitting nostalgia whore.

It's a few days before the tax deadline, so the foyer is still packed with forms. I pick up an automatic extension, because if someone's offering free time, I'm taking.

The internet stations are lovely things, with sharp, thin monitors and keyboards that give out tasty popcorn clicks when you type on them. I also enjoy the printing policy, which operates entirely on trust. It's ten cents a page, which you deposit in a clear plastic box. The bottom of the box is cushioned, to prevent the disruptive clatter of quarters.

I find a corner cubicle, enter the number on my library card, and immediately have my answer – revealed by the news capsule on the search engine page: *Soldiers Sentenced in Civilian Killings.* I have learned to hate headlines; their brevity constantly misleads. This one makes it sound like Conrad and Kai carried out the killings themselves. The headline is technically correct, but it has a rotten soul.

I click the link, my heart tapdancing. Half a second into my download, I learn that Conrad got a year in prison – for the coverup, for being the commanding officer. For faking Harvey's suicide. I scroll down until the second shoe drops: Kai, suspended sentence, regular psychiatric evaluations. Because his was a noble act. Because of his mental state after killing his best friend. Because he *wasn't* the commanding officer.

In essence, Conrad has done what a good leader does – taken the brunt of it for an injured subordinate. I decide that I will track down Becky and see how she's doing – and find out if I can visit him.

Naturally, I thought I might hear from Kai. It's been a month since the trial. Becky hasn't heard a thing about him; I feel guilty even asking, my ulteriors showing through like a cheap slip.

It's May. The trees have dropped all their blossoms, are beginning to green up. Life is passing at the rate of freeway traffic, and I have arrived at Monday morning, on the shore of a three-day karaokeless ocean. I get up. Java has made no magical appearance. I manage to shower, and groom myself, and dress, just like a person who could be seen in public with other persons. I stare out my French windows at my too-familiar backyard: the Doug fir that leans in like a gambler peeking at his neighbor's cards, the tiny hump of faraway ridgeline that rises over my fence. And ridiculous, overzealous sunshine, everywhere. Oh God oh God, it's noon. I will remain here all day unless I can manage to kick my ass off this bed. There's only one thing that will do the trick: drive. Drive like crazy.

I traverse the Narrows, glancing across at enormous sections of roadway dangling from what look like kite strings. Highway 16 doglegs to the asphalt Mississippi of I-5, heading south. But the roadside clutters up with bad memories: the Nisqually Delta keep driving the Olympia marina keep driving. I spot the ramp for 101, a binary sandwich of a number whispering promises of the Pacific Ocean, so that's where we're going.

An hour later, I'm cruising a long, lush valley past twin nuclear towers – coolers for a power plant that was never completed. I see a sign reading *Ocean Shores*. It sounds like a generic product: *Toothpaste, Light Beer, Ocean Shores.* So okay, I'm buying.

I wind through the harborside towns of Aberdeen and Hoquiam, then follow a road along the tidal flats – which right now contain about ten million pounds of hideous muck. Escape arrives on an evergreen ascent, which flattens out along a peninsula, and soon I'm turning left onto the main strip of Ocean Shores. An Irish pub hooks me with a sign reading *Comfort Food*; I wander in on road-stiff legs and order a potato chowder as thick as tapioca pudding, topped with starry flakes of parsley. The bread is dark, chewy and mysterious. I was *so* right to kick my ass off that bed.

Roundly fortified, I head into town, take an oceanward right and spy a municipal-looking restroom between two enormous hotels. I park there, trek a wide swath of dunes and discover a beach that runs a mile across and three eternities to right and left, composed of damp slate-brown sand. I'm a little alarmed when a car passes in front of me, a hybrid compact filled with gray-haired passengers. After a half-mile of northward walking, I come upon a college-age boy and girl, tossing a Frisbee, and give a smile as I pass. The sun is to the south, so my shadow precedes me on the sand. I hear the girl exclaim "Oh!" and then I find a small, dark oval hovering over my shadow. I raise my left arm, turn my hand so it faces behind me and close my fingers on the rim of the disc. I'm running a fingernail over its ribbed surface when the girl, an energetic lankiness of elbows and knees, rushes up.

"Holy shit! How did you do that?"

I guess I'm in a mood. I give her a perfectly serious look and say, "The secret is to let the Frisbee do what the Frisbee *wants* to do."

Carye takes a second to consider my wisdom and then explodes in laughter. An hour later, we're gathered at a driftwood fire – more for atmosphere than warmth – and I have just finished relating the Tragical History of Harvey.

"Shit!" says Joe. "Shit!" He brushes away a hank of hair that seems irresistibly drawn to his eyelashes, then takes another toke and passes it my way.

Carye says, "We came out here because Kurt Cobain grew up here."

I'm looking for a segue – suicidal young men? – but then, we're smoking. Segues are not required.

"Hoquiam or Aberdeen," says Joe. "Depending on who you ask."

"They seem to be having a debate about it," says Carye.

"Come to the town that sucks so bad you'll want to blow your head off," says Joe.

Carye laughs wildly. "But not before writing some kickass rock."

I can see why Joe and Carye are a couple. They speak in a tightly knit tandem, like relay runners passing a baton. Or perhaps it's just the weed.

"We're from Humboldt County," says Carye. "In Northern California."

"Which is why this homegrown is so almighty powerful," says Joe, with a wheezy laugh.

"It gets pretty cloudy there," says Carye. "But we thought it would be cool to see how bad it gets in a place called the Rain Coast."

"Absolute bullshit," says Joe. "It's been like Laguna Beach all week."

"Where's Laguna Beach?" asks Carye.

"No fuckin' idea," says Joe. "But it sounds sunny."

"But *your* story," says Carye. "God, Channy... What a great name that is: Channy. You are *so strong* to have gotten through that. You are a *powerful* woman."

Carye's admiring look – plus, probably, the weed – fills me up to bursting. As if to disprove her conclusion I start to cry, and soon find myself wrapped in a Joe and Carye sandwich.

When I wake up, the sun is threatening the horizon. I'm curled up on a Mexican blanket; Joe sits cross-legged next to me, trying to spin the Frisbee on the tip of his finger.

"Oh! Hey, Channy. Wow, I've seen the herb take some bad shit out of people, but you just sorta collapsed."

I blink against the light and prop myself on an elbow. "How long was I out?"

Joe brushes his hair out of his eyes and squints in thought. "'Bout, oh, two hours."

"Really? Fu-u-uck."

"Ha! You talk like a stoner."

"Haven't smoked much lately. I've gone and turned into a lightweight. So where's Carye?"

"Went to the water to look for sand dollars. She *loves* those things. Looks like she's coming back, though."

By the time she returns, I have managed to shake the sand from my clothes and the cobwebs from my head. I give them my phone number and demand that they come for karaoke if they get anywhere near Gig Harbor.

"Y'got any Nirvana?"

"Let's see – 'Teen Spirit' and 'Come As You Are.'"

"Rockin'! I'm there."

I hug them both, and give them the look of an adoring aunt.

"I'm so lucky that you two were here."

"When you have the Jedi Frisbee Trick," says Carye, "luck you do not need."

"Ha! Well, thanks anyways. I feel much better. Bye, guys."

"Bye!" they say, in unison.

I walk toward the sun, stopping once for a final turn-and-wave. By the time I reach the parking lot, the sun has ducked under the horizon, which in Washington time means somewhere between 8:30 and 9. I'm about to get into my truck when I hear a jangle of sounds that resembles "Take Five" by the Dave Brubeck Quartet.

It seems to be live. I scan the hotel behind me and find a stairway leading to a well-lit pair of glass doors. I have just found where the action is, and so, like a good Jedi princess, I go there.

The doors bring me to a high-ceilinged hall, ringed with mirrored posts and mauve upholstery. The back is a long rectangle of booths, the near square a cocktail lounge with an open fireplace, a marbletop bar and a perimeter of small tables at the beachfront windows.

The afterglow paints the barback mirrors in salmon hues, and blasting away from a corner of the dance floor is a trio of upright piano, electric bass and green drums. The players are all big, like they really ought to be playing football.

The bassist stands about six-four, wearing a do-rag better suited to a biker bar. The pianist has a clean-shaven pate, in the modern rocker style, with a bandage over one temple. He's pounding a solo like a ham-fisted Fats Waller, then lifts up, studies his field and dances into a Mozartean flurry. How he does this all in 5/4 is far removed from the scope of my knowledge.

In the midst of my musical trance, I find a short, plump brunette walking my way, and feel a sudden need to ask a question. Any question. I lean into the fringe of her path.

"Excuse me, umm... Who are these guys?"

Who are these guys? What're you, high?

The brunette gives me a compact smile. "I don't think they have a name. But if you'd like an audience with the bassist, I'm on *intimate* terms.

I give her a puzzled look.

"Okay, he's my husband. And he's having a heck of a time faking his way through this one."

"Sounds fine to me."

"Yes, but he's scowling. Anyways, he's Jon, the pianist is Paul, and the drummer is Mark."

I laugh, a little too loud. "Aren't they supposed to have names like 'Razz' and 'Speed'?"

She puts a hand on my shoulder. "I think someone's been watching forties gangster movies. Hey, would you like to sit with me? I am a lonely band widow."

"Sure. But let me buy you a drink."

"I will just let you do that. I'll have a chablis."

I'm low on decision-making abilities, so I get a chablis as well. We're soon back at Pam's table, yacking like sorority sisters. It's easy to see why she struck me as approachable – she has large eyes and round, doll-like features. You might expect a squeaky Betty Boop voice, but what you get is a calm alto.

"So," she says. "What's your story?"

I can't help laughing. "That's a little complicated. Why don't you tell me yours?"

"Sure! We're from California, Silicon Valley. Jon wrote code for a high-tech firm that very rudely laid him off. He had a tough go with the job-hunting, so the guitar became a full-time pursuit: blues band, funk band, surf band. That *definitely* wasn't cutting it money-wise, though, so we sold our overvalued house and moved up here. I'm a CPA, so I can work anywhere. Then he met the guys, so now he's playing jazz. Paul's an English teacher, which puzzles me because he ought to be playing in New York or something."

"My thought exactly."

"And Mark is in real estate. He's getting over his divorce by singing Tony Bennett songs."

"Oh! He sings from the drums?"

"He says it's a matter of simple beats and good posture."

"So does he sound like Tony?"

"Not tonight. Poor dear, he's fighting some nasty bug."

Paul concludes a lengthy exploration of "The In Crowd" and takes the group into a wrap. The twenty folks scattered around the lounge respond with warm applause. Mark attaches a sheet of paper to the shaft of his hi-hat with a binder clip.

"That's his cheat for new songs," says Pam. "Although I always wonder how he can read when the words are bouncing up and down like that."

Paul nods them into a slow, bluesy intro, and then Mark comes in on "Do You Know What It Means to Miss New Orleans?"

"Wow!" I say. "He does a wicked Louis Armstrong."

"He's not doing Louis Armstrong," says Pam. "That's what he sounds like tonight."

"Yikes!"

"Hey!" Pam spots a couple at the door and waves them over. One's a burly, balding man with a thick mustache (Ocean Shores apparently breeds nothing but offensive linemen), the other is a fiftyish woman with a broad, generous face and a thick head of frosted blonde hair. They seem inordinately happy, or perhaps just drunk. After a round of hugs and greetings, they join us at the table.

"Channy, this is my brother Allen and his wife Sarah. They're winos."

"Please," Allen objects. "Connoisseurs."

"Okay, Mister Hoit du Toit," Pam says, exactly like a sister. "Where have you been? The gig started two hours ago!"

Allen and Sarah look at each other and smile. Allen says, "We can't tell you yet. Not till the appetizers get here."

"Better be a good story," says Pam.

"Oh it is," says Allen.

The song ends rather abruptly, and we give the band an applause laden with question marks. The players bend toward each other, conferring, then Jon takes the mic from Mark's boom stand. He holds it awkwardly, as if it's about to go off.

"Um, hi. I'm Jon, your bass player."

The relatives at my table shout, "Hi, Jon!"

"Um, yeah, hi. Our vocalist has given his all tonight, and by that I mean he's got nothin' left. The thing is, we promised the ladies from the dance class that we would play 'Mustang Sally,' and if we don't we might not make it out of here alive. Would anyone in the audience like to sing it with us? Because you really don't want to hear me or Paulie try it."

And I'm on my feet, walking across the floor. I don't know what's come over me. Maybe it's the pot; maybe it's being at the western edge of an entire continent, or the Jedi Frisbee Trick – but obviously I'm the one to sing this song. I take the mic from Jon and say, "Whenever you're ready, boys."

The surprising thing is, this is *easier* than karaoke, because in karaoke there's no give to the music. At one point, I'm pretty sure I'm way early on the chorus, but the band performs a quick shift and everything's cool. Plus, I've got a baker's dozen of seniors shaking their booties in front of me, breathing hard and utterly delighted by my rescue act. *This,* I think, *is why Ruby loves the stage.* After a bass solo from Jon, I repeat the call-and-response, and Mark marches us into a drum-break finish. *Sweet.*

Jon sneaks up to my shoulder and says, "That was great! Y'know anything else?"

I turn to Paul and say, "What about 'Great Balls of Fire'?" Which is like asking a dog if he likes steak.

"Oh, I am all *over* that," says Paul with a grin. "Just watch me for the start."

He gives a three-count, plays the four-step launch and I'm off. Somewhere in the midst of all that karaoke, I have learned how to front a band. The seniors are jitterbugging as Paul draws out his solo to Herculean proportions, kicking out a leg to play a few notes with his wingtips. He nods me back into the bridge, then to a chorus repeat, then a big fat splatter of an ending. Suddenly, I'm a Vegas emcee.

"Paul! Lee! Lewis! on the piano. Liquid Jonny on the bass! Frogman Mark on the drums!"

"How do you know all our names?" asks Jon.

"I've been talking to your wife."

"Ah! So what's your name?"

"Oh," I say, and turn back to the mic. "And I'm Channy from Gig Harbor, your emergency fill-in."

"Hey Channy!" says Paul. "Last song. You know something jazzy and slow?"

That one's easy.

"Misty."

I'm always having a love affair with one song or another, and this one arrived on the lips of Ruby Cohen. It's a lovely, joy-laced melody, like a falling leaf that keeps nearing the ground only to be swept back up by a gust of wind. It's also got a shadowy undercarriage, which certainly matches my romantic life. Ruby ran me through it after a handful of karaoke nights, supremely patient, because I think she knew what a stretch I was making.

Paul gives me a lilting, rubato intro. I scan the old couples dancing before me, close my eyes and lift the mic. The words come out of me like colored breath.

Toward the end, I already know I've captured it. Ruby calls it "inner applause" – the outer applause that follows feels like an echo. I turn to thank the trio, then head for my table as they begin breaking down their equipment. I find Pam and kin beaming at me over a tray of oysters and a bottle of champagne in an ice bucket.

"Well didn't I find a diamond in the rough!" says Pam.

"Thanks! I run a karaoke bar, so I guess I developed some skills."

"I'll say!" says Allen. He hands me a glass. "We saved the last for ya."

I take a sip. "Damn!"

"No," he says. "Dom!"

To perform a spit-take would be downright criminal, so I force down a fizzy swallow. "Perignon?"

"My little surprise," he says. "We went to the Quinault Casino this afternoon, and I won ten thousand dollars at the blackjack table."

"Holy shit!"

"He's taking us all to the Ocean Crest tomorrow for dinner," says Pam. "It's a five-star restaurant."

"Wow! What fun. Could you take me too?" I realize immediately what a presumptuous question this is, and I cover my mouth in embarrassment.

Allen, God bless him, lets out a broad laugh and says, "Sure! Why not? I think you've sung for your supper."

And now, I'm glad I asked. Because really, I need all the pleasure I can get.

I spend the night four blocks away, at Jon and Pam's. The bed in their guest room is extraordinarily comfortable; it's the best night of sleep I've had in months. I wake to the ching of pots and pans in the kitchen, and wander down the hall to find a plate of bacon, eggs and waffles with my name on it. It almost makes me want to cry. I marvel at the power of strangers to take me in like this – a thought that is due to return a dozen times over the course of the day.

Once we're all bathed and dressed, I follow Pam's Toyota along a golf course to Allen and Sarah's house, adorned with the latest accoutrements of new housing: sienna-colored stucco, ceramic roofing and variegated windows with bay, porthole and archway frames. To the right of the driveway is their apparent cash cow, a spotless mocha-colored truck cab. The house's interior offers every imaginable variation of wine art: a photo of cabernet grapes, a poster from a Yakima Valley wine festival, a cartoonish sommelier constructed of corks and corkscrews. The back window affords a view across Grays Harbor to the snub-nose pyramid of Mt. Rainier.

Allen and Sarah are still radiant from their Monday jackpot, although I'm beginning to suspect that their sunniness is a permanent condition. They pile into Pam's back seat and we caravan up the coast. Twenty miles along, we pull through a town called Moclips and turn into what looks like a modest motel court.

"We're a little early," says Allen, "so Sarah and I were thinking of walking down to the beach."

We all join in descending an impressively lengthy set of stairs to another limitless slate-brown beach. Pam and I are the only ones wearing casual shoes, so we leave the others on the viewing deck and take off across the sand. The findings are modest – crab shell here, half a sand dollar there – but interesting enough to spur a conversation.

"I was just thinking," says Pam. "You never told me your story. What brought you out to the coast?"

"Hard to beat a story with a ten-thousand-dollar jackpot," I say, knowing full well that I can. "But maybe I can shorthand it for you. Have you seen the stories about that soldier who went nuts and shot all those Iraqi civilians?"

"Oh! The trials at Ft. Lewis? Just recently?"

"Yes. Well. I'm the widow."

Pam stops and puts a hand to her solar plexus. "God! I... really? I'm so sorry."

"It's all right," I say. "I'm sure it's hard to know how to respond. But believe me, he was sane when I married him. He might even have been nice. So please don't think of me as a victim."

"I guess that's what war does to people." She reaches for a sand dollar – a full one – and hands it to me. "I can see why you wanted to get away."

"Yes. Little did I know the lovely distractions waiting for me in Ocean Shores."

"Gateway to the Pacific Storm Front," says Pam, then looks back toward our companions. "Uh-oh. Allen's pointing at his watch. I'm guessing that's a sign."

I study the long ribbon of stairs winding into the spruce trees. "Do you suppose they have an escalator?"

"I... get the feeling that burning a few calories right now might be a good idea."

After a brisk uphill climb, the restaurant host takes us through a low-ceilinged hall into a woodsy side room. The west-facing wall is all window, affording a bird's-nest view of the forest and beach below. A large pickup speeds by on the sand.

For a few minutes, I feel a distinct pressure to be on my best behavior, but once the appetizers arrive I lose myself in the raucous chatter all around me. Our carnivorous rapture begins with Alaskan king crablegs dipped in butter, continues with mushrooms, foraged in local forests, then proceeds to a cloth bag next to Allen's chair. He reaches in and pulls out a weathered-looking bottle, then hands it to the sommelier and asks, "Would you do us the honor?"

The sommelier's eyes get big (no small trick in a five-star restaurant) and he says, "I'd be delighted."

I turn to Pam and ask, "What's up with that?"

"It's a 1969 Cab from Napa. Allen got it at an auction."

The sommelier takes laborious care in removing the cork, then slowly pours it into a decanter, making certain to leave all the sediment in the bottle. He tips a small ration into each of our glasses, and we wait as Allen goes through the ritual of swirl, smell and sip. He breathes out, letting the flavor simmer on his tongue, then delivers a one-word review.

"Damn!"

Being a neophyte, I'm not expecting much, but much is what I get. My first sip delivers a smoky, fruity wave of warmth, with just a hint of ripe Bing cherry. It is the most amazing substance that has ever touched my lips. Except for the roast venison that follows. And the pickled cabbage. And the huckleberry crisp. Our table is a madrigal of groans and sighs, verging on an epicurean orgy. Between courses, Allen regales us with trucking stories, like the retired Soviet tank they delivered to a military base in North Dakota, and fills in the details of his blackjack odyssey ("I absolutely could not lose; I must have taken twenty hands in a row!").

Much too soon, we're waddling to the parking lot, and I'm hugging all these near-strangers like a long-lost cousin.

"Thank you so much for letting me impose on you," I say to Allen. "I really, really needed this."

Allen gives me a lopsided smile. "Pam tells us you've been through some trauma. I just hope this takes the edge off a little."

"Thank *you* for saving our butts last night," says Jon. "I really wasn't kidding about those blue-haired ladies and their Wilson Pickett. Maybe we'll give you a call if Mark gets sick again."

"Ha! I'll work on my drumming."

"You be careful driving back," says Pam. "And take care of yourself, okay? Don't think you have to wait till your next trip to the ocean to pamper yourself."

Under Allen's instructions, I head back into Moclips and take a landward left, on a road that claims to be headed for Kurt Cobain's twin hometowns. I think about Pam's phrase: *Take care of yourself.* It actually seems like that's *all* I've been doing; it was nice to let someone else have the job for a while.

Halfway home, I have to pull into a rest stop. The garnish on my venison inspired a debate about a "Rosemary" song from the sixties (Simon and Garfunkel excluded) which quickly devolved into a group case of "songstipation." As always happens, the answer arrives long after I have stopped thinking about it. Our problem came from trying to mash two songs into one: "Smile a Little Smile For Me (Rosemarie)" and "Love Grows (Where my Rosemary Goes)." As the VFW guys who hand out free coffee cast curious looks in my direction, I stand at the pay phone and sing the two songs into Jon and Pam's answering machine. Then I bundle into my truck and head for the darkening mountains, homeward bound.

THIRTY

I'm in a familiar position, fighting to kick my ass out of bed. But at least the *bed* is moving – coasting slowly westward along the Strait of Juan de Fuca. The departure from Seattle was spectacular; I don't know a city in the world that looks better from the water. After that, however, the long afternoon of lining up, checking baggage and presenting documents finally got to me. I managed to sleepwalk through the lifeboat drill, but after that it was back to the cabin. I turned on the TV to check out all the day excursions – kayaking in Ketchikan, whale-watching in Juneau – and immediately collapsed bedward in a blurry ball. I awake two hours later to the roar of a televised glacier shedding ice chunks, and peer out my window to see a land mass that's probably Vancouver Island.

It's seven o'clock. I'm supposed to meet Ruby at eight. I have no idea how this is supposed to occur, since my limbs have lost the ability to initiate motion. Through much grunting and lamentation, I manage to drag myself all five feet to the shower. The fluorescents reveal a basket filled with sampler-size toiletries. I pick out a shampoo, a conditioner, and a bar of ocean-scent soap that claims to contain actual sea kelp (and smells, thank God, more like the *idea* of ocean than the ocean itself). The shower heats up remarkably well, and soon I am swaying under the sprinkle, praying for the washing away of my anguish.

Yeah, that's what I said: *anguish.* Anyone who's been through my particular brand of hell deserves a pot of gold, a certificate of merit, a Nobel Pity Prize. I have spent so much time harking back to that weekend in Ocean Shores that it's getting pathetic – because I haven't done anything in the interceding month that's even worth mentioning. I try to find pleasure in the small things – fresh bread at Susanne's, a starfish under the Jerisich Dock. But it's too late for small things, dammit. I'm looking for something *huge.* Thank God for the cruise, but even here there's a downside. I'm all alone, not even Harry Baritone to hang with, and the singles game is as treacherous as oceanfront property on a glacier. That and the unsettling feeling of returning to my home state; no matter how temporary the stay, it feels like backtracking, and I *hate* backtracking.

Okay. Let's focus. Tonight you get to see Ruby's show. That is SO *worth the effort. Now get it together, ya big baby.*

Ruby was so excited about me coming that she took me to Seattle's downtown shopping district and made me her own personal Barbie doll. The result is a little red dress with spaghetti straps and a neckline that reveals cleavage I didn't know I had. She also got me a pair of red Italian pumps trimmed in black, and loaned me her prize necklace, a gold serpentine with a teardrop pendant of her namesake gemstone. I should have a bodyguard just to put the thing on. (I think she got it from Scootie, but I didn't think I should ask.)

An hour after the process began, I stand on my bed in order to get a full-length reflection in my cabin mirror. I like what I see. If I met myself in a bar, I might even jump my bones. And now I better go, before I lose this feeling. I grab my black Spanish wrap and head for the halls.

The ship is Uncle Al's main girl, evidenced by the super-size faces of Louis, Ella and Miles looming on the wallpaper. Between the elevators I find a Leroy Neiman of the Manhattan Transfer at the Monterey Jazz Festival, an explosion of fluorescent paints. As I'm waiting, a trio of college-age boys passes, trying hard to conceal their sidelong glances, then bursting into exclamations as they round the corner. I'm getting hotter by the minute.

I arrive at the second deck and try to recall Ruby's directions: right at the espresso counter, the windows filling up with an icy pink sunset. A straightaway through the slot machines (switched on the minute we entered international waters), then a right at the photo shop and proceed to the silver doors.

And *what* silver doors! A pair of them, each ten feet high and four feet wide. I begin to see figures, and I realize it's a frieze of a classic Cotton Club gathering: dozens of characters blowing trumpets, tapdancing, smoking cigarettes. The top of the doors form an arch, and in the swing of the arch are light-bulb letters spelling out *ASTAIRE'S.*

"So ya gonna go in or what?"

I turn to find Ruby done up in a long sheath dress of gold lamé. A slit runs the length of one entire leg.

"Jean fucking Harlowe!" I say.

She feigns disappointment. "I was going for Rita Hayworth."

"Hell, Scarlett Johannssen, Jessica Rabbit – I'll give you any sexbomb you want." I wrap her in a hug. "I can't *wait* to see your show!"

"Well – let's begin by entering Oz." She swipes a card through a reader and the doors click open.

"Gracious!" I say.

Inside, it's a Cab Calloway paradise. Little music stands for the players, baby blue with silver sequin treble clefs. A stage in three semicircle tiers, spilling onto a dance floor of gray marble with swirling streaks of snow white. The whole spread is backed by a proscenium arch with Greek columns and gauzy white curtains, and stage left plays host to an enormous white grand piano. As I drift over to inspect, I spy a silver star on the floor and quickly cover it with my red pumps.

"Always hit a mark," I recite.

Ruby laughs, then indulges my fantasy by delivering a stand with one of those old-fashioned squarish radio mics. I cup one side of it, try to channel my best Marlene Dietrich and gaze out at the tables, done up with silver lamps and backed by a velvet curtain along the back wall.

"Roo-bee? Why am I experiencing déjà vu?"

Ruby wanders to the piano and plays two rising chords, as if to say "Ta-dah!"

"Have you seen *Shall We Dance?*"

"Astaire and Rogers?"

"You remember the nightclub?"

"Omigod! So this is like an exact replica?"

"No. But have you seen *Top Hat*? *Flying Down to Rio*?"

"Um... yes?"

"Those movies too!"

I take a slow stroll and join Ruby on the piano bench.

"Honey? What the fuck are you talking about?"

She giggles with satisfaction at having screwed with my head.

"*Well.* When Al got the idea for this cabaret, he and the designer sat through *all ten* Astaire and Rogers movies, and then came up with this... Well, let's call it an *evocation*."

"How freakin' cool! So you're like... Ginger Rogers?"

"Let's hope I can sing better than *that*."

"Ooh. Harsh!"

"Hey, she ain't a singer, I ain't a dancer. All's fair." She points an accusing finger. "And stop using my word."

A bartender comes out to greet us, equipped with mutton chops and a black tuxedo. His name is MacLiver, which sounds like a horribly misdirected fast-food entrée. He brings us a pair of lemon-drop martinis, and Ruby fills me in on her brief seafaring career.

"It's nearly a religious experience sometimes. These folks grew up on this music – and they're already close to rapture just being on the cruise in the first place. When you plug into their memories with a favorite tune, this radiance comes over them. I get regular offers to stay at people's houses – I could string it into a national tour if I wanted. And so far, three proposals of marriage."

"No shit!"

"Although the youngest was sixty-two. Although he *was* loaded."

"Bad girl!"

"Would a good girl dress like this?"

We're interrupted by "The Lady in Red" chiming from Ruby's bag.

"Oh! 'Scuse me a second. This is almost certainly a business call."

She answers her cell, then stands and walks away as she speaks. I could swear I hear her say, "The fish are running." She returns a minute later.

"Sorry. The downside to being Uncle Al's pet project is the constant check-ins. It's sorta like having a jealous Mafia boyfriend."

"'The fish are running?'"

"Oh yes!" she laughs. "Isn't that a gas? It's some kind of maritime lingo for 'Everything's A-OK.'"

"Miss Ruby?"

It's MacLiver (he used to be a butler, which explains the formality).

"Yes, Robert?"

"I'll be opening up now."

"Okay. Thanks." She turns to me. "Part of the mystique. They like me out of sight during happy hour. Will you be able to entertain yourself?"

I smile. "The fish are running. Break a leg, sweetie."

Ruby immediately starts busting up.

"It's a theater expression," I say. "Isn't it?"

"Sorry. You reminded me of... Well, I was talking to one of the showgirls. She used to be in a ballet troupe, and what they used to say, right before they went onstage, was 'Merde.'"

"Umm, my French is a little rusty, but doesn't that mean 'shit'?"

"Yeah. Isn't that funny? And I asked her why they say that, and she said, 'I have no idea.' Well, I better go."

Ruby sashays away (which in *that* dress is her only option). I yell, "Merde!" She yells "Merci!" and gives me a Jedi Frisbee wave.

I turn to find MacLiver hovering over me (these retired butlers have ninja stealth).

"Excuse me, Miss Channy. Once I open the door, I'll have to charge you for the drinks."

He waits patiently until I manage to process his meaning. "Oh!" I raise my glass. "I'll have another of these. Thanks."

"My pleasure."

After delivering my lemon drop redux, MacLiver opens the great silver doors and a long train of elderly passengers scurries to the tables like '49ers staking out claims. I harvest a few phrases out of the chatter, and gather that the evening meal was exquisite (I'm feeling stupid and hungry for missing it). When I turn back to my drink, I find that another ninja has stolen up on me. He looks about forty, with sharp light-brown eyes behind gold-rimmed spectacles.

"Pardon me but... I'm here by myself, and I'm wondering if I could sit with you? I hate to use a whole table just for myself."

"Oh, um... Sure. Have a seat. I'm Channy."

He takes my hand and sits. "I'm Donald. Donald O'Connor."

"Oh! Like..."

"Yes, yes. *Singin' in the Rain*. 'Make 'em Laugh.'"

"I guess you get that a lot."

"It's okay. Be worse if I was Ronald McDonald." He gives me a nice smile, and I catch a bit of his cologne, which is spicy but subtle. Donald O'Connor has possibilities.

"So where do you hail from?" he asks.

"Gig Harbor. It's near..."

"Yes! That new Tacoma bridge. You know, they're talking about installing low-level lights along the suspension cables. They would be powered completely by solar, and create an outline of the bridge at night. It's a marvelous idea. Lord knows, Tacoma could use some civic identity."

"I'll say! All it's got now is that Steve Miller song – and he probably only used it so he could rhyme 'Arizona.'"

"Actually," says Donald, "I think Miller lives in the Northwest, so it might have been vice-versa. You know the theme from *Hawaii Five-Oh*? The Ventures? They're from Tacoma, too. How does a band from Tacoma end up writing surf tunes?"

This *might* seem like a normal conversation between two strangers, but after ten minutes I realize that trivia is Donald's only mode. The more I try to steer us in another direction, the more he staples factoids to the ends of my sentences, and soon this good-looking, nice-smelling man – who sat down with even odds at bedding a desperately horny, down-on-her-luck widow – has utterly blown his chance. Fortunately, we're interrupted by MacLiver, who is evidently pulling double duty as an emcee.

"Ladies and gentlemen, welcome to Astaire's, the finest floating nightclub on the seven seas!" He reaches under the bar to adjust the sound. "And now, would you please welcome your chanteuse for the evening, the siren of the Inside Passage, our very own Ruby Cohen!"

A spotlight lands on the gauzy curtains, and Ruby flings them apart, vamping down the three-tiered stage with a brilliant smile. The horns and piano kick into a bouncy swing, and arrive at a big fat stop just as Ruby nears the microphone. She waits a couple beats, then hits the opening of "All of Me." It's a perfect welcome, a way of offering herself, parts and all, to her audience.

And Donald's only a step behind. "Did you see that movie, *All of Me*? That was so brilliant, the way Steve Martin was able to divide his body into male and female sides like that."

"Uh-huh," I say, as flatly as possible. My aim is to discourage further commentary – and it seems to work, but I can feel his frustration across the table, the stupid prick. And now I have to silence this irritating monologue running through my own head. *Pipe down in there!*

Ruby perches on a stool for a medley of Rodgers and Hart: "Lover," "Let's Fall in Love" and "A Small Hotel." It's great that she gets to include lesser-known songs; I suspect this is the work of her jazzophile boss.

She waits for the applause to die down, then says, "A couple of the dancers from the stage show – and I'd really suggest you check that out, they put on some *amazing* performances. Anyways, Marlena and Josh used to be in a Fred Astaire tribute show, and tonight they'd like to perform a number from that production. Give 'em a hand!"

The orchestra breaks into a romping version of "Begin the Beguine" as our dancers stride in stage-left. Josh is clad in a white tux with top hat and tails, while Marlena wears a flowing, cream-colored gown with silver-sequin angels and smiling moons. Marlena has thick, wavy blonde hair like Ginger Rogers (or an excellent wig). They hop to the high tier and rip off a couple of tight spins, then swirl up and down the steps in that springy Fred-and-Ginger fashion. They return to the main floor and break off for a side-by-side tapdance. It's absolutely top-notch, and I'm beginning to understand the religious fervor that Ruby was talking about.

Josh and Marlena take a couple of huge steps back to the top, where they negotiate a series of breathless in-and-out spins, Marlena's dress wrapping Josh in a circle of cloth. Josh picks her up by waist and thigh and lifts her into an arcing flight from one end of the stage to the other. As the orchestra slows, he dips her till her hair brushes the floor, sweeps her once around at that level and pulls her up hard. She jumps into his arms, the classic honeymoon-threshold posture, and the orchestra slams to an end. The place goes nuts.

"Josh and Marlena!" Ruby shouts. "Aren't they astounding? Aren't they ridiculously young and energetic? Don't you just hate them?"

She sits back on her stool and waits for things to quiet down, and then she gives a nod to her pianist, a tall black man with enormous hands. He starts into a march of single notes that begins to take on a melody. It's "Good King Wenceslas," heading into the same Nina Simone "Little Girl Blue" that she sang that first night at Karz. I'm afraid I might cry, not just for the memory but because this song is exactly how I *feel.* Ruby gives me a knowing look as she draws out the final line, then accepts a quiet applause.

"That song was for my homegirl Channy, who is seeing my show for the first time tonight. Channy, give the people a wave."

I hold up a stiff hand, like I'm answering a roll call.

"Don't believe the shy act. Channy runs the best damn karaoke bar in the Northwest, and she gave me a place to sing when I was pretty close to giving up music entirely. I paid her back by being a complete and utter bitch, but she was gracious enough to be my friend anyway. She has spent a lot of time lately being Little Girl Blue, but I'm hoping we can find a way for her to inhabit a universe more like the one in this next song."

It's "Misty." The piano sends down these paired raindrops, followed from beneath by the cello and violin. Ruby sings the first verse with a quiet sensitivity that my Ocean Shores version could only guess at. As it nears the instrumental break, they kick it into an easy bop, and our five white-suited waiters stream to the stage, straw boaters riding low on their foreheads. They form a line at center stage, one of them gives a four-count and they break into a softshoe, all the more charming because it's obvious that none of them are real dancers. The guy at the center seems to have a bit more elan than the others, so it's no surprise when they back off and let him dive into a time-step. This is about the moment that Donald O'Connor decides he can't hold it in any longer.

"There was this short film on Saturday Night Live once where they shot seven different New York lounge singers doing 'Misty,' and then they strung them all together so that..."

"Donald! Would you just shut the fuck up?!"

There has got to be a name for that phenomenon where you say something highly embarrassing at the precise moment that everybody else in the room clams up. Even the music has stopped. Even Donald O'Connor has stopped, and he's looking at something over my shoulder. I turn to find two hands the color of burnt wood, palms up, and a pair of generous lips around a blinding white grin.

Kai tips back his boater and says, "The fish are running, Channy. If you want this song to go on, you're going to have to dance with me."

I square my feet beneath me so I don't topple over, and I rise slowly, my gaze fixed on those dark, dark eyes. Kai kisses me on the cheek and says, "Just follow me. You'll be fine." He wraps a hand around my waist, I put a hand on his shoulder, and we take a step. The music begins.

About the Author

Michael J. Vaughn is the author of eight previous novels, including *Frosted Glass* and *Double Blind*. He is a frequent contributor to *Writer's Digest,* and a 20-year performing arts journalist. His poetry has appeared in more than fifty journals, including *Terrain.org, Many Mountains Moving* and *The Montserrat Review.* He lives in San Jose, California, and is, indeed, a karaoke addict, specializing in the songs of Frank Sinatra.

Lightning Source Inc.
LaVergne, TN USA
14 August 2009

154723LV00004BA/5/P